LOOKING UP

Caitlin, mother of four, nurtures her past as if it were another of her babies. But she is married to a man who resolutely neglects his past – until he finds an old girlfriend on a reunion website. As his attention turns away from the present, so Caitlin determines to find excitement in the here and now. All too quickly, everyone's future happiness – not least her children's – is under threat...

Rebecca Gregson titles available from Severn House Large Print

Hello You

LOOKING UP

Rebecca Gregson

Severn House Large Print
London & New York

This first large print edition published 2010
in Great Britain and the USA by
SEVERN HOUSE PUBLISHERS LTD of
9-15 High Street, Sutton, Surrey, SM1 1DF.
First world regular print edition published 2008 by
Severn House Publishers Ltd., London and New York.

British Library Cataloguing in Publication Data

Gregson, Rebecca.
  Looking up.
  1. Domestic fiction. 2. Large type books.
  I. Title
  823.9'2-dc22

ISBN-13: 978-0-7278-7887-8

Severn House Publishers support The Forest Stewardship Council
[FSC], the leading international forest certification organisation. All
our titles that are printed on Greenpeace-approved FSC-certified paper
carry the FSC logo.

Mixed Sources
Product group from well-managed
forests and other controlled sources
www.fsc.org Cert no. SA-COC-1565
© 1996 Forest Stewardship Council

FSC

Printed and bound in Great Britain by the
MPG Books Group, Bodmin, Cornwall.

For Mike, and also for Carol.
You both know why!

One

Saying it out loud was self-indulgent, she knew that, but Sheila Webb just couldn't help herself.

'There aren't many fifteen-year-old boys who would spend an evening with their grandmother out of choice,' she said, patting Kit's blond, furry arm.

'But then again—' Kit added in his new deep voice. He stopped mid-sentence. He'd been going to say there weren't many grandmothers who'd let their fifteen-year-old grandsons smoke, but a comment like that might make her think twice and it was Sheila's first thoughts he liked best. 'You're a one-off,' he finished.

He laid the cigarette paper carefully out on the old enamel-topped table in her garden room and lined up the tobacco.

'You'll apologize to your father then?'

'What for? All I did was add his name to a reunion site. You'd think I'd signed him up to a porn channel or something. He went completely apoplexic.'

'Apoplectic,' Sheila corrected, immediately wishing she hadn't. The boy had walked half-way across the city in the pouring rain to get

7

away from correction.

She watched him put another pinch of tobacco on to the paper, stopping herself from telling him he was overfilling it. At least the grand-mother role came more naturally to her than the maternal one had. There was no pressure to get things right, no angst when you got things wrong.

'What are you looking at me like that for?' he asked defensively.

'Your hair is sticking up in little peaks,' she said, but really, she was taking in the soaking tee-shirt, which was clinging to his torso and outlining some surprising contours.

'Oh, right. So why do you think Dad got so cross with me then?'

'You used his credit card without permission.'

'Seven quid,' Kit appealed. It was always worth appealing to his grandmother. She was the only adult he knew who didn't stick like glue to the first opinion that came out of her mouth. 'And it wasn't like I nicked it from his wallet or anything. It was next to the computer.'

'But you used it without asking.'

'To put him in touch with some old friends.'

'That's not the point.'

Kit couldn't see any point to his Dad's life at all at the moment. When Mark wasn't working, he was asleep. 'If I ever get like that,' he'd said to his mate Sully down the park, 'shoot me, will you?'

'You shouldn't have used his card. That's where you lose the moral high ground.'

Kit twitched a nostril in disappointment but felt his anger slipping away. Humble pie tasted so much better in his grandmother's town cottage than it did at his four-storey semi-detached home, where there was always a ready audience to watch him eat it. His three younger brothers were right there at the very first sniff of him screwing up. Sometimes, being the eldest felt like being under a giant microscope. He was always being *discussed*. 'You might be a learning curve for your mum and dad,' Sheila would tell him when he complained, 'but don't forget you're also a pioneer.' His reply: 'I never asked to be either.'

'Anyway,' Sheila said now, 'your father should be allowed to do what he wants with his free time. God knows he has little enough of it.'

'That's *his* fault,' Kit said. 'Mum's always on at him to take more time off, but he doesn't want to.'

'And tell me how he'd keep you lot in skateboards if he did that?' It was dishonest of her to pretend her son worked for the money. When Mark walked out of the house in the mornings, he metaphorically skipped. Kit's mother Caitlin, on the other hand, staggered out like a packhorse, laden with details of exam timetables, missing cricket boxes, guitar lessons.

'We've got too many skateboards as it is,' Kit grunted.

'So sell them on eBay.'

Kit laughed for the first time since bursting, like a big, wet, homeless dog, into her evening.

9

Grandmothers who let you smoke and knew about eBay really were few and far between. 'But isn't it a bit dodgy not to keep in touch with *anyone* from your past?' he asked. 'I mean, like not *anyone*?'

'Actually, I'd say it was standard male behaviour,' his grandmother replied.

In Sheila's experience, men weren't interested in the idea of preservation of any kind. Women noticed time passing before it even got there and men only regretted its going once it had gone. So it had been her who'd snipped off her babies' first curls, put their milk teeth in envelopes, dipped their feet and hands in paint and pressed them on paper for posterity. Her daughter-in-law Caitlin had done the same. Left to the men, six entire childhoods would have vanished without trace.

It was a very female observation and one she'd expect her son Mark, Kit's father, to denounce. Being a film-maker, he would point to his vast library of home movies to prove her wrong, but when was film ever an honest representation of anything? It was nonsense to claim that the camera never lies. She could pull out any 1977 snap of herself and her late husband Ken to demonstrate that. And just because you'd caught something in a lens, it didn't mean it was still *there*.

Mark might well be a walking film archive, but she'd be willing to bet she had a clearer mental image of his old school friends than he did, the lanky teenagers who used to clutter her kitchen with their huge feet and short fat ties, making fried egg sandwiches between jamming sessions in the garden shed. She had loved those days, when the house seemed permanently full, just before that coming-of-age starburst when each sparkle of youth had been projected, like Bonfire Night rockets, to a different compass point – Newcastle, London, Glasgow, York – fading so quickly to faint smoky trails.

'And your father's not really the old-school-tie type.' She saw the tie, black and gold with its interface innards hanging out as if it were yesterday.

'But you ask him about any of it, school, university – *any* of it – and he reckons he can't remember.'

'Of course he can.'

'In that case, he doesn't want to.' Sheila coughed to push herself through the moment. 'Perhaps he doesn't want you to know that he was a well-behaved, hard-working boy. Perhaps he'd like you to think he was a rebel.'

'Yeah, right,' said Kit, fiddling with the cigarette. 'Well, whatever it is, I hate his secrecy. It shuts us all out.'

Sheila couldn't have agreed more. Secrecy did shut people out, but occasionally it was worth it. She nearly said as much, but Kit was not the right ear for a confession. How she'd love to offload all that juggling and lying and over-compensating on someone, though. Sitting in a field on a hot day, she could still feel some of 1977's magic, as if the reality of it was close by

11

instead of in another country, another life.

'So what difference does it make to you who your father stays in touch with and who he doesn't?' she asked instead.

'It doesn't bother me,' Kit said, 'it bothers Mum. She wants a reunion for their fortieths.'

'Ah, their birthday.' Sheila felt like she'd just heard the crucial line in a radio play she'd missed the beginning of. So Kit had signed his father up to please his mum. Of course.

'*Birthdays*,' Kit said, emphasizing the plural in the Webb family way. 'Don't forget the "s".'

His grandmother got away with committing the deadly sin every year. She bought Caitlin and Mark joint gifts, baked them one cake, sometimes even made them share a card. In the early days of their courtship, it had seemed a sweet gesture. *Born to be together!* she'd write inside. Now, nearly two decades on, it looked lazy. She excused herself by saying it seemed profligate to do otherwise, but actually, it was her way of playing down the fact that Caitlin had no mother of her own.

Eighteen years ago, Mark had brought his young fiancée home as a fragile new orphan. The proximity of Caitlin's parents' tragic end had shaped Sheila's every reaction and she'd made a conscious effort to keep the spirit of Erin and John Rees alive, but it was difficult when all she had to go on were a couple of stock-still faces staring out from a handful of unremarkable photographs. She was no match for the real thing, though. She had seen the beautifully kept

12

scrapbooks, the annual work of adoring elderly parents. Caitlin's tenth birthday had been in Florida, her eighteenth in China, her twenty-first in New Zealand. Now, her birthdays were blots on the landscape and here, looming over a very foggy horizon, came the big one. Well, big to Caitlin anyway. Mark apparently couldn't care less.

'Their *birthdays* then,' Sheila said to Kit with false irritation. 'Anyone would think they were twins, the way they fight for individual recognition every year.'

'I wouldn't want to share *my* birthday,' Kit said.

'But a reunion? How can your mum have a reunion? There has to be a period of separation before there can be a reunion. She's still got all her friends from primary school.'

'She wants one for Dad.'

'Well, you've just told me he doesn't know anyone any more.'

'Which was why I subscribed to the website,' her eldest grandson answered, as if his argument had been with her. His rudeness didn't suit him and Sheila wondered whom he was emulating. This Sully character from the park, she guessed. The figure of Sully had begun to lurk in the wings of the Webb family theatre, waiting to come on stage in a sweep of his cape, to hisses all round.

'There's no need to be like that. And surely your dad's got enough friends as it is without having to dredge them up from the past.'

13

'Oh, right! That's where he gets his reluctance from. It's genetic.'

Kit put the roll-up to his lips and took it out again, picking a stray filament of tobacco off his tongue.

'Shee, would it be OK if I borrowed one of your filters?'

He'd only ever seen his grandmother smoke a handful of times, usually on the bench by the dwarf apple tree. It was her little treat, she said.

Sheila peered over her glasses. Calling her Shee was as new and revealing as the six-pack under his shirt.

'Whatever happened to good old Granny?' she asked.

'I think she was eaten by a wolf, wasn't she?'

Rather thrilled by her grandson's quick wit, Sheila disappeared through the heavy denim curtain that divided the garden room from the kitchen. It was called the garden room because it grew things, like fungi around the window frames for example. The Witch's Butter used to be her favourite, a burst of folded orange caps that was making its way impressively along the sill. Once, when she had spent too much time alone, a ludicrous but tenacious thought popped into her head that when it reached the end of the sill, she would die. Never mind that she was only seventy-one and looked and felt ten years younger, she'd been keeping half a superstitious eye on its progress ever since.

Beyond the curtain, she dialled Mark's home number. 'Only me,' Sheila said quietly. 'Just thought you'd like to know he's here.'

'Oh, thank God,' replied Caitlin. 'I had my money on the park again. Is he OK?'

'He's fine. Soaking wet and a bit bolshy, but he'll get over it.'

'What's he doing?'

'He's ... I'm ... I'm allowing him to roll a cigarette.'

There was a silence, which Sheila broke first. 'He asked, and...'

'It's just that if Mark ever knew...'

'I thought he might as well do it here than on a street corner...'

'He would go absolutely spare.'

'Or the park of course...'

The second pause seemed to go on even longer.

'Oh, what the hell. We all know he does it,' Caitlin said finally. *As long as that's all he does*, they both thought simultaneously. 'Can you get him to do some homework? He hasn't even looked at it tonight.'

'I don't think he has his bag with him.' Sheila's voice dropped even lower. 'I'll bring him home in an hour or so, when he's stopped being indignant. I don't think he should know I've phoned.'

'No. Thanks, Shee.'

'For what?'

'For being his sanctuary,' Caitlin said, desperate to clutch her son back and make the privilege hers again. 'Try and get him to clean his teeth or something before he comes home. If Mark

15

catches smoke on...'

'Bye, love.'

More secrecy, Sheila thought as she replaced the receiver. Are we all more alive in deceit?

In the garden room, Kit had only just realized his grandmother had gone when the curtain flapped again and she reappeared to hand him a battered oblong tin with the ghost of a Dutch windmill on the lid, given to her by someone once as a joke. As he opened it, Sheila smelt a perfume a quarter of a century old – an abandoned railway waiting room, a wildflower meadow by the side of the old trackbed, a private picnic in a goods shed.

'I can see you thinking I shouldn't be doing this,' she said. If he'd wanted to smoke a packet of ready-made cigarettes, that would have been a different matter, but she was a sucker for watching the construction of a roll-up.

With his hair dry, Kit looked younger – fluffier – again. She wondered if her lenience was a few years too premature.

'I wasn't thinking that actually,' he said. 'I was thinking that I like being treated as an adult.'

He took one of the little white filters out of the tin and butted it into the baccy, but it refused to go. He pulled some of the dark saffron strands away, put them carefully back in his pouch, ran the paper along his tongue and rolled it tight. Sheila watched him, and tried to remember the Kit who not so long ago had licked cake mixture, or rolled plasticine.

'You know what?' he asked rhetorically. 'Dad

16

says you never treated him like a kid. He says you even refused to dress him on his first day at school and so he went without any underpants on.'

Sheila winced. She could remember Mark hanging to the black railings of the playground as well as she could the fried egg sandwich brigade.

'But I bet he hasn't gone without them since.'

'Maybe he should. It might make him feel young again.'

'Forty *is* young!'

Kit looked up doubtfully. 'Yeah, right. Well, it would be nice if he could stop treating *me* like a kid.'

An image of a mantelpiece full of trite greetings cards filled Sheila's head: the relentless, unfunny jokes about baldness and impotence and sagging bodies on the front, the desperate and ineffective consolations written within. She would give anything to go back there herself.

'Life doesn't really begin at forty you know.' Hers, in one way, had peaked.

'I never thought it did.'

'You've got to be either under thirty-eight or over forty-two to enjoy a fortieth,' she told Kit. 'Unless you're me. Grandpa was eleven years older than me, so I felt permanently young. It's a very good move to hang out with people older than yourself. And I don't mean at your age, before you start defending this Sully creature and the park again.'

'He's not a creature, he's all right.'

Sheila ignored him and reflected on what she had just said, realizing both how false and true it was. Nobody wanted to be forty really, apart from in retrospect.

Ken would have been eighty-two this year, so maybe the spring chicken effect would have gone into reverse by now. Maybe they'd both have been silently watching the Witch's Butter together, between their naps. And maybe she would have been tempted to break the silence with an eleventh hour admission. It was odd, how the need to acknowledge her ancient disloyalty had come upon her lately. What was she after? Absolution?

'Take it from me,' she said. 'Every girl wants an older man.'

'What about Auntie Ali then? Her boyfriend is only twenty-five.'

'Yes, well, she's always been a contrary soul, right from the day she was born.'

'What about Mum then?'

'She wouldn't swap your dad for all the tea in China.'

'She doesn't drink tea. It reminds her of morning sickness.'

Kit was quick these days!

'Don't forget to take this with you when you go,' she said, tugging at a jacket on the back of a chair. 'Your mum's...'

Kit took a quick look. 'Dad's actually.'

'Oh? What *is* it with your parents and black linen?'

'Twins,' Kit said. 'Separated at birth.'

Two

South of the river in the four-storey, red-brick family home that Kit had taken his noisy leave from an hour and a half earlier, his mother Caitlin wasn't feeling genetically linked to anyone. Nor was she one half of a whole. If she was part of any fraction, she put herself at an insignificant sixth, the only pink slice in a pie chart of blue. When the testosterone levels were up, like they had been in the house tonight, she felt cheated. It was fate's, God's, Mark's, anyone's fault but her own that she didn't have a daughter.

Lately, she found she could weep with the lack of a blood-related female to talk to. Sheila did such a good impersonation of one that it seemed churlish to complain but every now and again, all this maleness just got to her. Tonight was a case in point. She'd been in her bedroom when the row between father and son had erupted beneath her feet, making her slam the lid of her mahogany box so hard she'd had to open it again to check its hinge was still intact. And if she'd broken it, that would have been Mark's fault too.

She kept the box on her dressing table for all

to see and yet she was the only one who ever lifted its lid to sift through the yellowing scraps of handwritten notes that in another life would have passed for rubbish. *Caitlin phoned. She is coming home at the weekend. Dry-clean navy suit for Caitlin's graduation. Check tyres on Caitlin's car.* She knew them word for word.

But she was in her kitchen now, looking at her crowded calendar. Biro, felt pen, coloured pencil, arrows, crossings out – she was already working a month ahead. She imagined other people must rather like October, with its shiny pumpkin glow, its sugary whiff of half-term Hallowe'en marshmallows and mellow fruit-fulness, but she hated it. October blew things away, like leaves off the trees and parents off the planet. Tomorrow, however, was only Wednes-day, September 18. Wednesday was one of her three days a week as a job-sharing education officer at the city museum. 'Is it your day off today?' her youngest son Rory liked to ask. 'It's my day at home,' she would answer carefully.

A class from a rural primary school was coming in for an Ancient Egypt workshop, which, thanks to the good old National Curricu-lum, she could almost do in her sleep. Apart from that, there was rugby for Dylan, swimming for Rory, a trip to an organic dairy farm for Joss and a parents' evening for Kit. Not much then.

September 17, she thought, opening the huge fridge. Three days short of three months before she and Mark kissed goodbye to their thirties and exactly one month until the nineteenth anniversary of her parents' fatal accident. One juggernaut, two sleepy drivers, four returning holidaymakers, two coffins, one orphan.

She was doing the counting thing again. During the funeral, she had computed the number of panes in the stained glass windows, the average age of the choristers, the amount of money a collection would raise if everyone donated one pound twenty-five. And now she and Mark were nearly forty. As she put an apple in each of the four lunch boxes she wondered where the time had gone.

At this stage of their wedlock (not deadlock, not yet), Caitlin thought she and Mark were more easily defined by what they didn't do together rather than what they did. He filmed, she preserved, he cut, she archived, he binned, she collated. She suspected there were more things they didn't know about each other now than when they'd taken their vows.

Getting married in the double-glazed, air-conditioned registry office, Caitlin hadn't even known Mark's parents' names, although that hadn't mattered as neither Sheila nor Ken Webb had been present. Nor had anyone else, unless you counted the female registrar, the two random witnesses dragged in from the neighbouring supermarket and the spirits of her own parents, one year on from their deaths, streaming in on a sunbeam through the high, narrow skylights.

Fantasies like that were private things now, along with all the other passing insecurities of life, like her irrational fear of breast cancer, her slowly diminishing libido, her craving for the children to stay young. No doubt Mark had a list of his own, too.

In the beginning, the gaps in their knowledge of each other had been caused by big things. Now they didn't know the minutiae. Did she, for example, know where he'd had lunch today? Had she told him about her dentist appointment? Being a social historian, Caitlin believed it was all in the minutiae.

The four lunch boxes lined up on the kitchen table were proving her point. Four apples, but only three salami sticks. Two rolls with cheese, two with ham. One with a little note saying, 'Look for your flask, Rory.' Three with one flapjack, one with two. She knew her boys inside out and there you had it – the state of her marriage was a trade-off with the kids.

She carried another pair of trainers to the stairs, which were permanently lined, in the same way that the Forth Bridge was permanently being painted, with things waiting to be put away. Today, with a chemist shop trip under her belt, it was the nit shampoo, the verruca cream, the cold-sore lotion, and a box of tampons.

'Don't go upstairs empty-handed,' she shouted at least once a day per pair of trainers. The trainers would go, but the tampons wouldn't. The boys treated them like they were radioactive; not even Mark knew where she kept them (or even precisely when she needed them) any more.

Passing the study, she saw that one of the boys had pinned a notice – 'Caution: Exclusion Zone' – to the door. She hadn't been intending to go in but a niggle of paranoia propelled her through the door. Her three youngest boys were crowded around a monitor, jostling for mouse control. They were playing God with their latest strategy game, creating virtual families, building them homes, finding them jobs, giving them off-spring, and then, because it was fun and they were boys, embarking on a programme of wilful destruction that didn't stop until their fictional families' lives were ruined. They all thought she was ridiculous for getting upset about simulated babies being neglected by simulated parents and carted off by simulated welfare officers. It's a *game*, they kept telling her.

'I hope you're not killing anyone,' she said. It was a mantra she had chanted for years and it came out in time to the snap and clack of her beaded flip-flops (which she had put on to remind her to remove the remnants of summer varnish from her toenails) against the wooden floor.

'We're not,' said Joss.

'He's on fire!'

'Put him out, you twat.'

'Dylan!' Caitlin said sharply. 'I won't have you using...'

Their father appeared not to hear. He was hunched over the other screen, editing at his iMac, leaning so far towards it that his rib cage was against the desk, his nose a ruler's length away. Caitlin went over to him and ran her hand down his back.

'Would you know what to put in a lunch box for me?' she asked.

'What's that?' He was aware that his wife had spoken but he hadn't bothered to register her words. When the house was full, there were too many words shooting out of too many mouths to digest them all.

'I was just packing the boys' lunch boxes and wondered...'

'Hmm?'

'Oh, it doesn't matter. What are you doing?'

'Trying to sort out some of the holiday tape.'

'Don't you do enough of that during the day?'

'Someone's got to do it.'

'No, they haven't.'

She stood with her arms folded, one hip lower than the other (a habit reinforced with each baby) and fought not to feel surplus to requirements. It was difficult to have a meaningful exchange over the cheap melody of the computer game's soundtrack.

'You're right, it does sound like soft porn,' she said to Mark.

'What?'

'Although how would we know?'

'Know what?' Her husband's lips were moving and sound was coming out but that was where the similarity with conversation ended.

'We haven't exactly seen enough to ... well, I haven't, anyway...'

'Sorry?'

'You know the other day you said you thought this music sounded like...'

'What?'

She shook her head of sandy hair and concentrated on the footage rolling across Mark's split screen. There was Rory wearing armbands, Kit and Dylan still looking like children, Joss dressed as a medieval knight, all four in canoes, on bikes along a river path, on the windy roof of a chateau.

'Was I actually on this holiday with you?' she snapped.

But no sooner had the ugly question left her lips than up her image flashed, red and scowling from a lounger, waving the camera away with her book. *Oh, sod the lot of you,* she thought, turning to go back out. She was unsettled not because she was superfluous, not because she no longer attracted the same level of attention she'd been so used to as a child, and not even because she and Mark had grown older, but simply because Kit was at Sheila's. Again.

Or at least, she'd thought he was. Suddenly, he was in front of her in the study doorway, inadvertently blocking her path and wearing an expression so familiar that she wished she could throw her arms around him and lift him to the sky.

'Hi,' he said, his lips curling uncertainly. He was getting so tall he almost filled the frame, blocking the light from the tiled hallway.

'Hi,' said his father first, hearing the petition for amnesty in his son's voice.

'Hi,' said Dylan, Joss and Rory.

It was the Webb family version of a powwow and they all knew the argument was over.

'You're back,' said Caitlin pointlessly, feeling his shirt to see how damp it was. All the time he'd been gone, the rain had smashed against the windows.

'Ali gave me a lift from Gra ... I mean, Shee's.'

'Ali!' said Caitlin, catching sight of Mark's younger sister behind him. Ali's presence was often a mixed blessing – she seemed to have a radar for tension – but tonight, it was approaching a comfort. 'Things any better?'

Ali shook her groomed head. 'He's playing squash again.'

'That's what you get when you shack up with toy boys,' Mark said unhelpfully. 'If you had someone your own age, they'd stay in every night.'

'Yes, playing on a bloody computer,' Caitlin added.

Ali was already regretting her generosity. Mark's home, although located in an area of the city increasingly associated with the trendy poor, screamed success. Her brother belonged to a clan she used to belong to herself, but her membership had somehow lapsed without her realizing exactly when. Being in this house in Dryhouse Lane always exacerbated her self-pity. It had substance, practical things, space and clutter. Its rooms had roles to fulfil, people to fill them. It was in a street with a real name, not conjured up by developers but born of the city's history with tobacco. The street had been there long before middle-class poverty had become a lifestyle choice. Mark and Caitlin lived in the heart of something, and she lived at the edge, literally, a waterfront apartment in a converted warehouse renamed Standpoint. 'What's-the-point?' was more like it. She could tinker around with all the lacquered bamboo plates and rattan footstools she liked, she still wouldn't be living in what anyone could call a home.

How, with just three more years under his belt than her, had Mark managed to build such an empire? At what point had their destinies split, his world to increase and hers to diminish? Why hadn't she seen any of it coming, acted before it was too late? Out of the corner of her eye, she noticed Caitlin's gesture to Mark, a three-line-whip nod for him to get up and be pleasant.

'Glass of wine?' her brother asked.

'No, I won't stay.'

'OK.' His acceptance of her refusal was too quick.

'Oh, go on then.'

He walked sideways past his wife and sister who were still in the doorway, his arms out-stretched so as not to touch them. Ali's trim breasts jutted out under her neat white tee shirt and fitted cord jacket. Caitlin's were hidden by a slate-coloured jumper that even she knew was incongruous with a summer skirt and flip-flops. Their height difference was down to the heels on Ali's wedge sandals under her black cotton jeans.

'What are we, toxic?' Ali said.

'I wouldn't,' Caitlin warned as Kit immediately filled his father's chair. 'You can see he's in the middle of something.'

'I wasn't going to. Oh God, is that last year or the year before? I look like a geek.'

Kit's brothers moved from their screen to his. Kit a geek? Excellent!

'Where? Where?' Rory shouted, pushing his body into a gap between the assorted thighs.

'Don't touch.'

'I wasn't going to!'

Mark came back in, handing his sister a glass of red wine but Ali didn't want red, she wanted white.

'So are you two going to have this reunion party or what?' she asked provocatively.

'No, we're not.'

'Why not? You've got to do *something* to celebrate reaching forty.'

'Says who? Come on kids, get out of my chair.'

'Kit says you've got a problem with the idea of contacting anyone from school.'

'No problem, just no desire. Look, you lot, if you touch anything, none of you will be back in here for a fortnight.'

'There must be someone from your past you're intrigued about.'

'I can't think of anyone.'

But Ali could. 'Look up some of his old university friends,' she told the boys.

'Dad?' asked Rory hopefully. He wasn't interested in which website they looked at, he wanted *any* website. 'Can we?'

'You don't want to make an issue of this, Mark,' Ali said.

'Oh, all right, for God's sake – but do it on the other machine.'

Rory didn't need to be given permission twice. He beat the others to the chair, pushed up his sleeves and moved the keyboard out of the way. With the ease of his generation, he cupped the mouse, gave it a shake and clicked. Too fast for any of the seven pairs of eyes to keep up, the computer responded and there it suddenly was, like a silvery bolt across a thundery sky – a school, a list of names, a university, a past – Mark's past, up for grabs.

Looking back, what Caitlin remembered was sensory. There was no portal her husband walked through, nor any cold chill as it opened and shut behind him, but she recalled shivering as he saw the name and wandered into a world she did not inhabit. Two words were all it took, and they weren't 'open sesame!'

'Nina Wills!' he murmured. Not John Goodridge, or Duncan Cleeves, or Julie Merrick or Andy 'Smeg' Davison, who were all there too. Not them, for they were names without the power of the portal. It was Nina Wills who had the power.

'Who's Nina Wills?' shouted the boys. 'Was she your girlfriend?'

29

But all Mark could do was repeat her name over and over again as if a rare bird he'd never really believed existed had just flown up and fed from his hand.

Three

Salt Peter Productions, Mark Webb's independent TV production company, had offices on the second floor of a former tobacco factory in the city's student quarter. Modest by nature, when people rang and asked to speak to Peter, Mark was always the first to say that if Peter was anyone, he was Chris Jones, his business partner.

The name had come to Chris four years ago when they had been plain 'Webb and Jones', working from the kitchen in Dryhouse Lane with two phones, a colossal email habit and a very useful contact in the ITV commissioning department. One day, Rory, who was then aged four, spilt orange juice over a camera and while Mark cleaned it up with plant spray and a hairdryer, Chris took a call that changed their fortunes. Were they interested in a lease on an old Wills cigarette factory? Mark said yes they bloody were, and as Chris lit up one of the thirty daily Marlboros he used to smoke back then, it hissed and sizzled portentously. 'That'll be the saltpetre,' he said.

So the directors of Salt Peter Productions took up residence in the cleaned-up former fag factory, and business, it had to be said, was good. The company had gone from strength to strength, which was not solely down to Chris's sharp marketing skills. Mark was an effective programme-maker, quick to recognize trends before they became issues. Those in the industry took him seriously and his name now carried enough weight that he was consulted by the same people who'd not so long ago forgotten to return his calls.

Neither of the men much liked the outside of the building, though. They were uncomfortable with its gleaming façade, which Chris maintained was like drawing on a menthol cigarette – the idea was there but the experience wasn't.

'But as our own documentaries keep telling us, regeneration is the thing,' Mark had pointed out.

This morning as he walked towards his shiny office, he felt a little regenerated himself. He was tired, but in a less self-pitying way than he usually was. You were late to bed, Caitlin had remarked as she'd stood on breakfast duty at the six-slice toaster this morning. Nina Wills kept you up, did she? Kit had smirked at his father, his aim off target as usual. But his son had been surprisingly close to the truth.

On the ground floor of the old factory was a large, open-plan bar where every morning, Mark read the newspaper, ate a pastry and drank a double espresso before starting his working day. Never mind that the newspapers ran stories he had seen the evening before, or heard on the radio half an hour ago. He needed his uninterrupted peace as much as he needed the caffeine.

He bought his usual fare and sat in what he considered to be 'his' place, feeling at home under the silver grey pipes that ran criss-cross over the concrete ceiling. He no longer noticed the rubber floors, steel doors, bentwood chairs or leather sofas. This month's painting exhibition hanging on the exposed brick walls – dismal portraits of grimy men in cloth caps in front of belching chimneys – might as well have been Blu-Tacked posters of football stars for all the attention he paid them. He cared not for his surroundings. It was simply where he went to enjoy a more peaceful start to his day than he could get at home.

No need to take a newspaper from the bar today though. His mind was busy, flashing with reclaimed snatches of his younger life – a local radio reporter, keen as mustard, bursting with flimsy opinion and thin confidence. The exact detail of the demo on the city's cathedral green he'd forgotten – was it the poll tax? Whaling? Blood sports? – but he could summon his interviewee all right. With her cropped hair and street warrior clothes, he'd described her on air as 'an elf in combats'. He still couldn't smell patchouli without wanting to get closer to it.

Mark shifted in his seat. It was hypocritical of him to be so immediately fascinated. In the early days of his marriage, his dogged refusal to import his past into his present had been the subject of many an upset. 'Why not invite these people?' Caitlin used to want to know. 'What are you ashamed of? What are you frightened about? Disappointed by?' But it was simpler than that. It was just that he didn't feel the need. Or used not to. So why now?

'You don't remember me, do you?' Nina Wills had asked him when she'd turned up at the harbourside radio station God knows how many years ago.

'Course I do. You're the elf in combats from last week...'

'No, I mean at uni. I used to come and watch your band play in the union bar. You all wore matching tee shirts.'

The band! Nina Wills! Our tee shirts! Out of character though it was, Mark was completely lost this morning in his own nostalgia fest. *Who remembers Vortex?* he'd read to his absolute amazement on the student reunion website's message board last night. *Vortex – the tornado of sound!*

In his thrill, he'd called for Caitlin but she'd gone to bed. With his first foot on the bottom stair, carrying his laptop in front of him like a thoughtful tray of medicinal soup for a recovering invalid, he'd realized the futility of including her. Why on earth should his wife be restored too? She knew nothing of his student years.

Vortex! The final name for their band had been

his inspiration, mainly to make use of the black tee shirts with the red 'V' they'd bought for a quid each at the market. They played cover versions from an era even then already gone – Deep Purple, Led Zeppelin, Free, King Crimson – but Mark had been most proud of their own material, a cringing smorgasbord of literary and political pretensions put to basic riffs. Well, what else would you expect from students of English and Politics? Maybe their best home-grown stuff had been the simple romantic ballads. His favourite – everyone's favourite actually – had been one he'd written called 'Long Term Love' which meant something very different at forty than it had at twenty.

One night, a girl had come up to him afterwards and given him a silk scarf. Not Nina Wills, someone else, someone forgotten, but *Nina Wills, Nina Wills, Nina Wills.* What a name it was, alphabetically disadvantaged at the bottom of the register but rendering the other names on the list immediately dull, like unplugged Christmas tree lights.

Would it be fun to get back in touch? What would he want from it? A fillip to his dwindling self-esteem? A chance to retrieve some memories before they faded altogether? A spot of flirtation?

But Nina hadn't much fancied him then and probably wouldn't fancy him much now with his balding head and widening girth – not that he needed or wanted to be fancied, obviously. But that was the whole point of internet reunion, surely. It allowed you to live the fantasy, to believe that you were still the floppy-haired guitarist to whom girls gave their scarves, even when you clearly weren't, even when you didn't really want to be any more.

Wills! He'd never before been struck by the coincidence that his ex-girlfriend shared her surname with the tobacco factory and it made him feel momentarily shaky, as if the writing had always been on the wall.

Wasn't the long-haired drummer called Gibb? someone on the chat board had written. Yes! Pale and spooky Gibb who had wanted to call the band Whirlwind. Too much like Hawkwind, the others had all argued. The Cyclonics then. No, we're rock, not Motown! Charybdis? Be serious, Gibbo!

And what would Gibbo look like now? Mark's own hair had fallen out long ago (the only thing for it these days was a number four all over) and his guitar lay in the loft like an outgrown toy. How *could* have all this been in his hard drive for so long without him needing it? Gibbo, Nina, Nina, Gibbo.

He suddenly couldn't face his Danish pastry. There was something else, something unfinished, connected to the memories. His thoughts had started the sort of restless hunting that goes on when you are not yet prepared to accept something is lost, the going back to the same drawer, the same handbag, the same coat pocket, just to check it isn't there. But sometimes of course, it is and then you can't believe you missed it.

Nina had announced she was leaving him in the radio station's dockside reception area. Dwarfed by a huge backpack, she had told him she was going travelling. 'Can't you wait until we're sure?' he'd begged. 'We're already sure – we've agreed we wouldn't want to keep it anyway would we?' 'I'd still like to know,' he'd said. 'Then I'll call you,' she'd promised, pecking him on the cheek, but she never had of course. So he'd been left to guess how their commonplace little drama had ended. It must have been a false alarm. She would have told him, he would have heard.

Mark finished his coffee and breathed out slowly. Would the chivalrous thing have been to stop her from going? Had she expected him to? But the longer he hadn't heard from her, the better it had been. There had been no baby then, no termination, no need to feel a shit. He was entitled to enjoy the thrill of finding her name again. It had all worked out for the best. If he'd persuaded her to stay, he'd never have met Caitlin, and Caitlin – he really did believe this – was the love of his life.

He got up from his table, walked through the swing doors marked Private and went straight up the metal stairs without making eye contact with either the bar staff or the other customers. He didn't stop at Jenny's desk or look at his post but went straight to his cobalt blue-painted office and knelt in front of his rarely opened corner cupboard. Lifting out its contents, he could manage about ten of the shallow white cardboard boxes at a time.

His prehistoric collection of 7-inch reel-to-reel radio tapes represented his earliest programme-making efforts. The boxes were dusty and some of the joins had split since the last time he'd moved them. Now, sitting on the carpeted floor, he began to open the lids, check the labels and close them again. It was incredible that these clumsy brittle spools represented the technology of less than twenty years ago but equally, where had all the time gone?

'I hear you and Caitlin are thinking of having a party,' his business partner Chris said, putting his head round the door. A lad Mark hadn't seen before was hanging around behind him, looking awkward.

'Caitlin might be...'

'Ashley, meet our resident miserable bastard. Mark, meet Ashley. Ashley's with us for a few days.'

'Work experience?'

'That's the one. What the hell are you doing down there?'

The teetering columns of flat white boxes surrounding Mark looked like the ruins of an Ancient Greek temple.

'Trying to find one of my old radio pieces.'

'Creative genius,' Chris said to the work experience boy. 'Oh, before I forget, Lou wants to know if the Webb family are free to join us on one of her freebies next weekend. She's got to do an ecotourism piece on a green holiday village or something.'

'I'm not milking any goats.'

'The kids can do all that. We can watch the rugby.'

'Why don't you get Lou to call Caitlin?'

'That's what I said you'd say.'

Chris and his shadow disappeared and Mark clicked the clear spool he'd had in his hand for the last five minutes into position in the old leather-cased recorder. Winding the yellow leader tape through the reel mechanism, twisting it round the empty spool, feeding the end through the plastic slit to secure it – it was like riding a bike. He shut the lid, pressed down the silver tombstone that was the 'play' button and, with the introductory 'flick-flick-flick' of the stray end of leader tape hitting the casing, he set his emotional alarm for three seconds.

'Could you just give me your name for sound level' – *'Nina'* – *'I need a bit more than that, tell me something about yourself'* – *'I'm twenty years old and I'd like to say that squatting is a cultural challenge and a revolutionary force. It puts housing at the top of the political agenda and...'* – *'Thanks, that's great.'*

Chris was back, plonking two blue carrier bags on to the frosted-glass desktop.

'Squatting? Is this your next gritty documentary proposal? What's in the bags? Stan from the telecine firm has just delivered them.'

'My videotapes transferred to digital. I've had them done for Caitlin's birthday present. I'm going to put together a sort of retrospective.'

'What, like an obituary?'

38

'She's always accusing me of only filming her when she looks rough so I thought I'd put together something that makes her look...'

'And this is her birthday present?'

'One of them.'

'Make the other one a diamond then, for God's sake.'

When Chris had gone again, Mark stacked the radio tapes quickly back into the cupboard, and put the recorder, with Nina still spooled up, on his desk.

'Open her notes, Dad,' his sons had urged. 'Go on, click on her notes. If you click, you'll find out what she's doing. Why don't you click?'

'I'm just not interested enough,' he'd told them but that, clearly, was a lie. He was suddenly like a moth to the flame, and if he went too close, he might get burned alive.

He pressed stop. This was ridiculous. Wasn't he the man who claimed that an obsession with the past was merely a boredom with the present? His hand hovered over the play button. The thing to do was to ensure one's contemporary life was interesting enough. The polished steel was cold against the pressure of his finger. Then again, he might as well listen to the whole thing, now that he'd gone to all this trouble. It couldn't do any harm – and anyway, who said anything about obsession?

At Dryhouse Lane, in the garret bathroom referred to as 'the apothecary', Caitlin Webb eased her work-weary body into the hot, aromatic water. She rested her head against the inflatable cushion shaped like a shell that her third son Joss had given her last Christmas and let out a long, low sigh.

On the back of the door were a light blue waffle bathrobe and a silver mesh bag containing a pair of soft, lilac suede mules, which in twenty minutes she would put on for the butterfly-like flight to her bedroom, leaving a dark chrysalis of clothes in a lump on the floor behind her.

This was the only space in the house she claimed entirely for herself. It was here that she indulged her desire for order and peace and exclusive ownership of things. It was here she carried out her depilation, washed golden tones in to her sandy hair, applied fake tan to her fair, freckled skin, plucked her light eyebrows and painted her square toenails. She alone recognized it as a grown-up version of her childhood bedroom where, as queen of all she surveyed, she sorted, categorized, filed, graded and displayed her possessions.

And here, on the individual white box shelves against the indigo wall above the bath taps, were her adult potions – a tube of shea butter hand cream and a pot of energizing sea moss scrub in one, a chunk of handmade soap and a heavenly scented air candle in another. She loved their promise of alchemy, twinkling with the possibilities of improvement and as she lay in the bath, she would visit them one by one. There was comfort in remembering who gave her the

Coco de Mer body lotion, wondering where she'd bought the grapeseed pure retreat gel, deciding whether she liked the exfoliating properties of the Dead Sea mineral salt brush or the organic lavender sugar scrub best.

Even the towels in here were hers and only hers. White and linen-trimmed, they were kept separate from the rest of the household laundry to ensure they never saw the insides of a damp kit bag or the floor of a swimming pool changing area.

Sometimes, Mark would come and wash her back for her. She enjoyed sitting revealed for him, wet and warm, because she knew her body – even puckered around the tummy like an old swimsuit – was still lovely to him. But those times were blue-moon times, and tonight, she was thankful for the solitude.

'Mummy?' came Rory's inevitable voice through the closed door. He was the only one of her sons still young enough to be oblivious to nudity, privacy, a woman's need for pampering. 'I've got something to show you.'

'Can it wait?'

'It's a present. I bought it for you on my school trip.'

A 'safe keeping' drawer next to her bed was full of gifts from zoos, museums, aquariums, camp shops – a plastic dolphin mounted on mirrored glass, a steam train in a bottle, a small rubber pink flamingo, a bendy pencil. She sat up, feeling guilty as only mothers in baths can.

'In that case, you can definitely come in!'

41

His glance took in her naked body. He had only last year stopped nuzzling her unimpressive breasts or reaching up to put a stubby finger on a nipple. Caitlin had got a pleasure from his interest that she couldn't quite grasp. It obviously wasn't sexual, and yet it wasn't entirely maternal either. It was derived more from a sort of selflessness; she was prepared to let him take advantage of her ordinary nudity like this so that one day some other woman could reap the benefit.

Rory handed her a green eraser with a picture of a tall ship on it.

'Thank you, that's lovely! Shall I take it to work or keep it here?'

'You could keep it here, for a sort of homework rubber if you want.'

'Yes, let's do that. You could use it too then.'

'OK.' He shrugged as if it were of no consequence. 'Can I put my feet in?'

Caitlin moved her legs to make room, and immersed her shoulders beneath the bubbles while he, sitting in his boxers and school shirt, regurgitated facts about the world's first great ocean liner taking famous cricketers to Australia to dig for gold. A wave of love came over her for her haphazard little inquisitor.

Each of her children was so different to the last. Kit, full of growing wit and burgeoning sexuality; Dylan, the classic second child, always on the lookout for opportunity; Joss, the freckled worrier so like herself; and this one, Rory, who could run the gamut of emotion from elation to despair before breakfast.

A loud clatter came from the roof space and she sat up in the water again, exposing her breasts, which were no longer interesting to Rory.

'Is there someone in the loft?'

'It's Daddy.'

'He's back from work already? What's he doing in the loft?'

'Getting his guitar,' Rory said, looking at his mother with his head to one side, as if to say, *since when did you care?*

Downstairs in the study, in the tight floor space between the two computer desks, Mark held the grey electric guitar with the white scratch plate close enough to feel the familiar solid body of wood against his stomach. There was a little more padding than there used to be, and his snake hips – the ones that used barely to be able to hold up his jeans – had entirely disappeared under a layer of good living. The guitar strap was his old black-and-gold school tie with a hole in each end, forced over two metal nuts, one to the left of his chest, the other at his right hip.

His fingers plucked randomly at the strings and short unamplified bursts punctuated the air. Dylan and Joss made faces at each other and their father, suddenly shy of his talent, rubbed his fingertips with his thumbs.

'The strings need changing. They've oxidized or something. They feel horrible.' He ran his hand over the guitar's dusty body. 'I should probably take it to a music shop, get it tuned properly.'

'Go on, play something then,' Dylan said.

'I don't know if I can remember ... look, see this?'

Mark pointed to a hand-painted flourish on the head stock, an amateur attempt at forgery. 'It's not really a Fender. I put that on, with paint from my spitfire models. It's a Japanese copy really – a Kasuga – so I sandpapered the name off, and repainted Fender...'

'You faker!'

'My mate Coxy told everyone.'

'Who's Coxy?'

'He used to say he was the nephew of the lead singer in Status Quo.'

'Status what?' Joss asked.

'They're like headbangers,' Dylan said.

Mark laughed. Just holding the guitar again made him feel happy. Vortex – the tornado of sound, silk scarves, Tuesday night in the union bar!

'I so wanted a Fender Stratocaster.'

'Why? How much are they?'

'Now? About eight hundred quid.'

He bent down and fiddled with a small practice amp at his feet.

'I used to want a proper amp as well. A Marshall. Jimi Hendrix played through a Marshall.'

'Purple Haze,' Joss said. He'd seen it on his iPod.

'Good boy!'

'Turn it right up,' Dylan said. 'Play something

44

really loud.'

'Not on these strings.'

'Try.'

Mark took the tortoiseshell plectrum he'd found in a dish on the sitting room mantlepiece out of his trouser pocket and put it in his mouth. Plectrums had been knocking around the house for as long as anyone could remember. They turned up every now and again in toy boxes or pencil pots, giving the (up until now) false impression that they were a part of what went on in the house. Joss had never been entirely sure what they were.

The sliver of pointed plastic felt familiar between Mark's teeth. 'OK, there are two things sad old gits like me always play in music shops – "Stairway to Heaven" or "Smoke on the Water". Thing is, "Smoke" needs maximum distortion...'

Mark cranked up the volume. From the tiny box came an explosion, a harsh blast of sound that rocked the walls, and sent Joss back towards the door. Mark mouthed the notes as he moved his fingers around the rusty strings.

'G to B flat to C to G, B flat, C sharp, C...'

Three storeys up in the apothecary, Rory whipped his feet out of Caitlin's bath.

'Is that Daddy?'

He lunged for the door, leaving wet marks across the white boards.

'I guess so. Unless Jimmy Page has come round.'

'Jimmy who?' Rory shouted, thumping down

45

the stairs.

Alone again, Caitlin sank beneath the water. She recognized the riff; she just wasn't sure she recognized the player.

Four

To a casual observer, Ali Webb may well have looked like a woman in control of her life. Her movements and clothes were perfectly co-ordinated as she jogged along the cobbled back streets of the newly sanitized docks. Her face was showing just the right amount of exertion to suggest fitness and stamina and it was in the borrowed style of her personal trainer that she exhaled carefully through the neat little circle of her UV-protected lips.

In fact, she was more out of control than she had ever been. A quarter of a mile away, behind her front door, lay the broken squash racquet of her much younger boyfriend, its strings slashed. Her facial glow, suggestive of long-distance running, was actually the aftermath of un-speakable rage.

She puffed into her mobile.

'Could I speak to Erica, please?'

The receptionist on the other end of the phone was accustomed to the sound of raw panic.

'She has a client waiting just at the moment,

but let me see if she's free. It's Ali Webb, isn't it?'

'Yes.'

'I'm beginning to recognize your voice. Hold on, Ali.'

Ali continued to pound the cobbles. The bigger the distance she could put between herself and her flat, the better. Behind that door, along with the irreversibly damaged racquet, lurked the memory of a woman so deranged, so consumed with jealousy, that she was – apparently – capable of inflicting serious harm on an inanimate object with a kitchen knife.

One minute she had been performing the sane task of unpacking the dishwasher, and the next, she'd been hacking uncontrollably at 120 pounds worth of titanium graphite and gut string. With one simple text message from Rob she had become the stuff of fiction – the bunny boiler, the shower curtain slasher, the jailed spurned lover on page five. And yet in those few violent seconds – no more than thirty – she had savoured the most delicious ambrosial power.

Erica's measured therapist's voice suddenly soothed her.

'Having a bad day, Ali?'

'Oh, Erica, I'm sorry to trouble you. Are you free any time soon? Only I think I'm ready to tell you.'

Erica said nothing.

'About my father.'

'Uh huh.'

'I mean, he's been dead for years. I don't

know why it's taken me so long.'

'No one's parents ever really die, Ali.'

'Can you see me this morning?'

'Impossible I'm afraid. What about tomorrow? Say five o'clock?'

'I was hoping for something this morning.'

'No can do. Sorry.'

'Oh. OK then.' Ali stopped running, wiped her eyes on the sleeve of her pale grey and pink zipped tracksuit jacket, took a deep breath and dialled another number.

'Caitlin? Can you talk?'

'Not just now, Ali.'

She tried another.

'Mum?'

'I've got the painting group here, darling. Can I call you back?'

Ali put her slim phone back in her pocket and leaned forward, her hands on her knees in the style of a genuine jogger, and briefly thought she might be sick. The image of the racquet immediately returned.

It had been leaning provocatively against the hall wall all morning, glinting and sparkling with the kind of confidence she saw in the young women who hung around the cobbled piazza outside her flat, pretending not to be interested in the young men who were pretending not to be interested in them back.

Rob had promised to help her build the bookcase that had been sitting in its flat pack for a fortnight. The marinated chicken breasts and the wine were already in the fridge. They were going to have a cosy evening in, doing the sort of thing that couples building a future together do. She'd even bought him an electric screwdriver. And then her mobile had gone off. *Just realized it's the first round of the tournament tonight, so shelves will have to wait. Sorry x.*

It had all unravelled in such a frenzy. She knew she had thrown her apparently indestructible phone across the units so hard it had ricocheted off the kettle and shot across the beech surface before falling on the floor. She knew she had picked the sharpest knife from the steel block. She knew she had screamed some sort of battle cry. But what force had propelled her down the hall? What voice had persuaded her to make the first cut? What screw had finally come loose?

And where was the consistency in her unreason? Instead of fleeing in whatever clothes she had on like any other normal mad person would have, she had calmly walked into the laundry room and changed into her running gear, discarding one top, searching for another, wiping a wet cloth over her white trainers like she always did.

As she began to run again, her head span with snapshots of the last half an hour. The knife, the empty hallway, the evidence of her insanity lying on top of Rob's sports bag like a murder victim waiting to be discovered.

Self-preservation suddenly kicked in. The thought of him coming home unexpectedly, the prospect of even beginning to try to explain to him what she had done, spurred her on. She started to run faster across the footbridge, away from the docks and into town. By the time she reached the sports shop, the exertion in her face was genuine.

'Do you stock Head squash racquets? Have you got the Intelligent range in stock? ... Thank God for that.'

Ten minutes later, with the new love rival in her hand, she felt better. She even had the nerve, just for a moment, to feel cheated. Her purchasing power was one of the things about her that Rob found sexy. It was the only advantage she had over women his own age, who were still renting rooms with shared bathrooms, still taking holidays in two star hotels, still driving wrecks. He'd be turned on by the idea of her shelling out more than a hundred quid on him just like that – except she wouldn't be able to let him know.

She replied to his text. *No worries, shelves can wait. Enjoy xx.* Soon, it would be almost as if the 'accident' had never happened, like the time Caitlin ran over their six-week-old kitten and had another one from the same litter in its basket before the boys were back from school. *We all do it,* she comforted herself. *We all try to hide our mistakes. I'll be able to laugh about this one day.*

Nina Wills didn't recognize the smiling jogger as she drove past the same car park for the third time.

'This city never used to be so full of runners,' she said to her daughter Chloe.

'For God's sake, Mum, it's years ago. Admit it, you don't know this place any more.'

'I do, I do, I just need to get my bearings.'

'We're lost.'

'No,' Nina said, shaking her newly tinted aubergine hair, 'it's around here somewhere. The man on the phone said it was where it's always been.'

'Except you can't remember where that is. You should have asked him for directions, but you were so keen to let him think you knew, you couldn't bring yourself to.'

Chloe wobbled her head as she spoke so her curtain of glossy hair swung around her olive face.

Nina laughed, even though she wasn't entirely sure her daughter had meant her to. She was even more pleased to be back than she'd imagined, although some parts had changed so much it was like looking at a digitally aged image of one's own face. A quick glance and the place was a stranger, a second look, and that bend in the river or that painted Georgian terrace smiled back at her. Today though, the city was playing hard to get.

'OK, so it's not down here. It must have been that turning back there. Is there anything behind me?'

'Can't we give this up and go and have another look at the school? Just from the outside?'

'Why do you like that one so much?'

51

'People come out smiling.'

'I'm glad to hear you attach so much importance to that activity,' Nina said pointedly. As she groped for reverse on the five hundred pound car she had bought the day before from an advert in the local paper, she took the opportunity to check on her daughter's reaction. She never knew these days quite how much parenting she could still get away with.

Maternal instinct hadn't always eluded her. In the Greek hospital in the first days after Chloe's birth, her belief in herself as a mother had been strong enough to break rules that were as old as the whitewashed walls that imprisoned her. Even through two closed doors and against the backing vocals of twenty other hungry newborns, Nina had been able to pick out her own baby's cry.

'I'm her mother,' she'd said defiantly to the stout midwife with the moustache and permanently folded arms, 'and I feed when I want, not when you say.' It had been a statement more effective for its emphasis than its vocabulary. She'd never mastered much Greek, not in five years of living there. Nor Turkish after living in Turkey come to that, which was even more shameful, given the time scale.

These days though, she had only a vague idea what was going through her daughter's mind. For example, was Chloe really sulking now or was that tendency to curl the bottom lip genetic? If she *was* sulking, what was it about? And if she wasn't sulking, whose gene was it?

'You *must* know!' Nina's disgusted father had snapped at her sixteen years ago when Nina had called Newcastle from Paros with the news. 'How can you not know?'

And Nina had told her father he would have to work that out one for himself, after which the phone line had gone stone dead. The lines of communication had never been properly restored, and to compensate, Nina made much of the fact that the only people she and Chloe had to please were each other. On days like today, it seemed trickier than it should be.

'It's round here somewhere,' she said. 'Give me five more minutes.'

Chloe set the timer on her resin-strapped shock-resistant waterproof watch with alarm, data bank and tele-memo.

'This is so stupid. Let's go to Ikea,' she hissed through her brace.

'We don't have the money for Ikea.'

'Mum, *everyone* has the money for Ikea.'

Nina bit her lip. It was her fault Chloe laboured under such misconceptions. She should have stood her ground and sent her to the village school in Turkey like she'd wanted to. 'Making do' was no more than an embryonic sensation for Chloe, gained by osmosis while still in the womb as her mother had rinsed out the dregs of retsina from narrow-mouthed glass jars and swept sand off the floor. By the time Chloe had been old enough to have memories, money had been no object – Rauf's money unfortunately, even though it cost her dear to even think of his

53

name. Anyway, they were properly poor again now.

The two of them could have chosen anywhere in the world to make their fresh start. It wasn't as if either of them had any attachments. Having another go at Greece had been one option. Staying in Turkey had most definitely not been another. But Chloe had said all she really wanted was a home in England, with her own room, painted lime green, and her mum on tap. No more having to share a dorm with spoilt kids you couldn't stand, no more having to share your school holidays with a hundred sunburned guests in Marks and Spencer sarongs, and no more having to share your mother with a psychopathic hotelier who used to try and pass himself off as either your boyfriend or your father, depending on whose approval he craved.

This gentrified port in south-west England would do nicely for them both. It was a city that, according to Chloe's internet research, was a city of culture, of skateboarders, a media city, a city teeming with creativity and history, but more importantly, it was a kind city that had once treated Nina well.

'Bingo!'

On their right, under the brick arches of a gargantuan dockside warehouse, was the second-hand furniture place she'd been looking for.

'*That*?' Chloe said, screwing up her nose. 'We've spent an hour driving round in circles for *that*?'

'You wait,' Nina said. 'You'll see. You won't

want Ikea after this.'

'I'm not sleeping in a bed someone might have died in.'

'New mattresses, I promise.'

Above the opening was a huge woodchip sign roughly cut in the shape of a genie's lamp painted with the words 'Lad in Cave'. The biggest, and Chloe hoped, ugliest, furniture was crowding the pavement outside. Just inside the door, an elderly man sat in a burgundy mock-leather armchair reading a newspaper.

'Don't tell me *he's* the lad?' Chloe said, staring in disgust.

Nina sneaked another cautious look at her daughter as she parked the car, but this time, the pout was not the thing. Chloe tucked her straight hair behind her studded ear and in doing so, revealed the ghastly coral gash along her cheekbone.

Nina was surprised to realize that what the bright pink tramline (since Chloe had peeled off the scab) had come to represent now was no longer her failure to protect her only child, but their joint passport to freedom. Intriguing though the mark was to new acquaintances, neither of them noticed it much any more, other than to keep an eye on its recovery.

Chloe felt the observation but didn't intend to do much about it. She had managed without parental scrutiny at boarding school for the last seven years, and she wasn't in the mood to start encouraging it now. What she wanted these days was freedom. Freedom to wear what she liked

55

without Rauf accusing her of loose morals, freedom to say what she thought when she thought it, freedom to go to bed, get up, go out and come in whenever she liked without Rauf continually threatening her with this punishment, that punishment. The way she saw it, her mum owed her at least that.

She carried on looking straight ahead. A squat male figure was walking towards their small, red, slightly rusty car. For a split second, Chloe's instinct was to bolt out of the car and stand up to him (or even tower over him) and shout, 'You tiny control freak! You vain bully! You ostentatious dictator! Look at me, I'm taller than you now! And my pierced navel, how do you like that? Go on, have a good old look!' (Only she knew how much Rauf liked good old looks.) Her hand flew to the door.

'Hang on,' her mother said obliviously. 'Let me just straighten up.'

Chloe's second instinct, one that skimmed off a sore memory of a ringed hand against her cheek, payment for a solitary walk in shorts on a beach at dusk, was to loosen her grip on the handle and shut her eyes.

When nothing came other than the wrenching noise of the handbrake, Chloe opened her eyes again and took stock. The man walking towards them was not Rauf Abaz. He was not unlike him, with his steel-coloured hair and darker moustache, but he was missing the pitted weathered skin, and the ring. So why was he coming straight at them?

The cobbled street, flanked by the old brick warehouses on one side and a railway sleeper fence on the other, was blocked by three bollards, beyond which there was only a grey expanse of dock water and the late September sky. A battered white delivery van was blocking most of the remaining available space. The Rauf impersonator was an innocent office worker taking a midday walk, and the route he'd chosen was his only option. He smiled briefly as he held his suit jacket against his business-lunch tummy and squeezed past the driver's door. Chloe was unable to rein in a rapid nervous giggle.

'God, I thought that was Rauf for a minute!'

'You don't need to worry about him, he's history.'

'Yeah, I know, but...'

The man in the burgundy armchair outside the shop put down his newspaper and nodded chivalrously, as if he weren't really sporting two day's worth of stubble and carpet slippers, but a neatly trimmed moustache and polished brogues.

He'd been trying to work them out as he'd watched them park and walk arm in arm across the cobbles. The older woman's clothes suggested an income the car did not. There was wool, and then there was cashmere and Lad could see even from here that the deep violet sweater that stretched across her obvious breasts was not pretending.

He could see the age difference more clearly now. It had been the mother's hair that had thrown him, one of those intentionally unnatural shades cut to look messy. She looked like a woman who had once relied entirely on sex appeal and for whom, on that count, time was running out.

'Have a good look round,' he said to them, by way of a welcome.

'Thank you, we will.' Nina smiled with a low-level flirtation she just couldn't help.

As they moved further inside, the smells of cats and old age and village halls tickled their noses.

'I furnished my bedroom in the squat from here,' Nina said, smoothing her hands over a flimsy Formica unit.

Chloe gave her a withering look. It was the sort of self-conscious comment her mother made all the time recently. Since leaving Turkey, Nina had talked about her previous 'deprived' life in the kind of evangelical terms that made it sound as if everything was so much better then, as if having money made you less interesting, as if her years abroad had been *all* bad.

'Some of the others used to get cross whenever I came back with something, as if wanting to have nice things was in some way wrong.'

'But that's exactly what you're making me feel like now.'

'One bloke, Mick, who had a gold tooth, actually set fire to a tablecloth I'd come home with. He said it was spoiling his experience, claimed I wasn't trying hard enough to embrace a new form of living...'

'You've told me all this before.'

'I had this boyfriend, a radio journalist...'

'Yes, yes, heard it, heard it.'

'He used to stick out like a sore thumb in the squat. He used to wear polo shirts and everyone used to laugh about him when he'd gone.'

Nina opened the glazed door of a light blue kitchen cupboard to banish the feeling of guilt that surrounded her memories of Mark Webb. The shelf was full of mouse droppings. She rocked the top of a narrow welsh dresser to check its relationship with the bottom, but discovered there wasn't one.

'If it was so good, why did you leave? That's the one bit you haven't told me.'

'It's a good question, but one I can't remember the answer to. I guess I just woke up one morning and realized I wasn't happy.'

'So you dumped your entire life and left the country?'

'That's about it.'

'OK...' Chloe said slowly, narrowing her green oval eyes and sucking through her brace, 'I see a pattern emerging.'

Lad got up from his chair, a well-worn sales patter on the tip of his furry tongue. He could hear the rustle of tenners in his money belt. Drawing in some of the powdery air through his teeth, he approached them from behind. *Reel 'em in, Lad, reel 'em in.* He didn't speak until he was right there, breathing down their necks.

'What are you after then, ladies?'

The way they both jumped, like you might if a

door slammed unexpectedly, puzzled him, until the younger one turned and he saw the scar.

I tell you what you want, he thought. You want a bloody big lock on your front door and an even bigger bugger on the back. You want to stop the bloke who thinks that just because he paid for your watches and your designer jeans that he bloody owns you from coming anywhere near you, that's what you want.

Five

'He should have been left where he was, he should,' a boy with broken spectacles said, nodding towards a 3,000-year-old mummy lying in its decorated sarcophagus.

Caitlin Webb immediately warmed to him. A child with an opinion was a godsend on a workshop like this. She always briefed her own four boys before their school trips.

'Ask questions,' she would say. 'Look interested.'

'What makes you say that?' she asked him.

His face reddened. He hadn't meant to speak out loud.

'Go on,' she encouraged. 'It's a very interesting thing you just said.'

'My nan says you shouldn't disrupt the dead.

You should let them rest in peace,' he whispered.

Through a finger-smudged sheet of safety glass, the mummy stared blindly back at him. Caitlin saw his head suddenly retract into his neck, like a tortoise reacting to a dog's inquisitive nose, and she moved forward to reassure him.

'Miss? What would happen if he came alive?' asked a girl with a ribbon at the top and bottom of each tight plait.

Caitlin was asked the same thing without fail every single time. It wasn't an original enough thought for her liking and she'd learnt not to encourage it.

'He could take the rest of the workshop and then I could go home,' she said.

Ancient Egypt had been on primary timetables for so long, she sometimes wondered if the National Curriculum itself had been mummified, but she hadn't yet tired of spotting the point at which school trip turned to time travel. When it did, a child's gaze would become fixed, his or her mouth would hang slightly open and the air around would snap, crackle and pop with insight.

She coaxed the boy with the broken glasses back to look into the display with her. Three original lotus flowers lay on the mummy's stomach, their delicate petals still impossibly blushed with a faint colour not unlike like the pot of yellow roses, now dried, that Mark had given her for her thirty-ninth birthday last

December. Mark's blooms were already parched and depleted, ready for the bin. It was only guilt at her lack of sentimentality that had saved them thus far. But the longer she looked at these desiccated heads, the less she understood. Should the toll of 2,999 years really be so undetectable? If so, how could a mere sixteen years show themselves so obviously in a marriage?

'What are you all thinking?' she asked, in an attempt to get some low-level debate going. It worked with some groups. Did they think dead people's bodies should be on show? Did they agree that the dead deserved to rest in peace? What about the mummy's expectations for the afterlife? Did they think this one would be angry or sad to find himself here in this museum?

None of them answered. Caitlin was good at pinpointing the fault line between interest and fear – if it opened up and any of them fell in, she'd never quite retrieve them. Occasionally, the odd child could become almost hysterical.

She had nearly lost the boy with the broken spectacles in an earlier chamber with her story of Ramesses VI, torn and hacked to pieces by tomb robbers who were after his gold. Nor had he been too happy about the nameless mummy in the brown bitumen-stained binding that had come away at the feet. Are those stumps his toes? What's the hole in the back of the head? Why isn't it lying down like the others?

Up close, the boy smelt of the school canteen, the same smell of overcooked vegetables or cake and custard that she noticed on Rory or Joss sometimes. An instinct made her put her hand out to touch him but he flinched and she withdrew.

'He looks like he stinks!' said the only child not in uniform, moving in to hang over the waist-high display case. She was wearing a sleeveless shiny blue vest with black velour leggings and school shoes, with a roll of white tummy baring itself between her clothes. Until now, she had been singing the same line of girl band lyrics over and over again.

'Well, so would you if you'd been wrapped in bandages for three thousand years,' Caitlin's colleague and curator Lesley answered back. Lesley was wonderfully ruthless with children. She had none of her own so she was able to detach herself from them in a way Caitlin could not. Lesley never went home wishing she had been more responsive to the girl with the bad teeth or the boy with bad hair, but then neither could she identify fault lines. Between them, they made an excellent team.

The girl with the plaits looked at her blankly and returned to her pop song. Lesley carried on.

'A man called Sir Flinders Petrie discovered this tomb in 1908. The X-rays show the body of a man about thirty years old, with his bones and teeth in good condition. We don't know what he died of but...'

'It's stealing,' the boy with the broken glasses interrupted.

Lesley rolled her eyes at the rest of the class

but Caitlin wanted to hug him. It *was* theft. These afterlives should be in pyramids, not under municipal roofs having undergone the indignity of being unwrapped by some Victorian showman as an evening's entertainment. She didn't really believe that if you messed with the past, it would rise up and grab you, but there was something wrong with the selfishness of the displacement all the same. It was the sort of thought museum workers were not supposed to have so she shook it away and tried to concentrate on Lesley's familiar counter-argument.

'Up until twenty years ago, Egypt Railways used mummies as fuel for the trains. In the Middle Ages, mummies used to be ground down for medicine. Charles the Second even used to rub mummy powder into his skin in the belief that he would absorb some of the spiritual goodness. Is being a museum exhibit worse than any of those fates? I don't think so!'

A child shuffled forward and a floorboard moaned beneath the thin carpet. To Caitlin and Lesley, it was the noise of a department that needed refurbishment, but to the boy in the broken glasses, it was probably the sound of a creaky coffin lid, a restless spirit coming to haunt its captors, a tortured groan from a tomb robber hanging in shackles from a pyramid wall.

The boy turned round and started to push his way out of the group. Ignoring the shunts and cries of indignation, his head bobbing above the sea of bright blue sweatshirts, he disappeared through an archway. He didn't know it but he

64

was on his way to the reconstructed burial chamber.

'I'll go,' Caitlin motioned to Lesley.

She felt a strange sort of relief flood through her as she followed in his wake, like she did when one of her own boys complained of feeling sick, and then was. If there was something inevitable on the horizon, she preferred to get it over and done with. 'So, to remove the brain,' she heard Lesley continue without a pause, 'they would push a hook up through the nose and draw it out bit by bit. It wouldn't all fall out at once obviously. There would probably be a lot of digging and pushing and...'

Caitlin smiled as the children mewled and puked behind her. Lesley was a star. In a minute, she'd be showing them her trump card – a Tupperware box full of mummified skin that she had come by in her previous job. The tar-black flakes she carried around in her briefcase were the sweepings from a hospital floor, collected by a spectacularly incompetent team of medics in the 1950s after a mummy they had been entrusted with had inexplicably fallen off an X-ray table. Lesley liked to offer them round, like crisps at a party, encouraging the children to touch and smell them. She had never suggested it in so many words, but some kids had been known to lick them. As far as Lesley was concerned, the past was there to be poked at, turned over, sniffed, rubbed (but not necessarily tasted). Not everyone agreed with her. Upstairs in her office was a thin file of complaints from horrified parents. To a large extent, Caitlin was with them. It wasn't the health and safety aspect that disconcerted her, it was the ethical issue about whether it was *right*.

She hurried through the maze of sand-coloured corridors after the boy. The Egyptology gallery – which was only half the size of its originally intended dimensions – had been constructed to resemble the inside of a pyramid. At each right angle turn, there was something to confront you – a towering cast of an ancient god, a faded hieroglyphic scroll, the enlarged X-ray of an early skeleton – but at this speed it was more like a ghost train. No wonder the child looked like a rabbit caught in the headlights when she found him.

He was pinned against a far wall next to what many visitors found the most disturbing exhibit of the lot. The Crouched Burial was alarming for its humbleness, its lack of panoply, its pitiful remains.

The boy's left arm was outstretched, as if shielding his eyes from a bright light.

'What's that?' he panted, pointing in the opposite direction to the one he was looking in. 'What's in there?'

Caitlin understood a little boy's need to hear the full story before bedtime.

The wooden box he was gesturing to contained the bones of an old man, once wrapped in linen, naturally preserved by virtue of having been buried in hot sand. The legs were pulled in close to the body, the arms hugging them. It took some careful study to make out a human skull, pelvis and thigh bones.

It was the position of the skeleton that so often disturbed people. Crouching was equated with hiding from danger. When the boy's own legs were tucked into his chin like that, he could hear his heart thumping against his ribs.

He wanted to know the answers to the same uneasy questions as most children did. What dark corner had the old man died in? Who was he concealing himself from? Were his hands above his head like that to protect him from the killing blows that were about to rain down on him?

She looked around the empty chamber.

'That?' she said in a light voice. 'That's Fred.'

Well, why shouldn't she baptise him? He deserved a name. She had given him other accessories over the years, like a wife and children, a job and a house – but Fred? Could she not have come up with something more appropriate? Asef? Nakht? Kaem-Na? Well, he would just have to grow into his name, like her second son Dylan had had to.

She held out her hand and touched the tips of the boy's fingers. This time, instead of flinching, he moved forward and squatted next to her by the side of the glass.

'He's not much to look at any more is he?'

Privately, Caitlin often tried to put her mummies in the context of their lives. It was her way of dealing with the injustice of their fate. Sometimes, when she was on her own with them, she even made a futile attempt at communication. If she stared at them long enough, she thought she might find out if they minded lying in such cramped conditions being stared at by semi-revolted kids. The problem was, the museum had very scant knowledge of this particular exhibit. The old man's place in history had been secured solely on the grounds of the nature of his burial. What could she tell the boy?

'We think Fred might have been an artist...'

It would have been a whole lot easier to make him a part-time priest or a scribe. She was making this difficult for herself. But as the boy cocked his head, she felt something release itself under her rib cage, like the unlacing of a boned corset.

'How d'you know?'

'We don't, not for sure, but rumour has it...'

For some reason, maybe because she was using her storytelling voice, she thought of one of the old books at home about a beach artist who carved a horse into the sand. With his one eye, the sand animal saw real horses, and he longed to join them, white and foamy, galloping in the waves in the bay. When the tide came in, his dream came true.

'Rumour has it that Fred was born in the ancient city of Thebes, the youngest son of four boys. At fifteen, he was asked to go and work on the pyramids, which was considered a great honour. So his family packed him off with the best tools they could spare and off he went into the desert where he worked on the pyramids all his life. Lots of men did the same.'

'I thought you said he was an artist.'

'I'm coming to that. In his spare time, he would carve animals out of the desert sand...'

'What sort of animals?'

'His specialities were sphinxes, cats and crocodiles. He was so good at them he became famous. Egyptians would travel for miles to see his creations.'

The boy looked at the pile of bones and tried to believe it.

'He kept working until he was very old. His last sculpture was an exact replica of the pyramid he had spent his whole life building.'

The boy put his warm hand on the glass where it made a steamy outline.

'And when he died, all his friends clubbed together to give him the best burial they could think of. They wrapped him in linen, put him in a coffin and buried him in the hot sand to preserve him for ever. You see? So he wasn't killed. He died of old age.'

'But why is he all scrunched up like that?'

Caitlin knew, with an instinct that Lesley didn't possess, not to bring the foetal position into it.

'Maybe he died in his sleep, protecting his favourite object.'

'What was that?'

'The chisel his mother gave him as a young man.'

'Is that true?'

Caitlin looked at the boy who was now floppy

69

with relief, like Rory on the sofa after school.

'Do you want it to be true?'

He nodded.

'Then who,' she said, still squatting on the floor looking at the miserable heap of bones, 'is to say it isn't?'

Later, Lesley, walking in from the museum's pedimented carriage entrance after seeing the class safely back on the bus, said, 'I don't know what you did, but that kid with the sellotaped glasses went home a different boy.'

'I told him the crouched burial was an artist called Fred who used to carve crocodiles out of sand.'

Lesley was still laughing by the time they were in the Great Hall again. Her throaty cackles ricocheted off the coloured stone pillars like pinball marbles, disappearing up into the glass roof. The steward on the cash desk looked up, saw it was Lesley, and looked down again.

'You know what all this is about, don't you?'

Lesley's eyes were wide with conjecture as they crossed the terrazzo floor. Above them, suspended from rafters in the cavernous ceiling space, was a gigantic replica of a Box-kite aeroplane made for a comedy film shot in 1963 about flying machines. Three separate couples were each looking up at it, as if it were a great feat of early engineering rather than a large film prop made of balsa wood. Lesley reckoned she could buy a five quid urn from a garden centre and people would still spend time looking at it as long as it was in a glass case.

Caitlin and Lesley were oblivious to the faint smell of institutional disinfectant and the building's impossible acoustics as they walked back to their office. The museum was as run-of-the-mill to them now as a local government office might have been. Its grandeur certainly had its limitations. You couldn't have a private conversation in the great hall even if you whispered.

'This is all about Mark and that website.'

A lone male student sitting on one of the original walnut benches glanced up.

It was Caitlin's turn to break the hushed tones. Her hoot of derision shook awake a pensioner at one of the café tables but his eyes were closed again by the time they mounted the marble steps that would take them up a floor.

'You can't fill in the details of your husband's past because he won't let you, so you're making do with a pile of three-thousand-year-old bones instead.'

'I was just trying to stop the poor kid having nightmares!'

'The boy was a strategic pawn.'

'Well, I think we should give them *all* names.'

Lesley pushed a card into a slot to unlock one of the doors that led from the public gallery to the offices. 'The only name you're interested in is Nina Wills!'

The temperature was always a degree or two cooler on the stone landings behind the gallery walls and as the door opened, a blast of cold air came at them.

'I've only mentioned it once!'

'Really? Then you've got to admit, it's one of those names that has a personality before it has a face, don't you think?'

'I wonder what she looks like.'

'I can tell you.'

All the way up her arm, Caitlin's skin produced goosebumps. 'How?'

'I looked her up for you. These are her notes.'

The sight of Lesley handing her the piece of paper caught Caitlin just behind the knees, in that vulnerable crease that can bring someone down. Her legs buckled and she crumpled ever so slightly, hitting her right shoulder against the door frame which she disguised as a deliberately casual move.

'Well, go on! Don't you want to read them?'

As Caitlin put her hand out to receive the information being offered, she thought of the alabaster Eve on the small section of medieval frieze downstairs, holding out her arm for that apple. She was striking a bargain with herself.

'I guess I'll take both the knowledge and the consequences then please.'

She opened the folded sheet. The page was empty aside from two lines of plain font at the top.

It's a long story but I'm back in Bristol after seventeen years running bars and hotels in Greece and Turkey. Single again, living in happy poverty with my fifteen-year-old daughter and just been offered a job working part-time in a junk shop! Successful career woman or what? Would love to hear from anyone who remembers me.

'Bristol?' Caitlin tried to laugh it off. 'She's here in this city?'

'I thought you ought to know.'

'Well, Mark will be pleased.' Caitlin handed the paper back.

'Keep it,' Lesley advised. 'Show him. I bet he runs a mile!'

'What if he doesn't?'

A gust of insecurity whipped around her ankles. She thought of the little boy with the broken spectacles and Rory at bedtime. Sometimes, you really did need the full story.

'Ali?' she spoke into the phone a minute later. 'Sorry I couldn't speak earlier. Do you fancy lunch?'

Six

'Truth or dare!'

Vanessa Jones got up from the floor in a movement reminiscent of infant dance lessons – 'imagine you are a tiny seed growing into a big tree' – and uncurled herself to take centre stage on the sustainably grown European softwood boards.

For a family of journalists, the Joneses were

such physical communicators. Vanessa's mother Lou, sitting cross-legged and bare-footed on a sofa opposite, smiled indulgently at her performing daughter, swept one side of her long, ash-blonde hair over the top of her head and took up her notepad. Next to her, Caitlin, being nosey, watched her scribble down two phrases – 'self-sufficient entertainment' and 'kids all exuding clean energy' – in her notebook.

Lou's contrived thoughts never made it as far as her final drafts. The travel articles that eventually appeared under her name in the monthly glossy for women of a certain age were sharp and uncluttered but, like her suitcase packing, Lou's jottings were always crammed with surplus frippery. She saw Caitlin taking a peek.

'They are though, aren't they?' she whispered to her friend, underlining the word 'kids'. 'Particularly Olly.'

Lou's fourteen-year-old son Olly hadn't yet mentioned the lack of his PlayStation. Normally, twice a day, with the lumbering resignation of a bored cow in a milking parlour, Lou and Chris's youngest child would plug himself into his console and fulfil his quota. He was the sort of teenager that parents brace themselves for – spotty, gormless, awkward around adults – and he made Kit and Dylan shine in comparison.

Lou peeled off the second of her three precautionary layers. Bare-armed now in a silk cashmere vest, she picked up her pen again and noted that despite there being no heating system, she was as warm as organic wholemeal toast in Britain's first purpose-built earth-sheltered self-sufficient holiday chalet. She smiled an 'I was right and you were wrong' smile across the room at her husband Chris. He half smiled back.

Lou had certainly cornered a certain travel writing market. It wasn't every freelance who could muster a party of ten adults and children at short notice. The chance to 'test dwell' this spanking new eco-building in the wooded grounds of a manor house near Bath had her name on it from the moment the non-toxic paint had dried.

'Learn how easy it is to live in harmony with the environment,' Chris had read from the brochure a week ago in a voice that suggested he'd rather not. *'Eat food produced from our own organic farm, or fish from our own lake. Electricity provided by the wind, heating by the sun, water from the rain* ... Freeze, starve or die of thirst in the dark with Holistic Holidays, oh God, do we have to?'

The question was fair enough. Lou's travel writing had provided as many uncomfortable, boring, exhausting and ludicrous experiences as it had luxurious, relaxing, delicious ones, but his wife was a persuasive Pollyanna. And there was always the promise of sex, which somehow was much more celebratory away from home.

'I really think Caitlin needs a break,' Lou had wheedled. 'She and Mark...' and as she'd rocked her hand as if searching for a balance, Chris had suddenly remembered his suspicion that he'd caught Mark in some furtive act at the office the other day – all those radio tapes on the floor, and his flustered explanation about some squatting archive or other.

'Go on then,' Chris had said. 'I'm game if the Webbs are. But is there a TV? I'm not missing the rugby.'

Thanks to Lou's travel writing, the two families were used to being thrown together on neutral ground at short notice. They did it with such ease and regularity that the discovery of private details like who wore what to bed had long ceased to be a revelation. Everyone knew that Chris never uttered a word in the morning until he'd had a cup of tea, that Lou stayed in bed until he brought her one, that Caitlin would be the first up but last dressed, that Mark was edgy and restless if he couldn't get a newspaper.

This weekend's break, though, seemed to be missing the usual predictability. Mass puberty had completely disrupted the familiar routine of sleep patterns and bathroom habits, and already, the reservoir-fed, heavily insulated hot water tank was empty.

'It won't do you any harm to go dirty for a day,' Caitlin had huffed at Kit when he'd complained about it. It wasn't so long ago that he used to wear his football-match mud on his shins like a trophy for days.

Still, they were all cosy and happy now.

'Come on, truth or dare!' Vanessa trilled again from the centre of her performing circle.

Before this sudden burst of animation, she'd

been sitting between Kit's legs, using his bent limbs as arm rests. Vanessa had draped and sprawled and hooked herself around everyone practically since birth, so no one thought anything of it. No one except Kit, that is.

Her sleepy audience stirred from the horse-shoe of red sofa beds and deep blue armchairs that separated one end of the chalet's open living space from the other. Rory, a chrysalis in a sleeping bag, twitched in his newly suspended consciousness, Joss was endeavouring to stay awake from his nest of cushions in front of the only non-solar source of heating – the wood burner.

Kit, Dylan and Vanessa's brother Olly were sitting with their backs against the sofas, their knees almost up to their chins, warm beer cans in their hands, superior in their late-night staying power.

Behind them, on solid biscuits of upholstered, natural fibre but sinking nonetheless, were their mothers who had spent the last hour enjoying the forgotten privilege of seeing the tops of their sons' heads again.

Caitlin noticed the swirl of Dylan's double crown, and remembered with a pang the bad-hair days of primary school, the wayward crests he used to sport at breakfast. He was always such a hot little sleeper. It was as much as she could do to stop herself reaching out and strok-ing him, but there were unspoken rules attached to these weekends and a ban on physical dis-plays of parental affection was one of them.

Only Rory sought her hand in a crowd these days.

Vanessa rotated on the balls of her pretty little feet, with her arms outstretched like a roulette wheel, as if there were some random element in the choice she were about to make. She was wearing a pair of mint green tracksuit bottoms with working side zips that ran from her ankle to her waist and were currently undone to the knee, and a fitted fluffy white gilet over a cap-sleeved yellow tee shirt. She looked like one of the fairy trumpets she used to make from dandelion stalks.

Her arrowed hands wavered desultorily between the adults and then swung back to fall on Kit, as he'd been expecting them to.

'Kit Webb!' Vanessa pounced. 'I choose you!'

Olly let out a moan of frustration. Kit was *his* friend.

'What's truth or dare?' Joss struggled to ask from his cocoon.

'You get asked a question, and you have to either answer it truthfully or do a dare,' Vanessa answered. 'Like this, look.'

She fixed her gaze directly on Kit.

'Kit, is it true you are a virgin?'

'Vanessa!'

Lou shouted so crossly that Mobo, their black Labrador, sat up and barked. Rory flinched in his bag.

Caitlin was grateful to be behind Kit just then. She looked across at Mark, who was red with anger. He got up and lifted the slumbering Rory over his shoulders like a fireman.

'He doesn't have to answer,' Vanessa said with a grin. 'He can always do a dare instead. You have to ask embarrassing questions or it doesn't work. Watch.'

She looked straight at Kit again, who curled one side of his mouth in uncertainty.

'Kit, is it true you like chocolate?'

'Only milk.' He turned the curl upwards into a smile.

'See?' Vanessa said, her arms outstretched and her palms upturned. 'Not exactly interesting, is it?'

'My turn,' Caitlin said sternly, hissing to protect her goslings. 'Vanessa, is it true you like being the centre of attention?'

'Of course!' Vanessa swayed in the breeze of disapproval. She thrived on ill winds lately. 'That means I get another go, so I can ask someone else a question. Caitlin, is it true you like Olly more than me?'

'Vanessa!' Lou shouted again.

'It's a *game*, Mum.'

'I like it,' Joss said from the cocoon.

'Joss,' Caitlin said softly, 'if you don't go to bed now, Dad might give Rory the top bunk.'

The ten-year-old, almost dead on his feet but doing his best to look reluctant, got up and followed his father.

'Good,' said Vanessa rubbing her hands, 'now we can get really serious!'

Chris shifted uncomfortably in his armchair and wished to God Lou had let the virgin question go. He didn't have the energy to get defensive on his daughter's behalf at this time of night. Of course they all championed their own children. Of course both couples privately condemned aspects of each others' parenting. Of course they all cast aspersions elsewhere. He just didn't want it to happen at this precise moment, when there was nowhere to run.

'Caitlin? Hesitation...' Vanessa teased.

'Sleeping plan flaw,' Lou jotted down in her notebook. 'Snared by circumstance.' The sofa beds that were supposed to accommodate the four teenagers were currently occupied by the wine-lazy adults, and one could hardly decamp to a bedroom without making a point, even though the master bedroom did house a large, energy-efficient plasma screen satellite TV recessed into the lagged and soundproofed concrete walls. 'Not suitable for warring families at Christmas,' she footnoted.

'No, it is not true that I like Olly more than you,' Caitlin answered curtly. She didn't like either of the Jones children much at the moment, but she used to, and she would do again. As the only girl among five boys, Vanessa could so easily have been out on a limb. Instead, she had constantly given an arm and a leg to be in there, and Caitlin had to give her credit for that. 'Now what happens?'

'I can challenge you,' Vanessa said. 'I say it *is* true that you like boys better than girls.'

'No, it isn't.'

'But I have evidence.'

'Hit us with it then,' Chris said too cheerily.

'When I was younger, Caitlin was always pregnant, and I used to ask you to try and have a girl, didn't I, Caitlin?'

'You did, I remember that.'

'So obviously you didn't try hard enough! If you'd really wanted a girl, you'd have got one!'

The room relaxed, but Vanessa immediately delivered another salvo.

'And furthermore,' she said, 'I heard you say so to Mum earlier.'

'Say what?' Lou asked twitchily.

'You were complaining about the amount of clothes I packed and Caitlin said thank God she didn't have any daughters.'

'No she didn't. She said there had to be some compensations for having all boys.'

'That's not saying she likes boys better than girls,' Dylan said from the floor.

'Yes it is. And I also heard her say she wouldn't want to be in Mum's shoes.'

'But I'd *love* to be in Lou's shoes,' Caitlin said, picking up a quail-coloured suede babouche, 'they're gorgeous!'

'So you must have been lying! I win! I win!'

As Vanessa hollered with victory, the row of teenage boys with their backs against the sofa began to bay, like politicians in the Commons, for blood.

'Dare! Dare!'

'Now you've got to tell us your most embarrassing moment, Caitlin!' Vanessa sat triumphantly back down on a large black cushion between Kit's open legs again. Olly scowled and kicked her feet away from his.

'Why d'you have to sit there?'

'I don't have to. I want to.'

'Kit might not want you to.'

'I'm all right,' said Kit.

'OK,' Caitlin started, thinking she owed it to the weekend to jolly things along a bit. 'You know when you take your pants and your trousers off at the same time? And you leave them on the chair in the bedroom and put them on again the next day? Well, when I was teaching, one of my Year Six kids started waving something red in the air, and shouting, "Miss, I've found a pair of knickers on the floor!"'

'No!' Lou mouthed at her, but it was too late. Kit and Dylan were puce. A dirty pants story from their mother!

'They had a Scotty dog in a tartan bow on the front ... they must have worked their way down the leg of my trousers...'

'A dog on your knickers?' Vanessa nodded approvingly. 'That is embarrassing...'

Dylan got up off the floor and took advantage of the space his father had left on the sofa bed. He took off his pungent trainers, laughed uncouthly when Kit and Olly hurled personal insults at him for his contribution to the chalet air, and stretched out.

'Sorry about all that,' Lou apologized, when Mark came back in.

'What we forget,' Chris said, more relaxed now that the tasteless stream of bad underwear and stinking body parts stories had run dry, 'is that this lot are the first generation to be weaned on reality TV. The promise of a nervous breakdown unravelling live on telly is their idea of a good evening in. It comforts them to know that there are people out there who are more mannerless and stupid, more emotionally underbred than they are themselves, it makes them feel superior.'

'Oh, thanks, Dad, that reminds me,' Vanessa said, 'Can we go and watch *Celebrity Little Sister* in your room?'

'Celebrity *what*?'

'The younger sisters of two boy bands are sharing a Caribbean beach house with their brothers and last night, one of them slept with both twins and I want to see what...'

'Three of them are gay,' Olly grunted.

'And one of the little sisters is pregnant,' Dylan said.

'How little?'

'They're all legal, if that's what you're asking.'

'God help us,' said Chris, shaking his head. 'You're all making me feel very, very old.'

An hour later, the three teenagers lying under the gloriously weighty feather duvet in Chris and Lou's room had an aggregate age of almost forty-six. Fourteen and a quarter of those years was asleep on the far side, in an alcohol-induced coma, head at the head, large feet at the foot, brain somewhere else altogether. Olly's beery dribble was already leaving a laddish stain on the unbleached cotton pillow.

Kit, representing fifteen and a half years, lay upside down next to his friend's bare toes in the middle of the bed, his chin resting on folded arms, pretending to watch the TV. The remaining sixteen years, embodied by Vanessa's stretched torso, was on the narrow margin of mattress nearest the door.

The side zips on her trousers were now undone all the way, and her alabaster legs seemed to be enjoying the freedom. As she rolled around like a cat near the catmint, her bare skin kissed the other fabrics nearby – the soft, brushed cotton of the duvet, the washed-out canvas of Kit's own trousers. The loose spearmint-coloured material of her tracksuit bottoms had bunched between her legs, where she felt padded and warm.

Fully dressed but crumpled under the feather quilt, Kit was cosy too. It was dark in the room save for the glow of the neat wide monitor set squarely into the back wall, and he felt more confident for being undefined. Every now and again, in the style of a 'Who is it?' round on a television quiz, glimmers and flickers from the plasma screen illuminated a cheekbone, an ear, a hand.

He and Vanessa were aware of lots of things – each other's proximity, Olly asleep next to them, their four parents in a room only a corridor away, like guards playing poker while the prisoners dug the tunnel. Escape, though, was not on Kit's mind. He was enjoying the captivity, hemmed in by inertia on one side and

84

restlessness on the other. He liked knowing he could join either one, whenever he wanted to. No pressure.

On the plasma screen, reality TV had lost out to fantasy. An American woman was working late in a high-rise office building. Her neck was aching so naturally she had to undo a tight French plait and bundle up her loose long hair with one hand before she could rub it with the other.

'She's going to have sex,' Vanessa predicted quietly. 'Any minute now, she's going to have sex.'

Kit kept very still. Her elbow was touching his. Elbows were not his favourite body part: the red rough pimples on his own sometimes spread to his upper arm where he squeezed them and made a mess. The way they poked unattractively out from tee shirt sleeves reminded him of embarrassed tortoises. But the prolonged connection with Vanessa's was having an effect.

'Who with?' he squeaked in a voice he thought he'd left behind.

On cue, a man in a suit appeared behind the woman and took over the role of masseur. She span in her plush leather office chair to face him.

'On the desk,' Vanessa whispered. 'What will you give me if it's on the desk?'

Kit pressed his body into the mattress. The woman, now spreadeagled against inlaid walnut, brought her legs up around her lover like a black widow spider catching its prey. Kit bit the skin on the back of his wrist.

Vanessa let her own legs fall from the air. The side of her right calf landed on the back of Kit's left. An hour ago, when she'd had an audience, her contact with him had been overt, pointed, showy. This was delicate, gentle, discreet. He remained stock-still, with the expressionless concentration of a joy rider contemplating driving over a cliff.

On screen, the couple embraced, entwined and engaged just six feet from his face. The woman had brown, hard nipples that were almost permanently in shot. The man had tight white buttocks with a dip in each side that suggested control. Together, they moaned and cooed and sighed. The woman's hair fell over the parapet of the desk, Vanessa's fell over the pillow. The man's head rocked above the woman's with the slow rhythm of experience. Kit's heart thumped at twice the beat.

Quickly, Kit pushed his forearms down so his head and shoulders were off the mattress and turned. He didn't quite know what he was going to do next, but it turned out not to be his decision.

Vanessa's reactions verged on the robotic. She lifted her face, parted her mouth and she put her lips between his. Suction happened.

Instantly, his world was reduced to a sensation of wet stirring. Their jaws circled, teeth clunked, tongues searched. His technique was rubbery and wet against her experienced direction but still he moved his lips round and round. The more he did, the hungrier he got. He wanted to peel her and eat her.

There were armholes but no flesh, material edges but no entry, straps but no bra. His hand pushed a clumsy way in, rubbed against mesh, a nipple, surely a nipple, trapped underneath. Where was the springy tenderness of her breasts he'd imagined? They were restrained or flattened by something stretchy which forced him to retreat. She stopped trying to undo his shirt and pulled something. A Lycra membrane flew above her head and suddenly, supple lithe skin slipped beneath his hands.

Sharp, painful pulses throbbed in his groin as he found a soft cushion of tissue and played with it. Should he squeeze it or stroke it? His body jerked in a desperate convulsion, a clueless thrusting. He cupped her breast, found its centre, lost it, tried to find it again with his mouth. Through the canvas of his trousers, she felt a hardness banging against buttons. He ran a palm up a leg and came across a wad of material, but she shifted and his fingers caught the teeth of a zip, a way in.

Then somehow his trousers were around his knees, his penis leaping out of the slit in his boxers like a greyhound out of a trap. She gripped it for a second and then he was on top of her, pushing, thrusting, heaving, pitching, tossing. The tempo of their own dance jarred farcically with the carefully choreographed one being played out on the screen behind them.

Vanessa was pushing her pelvis towards him. Pubic bones crashed against each other, folds of material and warmth and skin enveloped them, and then it happened. Fluid burst from him, over or into what he didn't know. As it kept on coming in short, exasperated spurts, she put a hand over his mouth to keep him quiet. When he collapsed beside her, feeling an entirely different sort of confusion to the one he had felt earlier, he noticed to his horror a pool of something from him in the dip of her navel.

'You *are* a virgin, aren't you?' she whispered.

He fell on to his back, feeling like a close second in a 1,500 metre sprint. If she hadn't asked him, he wouldn't have been entirely sure.

Seven

The picture postcard village's 'local produce sale', held every other Saturday under the tiled roof of the seventeenth-century octagonal Yarn Market, was even more conscious of its desirability than Vanessa, thought Mark as Lou led the way through the studiously chic stalls the next morning.

Caitlin and Chris had fallen behind, sidetracked by old postcards of the area – an ancient stone bridge once used by packhorses, a cobbled street, a gnarled old man with the kind of beard you never see any more. Mark knew Caitlin would buy one, and that it would end up in her already full desk along with all the others. He also knew that Chris wouldn't, not just because the thought of second-hand goods made him slightly squeamish, but also because for Chris to gain pleasure from acquisition, he had to feel the pain of a considerable hole in his bank account. These time-earned details of each other's 'little ways' peppered their mutual teasing but, for Mark at least, they also acted as buffers, a safe place to stop the advance of total intimacy. Mark had grown out of the need to know his friends' secrets at about the same time he'd grown out of a taste for six pints of lager and a doner kebab.

But what about *his* shopping list? Did he want *Smokey Joe's organic salmon, smoked slowly over naturally fallen oak from our own estate* or *Artisan English butter flapjacks – food artistry from the soul*? Some crunchy apples and a bit of cheese would do the job to be honest, but he had been partnered with Lou this morning, and Lou was on a mission.

As she said 'in the interests of investigative journalism', if these traders really expected to be able to sell their wares at London prices then they could jolly well answer a few London questions.

'What's the Tricklemore goat's cheese like?'

'Is the vanilla in your pecan cookies Madagascan?'

'This *confit de tomates fumées* ... is it more chutney than sauce or more sauce than chutney would you say?'

Mark found her pretence both amusing and

embarrassing but he wasn't sure which of the two he should display, facially speaking. Thinking it was safer to opt for neither, he remained expressionless.

'You in a bad mood?' Lou asked him when they had plonked their cloth tote bags – the ones they'd found hanging on pegs at the chalet under a sign that read, 'Take Me Shopping' – by the tiled well where they'd arranged to meet the children. 'You didn't have to come. You could have stayed at the chalet and read the papers.'

'Not at all, why?'

'You're a tad stony-faced.'

'Don't worry about that, it's just my way of disassociating myself from you. I don't want the locals to think I'm another of those up-country folk coming down here with their flash city ways...'

'You disassociate yourself from everything these days!'

'Like what?'

'Oh, you know, your best and oldest friends, your family, your...'

'Don't you start.'

Lou laughed and snapped a biscuit in half, giving him the bigger bit. She liked being with Mark when Caitlin and Chris weren't around. They enjoyed a sort of low level sexual teasing that she believed kept their four handed friendship a little edgy. Mark just believed she was an incorrigible flirt.

'It's true – you never used to be so detached...'

'That's my wife talking, is it?'

'Not this time, no.'

'What do you mean, detached?'

'It's like you're somewhere else half the time these days...'

'Where?'

'How am I supposed to know? It's just that you opt out, as if you're bored with it all...'

'I don't mean to...'

'I'm just telling you that's the way it comes across.'

Mark scratched the back of his neck uncomfortably. Lou's accusations made him feel bleak. She was confirming his own creeping view.

'Surely everyone gets a bit bored every now and again...'

'So you are?'

'Not bored exactly. It's nothing terminal. It's probably something to do with being forty.'

Lou brushed off the cookie crumbs from her sweater by pinching the delicate wool between her breasts and shaking it.

'You don't mind me saying this, do you?'

'I don't know what you *are* saying. You and Caitlin talk in riddles. I mean, exactly *how* do I opt out? Give me an example.'

He asked it like one of his sons might ask him for the meaning of a long word they hadn't heard before. Lou thought, not for the first time, how incredibly unaware he sometimes was.

'Well, you never used to stand back and let stuff happen but now you just sort of go along with the flow, you're happy for life to...'

'What sort of stuff?'

'Everyday stuff, you know, like this picnic. The idea of getting into a hired canoe, rowing across a man-made lake and eating lunch on a fake island doesn't appeal as much as watching the rugby with Chris, does it? You'd much rather cycle to the pub...'

'Put like that...'

'So, you should have said.'

'But then I really would have been opting out.'

Lou laughed. 'Bit of a flaw in my argument there!'

'You see what it's like for men? They can't win.'

'Chris does all right. He's doing his own thing this afternoon and no one is holding it against him.'

'He's not married to Caitlin.'

'When has she ever stopped you doing something you wanted to do?'

'Yeah, but hey, come on, we're on a family weekend away. I wouldn't be much of a father if I sat in front of the telly all afternoon...'

'The boys would watch it with you.'

'The younger two wouldn't, not out of preference.'

'But if you led the way...'

'It's not what I do...'

'That's what I mean. You let things happen to you, rather than making things happen. You're reactive rather than proactive.'

'But I've always been that!'

He saw a child approaching, wanting food or cash or an answer to how much longer they were going to be. It was all three of those things as it turned out, and by the time he'd dealt with it, his conversation with Lou had all but come to an end.

'I'm happy just mucking along,' he said, not wanting to leave things with him on the defensive.

'Then you live in danger of always being part of someone else's agenda.'

'And what if I don't have my own agenda?'

'Everyone has an agenda, Mark...'

'Do they?'

'Give over,' Lou said with a laugh, breaking a second biscuit, 'I'm not *that* stupid. Here, have this and cheer up for God's sake!'

The clay-lined lake – built into the contours of the land a year earlier by a fleet of swing shovels and bulldozers – still looked like a newcomer. Its naked sides had yet to disguise themselves with the bullrushes, gunnera and grasses that had been submerged in weighted pots around its edges and its central island was no bigger than the Yarn Market. There was nothing other than its mirror-glass calm to entice guests on to it but the children – minus Olly who was currently cycling along a towpath with his father to watch the rugby on a flat-screen TV in the local pub – were eager to cross.

'I've just realized there aren't enough adult life jackets to get you all over,' the young lad on canoe hire duty informed Lou nervously.

'How many are there?'

'Er ... two.'

'*Two*?' Lou repeated, secretly delighted to be able to find fault at last. Her articles were always better for that little gripe.

'We're not strictly open yet. This is just a press weekend.'

'Yeah, it doesn't matter if a few journalists drown...' Caitlin muttered.

'That's nice,' Mark said. It seemed to him that as far as his wife was concerned, he might as well not be here. She was either talking to Lou or Chris, or dealing with the kids. So far today, he couldn't be sure they had actually made eye contact.

'What? It was a *joke*...'

'Mark, you could always go and join Chris and Olly...' Lou suggested. 'The match hasn't started yet. Text them and tell them to wait...'

'No, I'm OK. I'll stick around here.'

Caitlin pulled the sort of face that Dylan made at Joss or Rory whenever they said something inept.

'What was that for?'

'I'm not sure that was a suggestion. I think it was more of a solution.'

'Only if you want to,' Lou said to Mark pointedly.

'I was being gentlemanly...'

'How exactly?' Caitlin asked.

'By giving you or Lou the opportunity to get out of it.'

'Get out of what?'

'Oh, you mean you actually *want* to row the world's most expensive picnic across a murky

94

reservoir to a patch of waste land?'

The children were already on a fleet of orange sit-on kayaks. Rory's red life buoyancy aid was up to his ears. The nose of Dylan's craft was touching the tail of Joss's, making it wobble. Vanessa was squealing to Kit like a damsel in not much distress.

'Of course I do. Why else would I be doing it?' Caitlin replied.

'See?' Lou smiled, tossing him her press card. 'Agendas.'

'What's this for?'

'Your pass to happiness. Free bike hire, free internet access, free drinks at the bar. Use it wisely.'

'Thanks, Lou.'

He slipped the card into his back pocket and went to kiss Caitlin goodbye but she was distracted by a playful scream at just the wrong moment. Oh, fine, he thought. The turn of her body away from him and towards the children just proved his point.

'Caligula!' Chris shouted that night, slapping his thighs with gratification. Mark clapped his hands, his feet off the floor for a split second.

'What a film!'

Since the children had dispersed, Lou had migrated to curl up with Chris but Caitlin and Mark remained a distance apart.

'It was awful!'

'But it worked.'

'Did it?'

She could hardly believe what she was hearing, but next to her on the foam sofa, the man she had shared a bed with almost every one of the last 6,000 nights of their marriage was admitting, in the way that she might discuss the merits of the Wonderbra, that porn did something for him.

'Too right it did.'

'Is this the beer talking?'

'He's only had half a pint!' Chris teased. 'Half a pint! And he turns up ten minutes from the end of the game! That's not watching the rugby!'

There was a game that her boys played called 'Trust Me', in which you fell backwards from a standing position, eyes shut, into the arms of your faithful brethren without bottling out. As catcher, Mark had just broken the golden rule and walked away from her, mid-fall.

When she'd boldly stated a minute ago that her husband came from the rare breed of men who genuinely preferred the real thing – even if that happened to be once a fortnight in bed with your wife – to some stratospheric scenario involving others, then she'd honestly not expected him to answer, 'Yes, I prefer the *idea,* of course I prefer the *idea,* but Chris is asking about being given a direct choice.'

In her stultified state, she had asked, 'So you *do* fantasize about other women then?'

The disbelieving peals of laughter from Lou and Chris on the other sofa hadn't helped. And now, as if all that wasn't bad enough, he was telling them, in the style of dinner party anecdote, a story she considered private.

'So we sat there in Caitlin's flat watching this film in the darkness, and her hand crept across to my lap, and just as I was thinking, this is the girl for me, she suddenly leapt up...'

'Mark, shut up...'

'A pervert I think you called me, didn't you?'

Mark gingerly attempted to put his hand on her thigh, showing he knew full well how thin the ice was he was skating on.

'I wasn't expecting it,' Caitlin said. The tips of her words were sharp with frost. 'I was young.'

'Caitlin! It was a film famous for women fondling each other...'

'It was a bit of tacky porn. How was I supposed to know that would turn you on?'

Chris brought his dad's smile out of retirement, the one he used to use for the children's endearing naiveties. Caitlin's puritanical streak made him curious.

'Would it still shock you now?'

'Well, for a start, we'd have to be sharing a sofa,' Caitlin rattled through a mouthful of ice cubes.

'We're sharing one now,' Mark pointed out.

'And I'd have to have my hand on his lap...'

'Hey, have you two ever read any Nancy Friday?' Lou asked quickly. She was beginning to feel responsible for Mark's behaviour.

'Nancy Friday?'

Caitlin guessed the name might have something to do with sex. She and Mark used to snigger about the slightly desperate way Chris and

97

Lou banged on about their life in the bedroom, but that was in the days when the two of them favoured discretion, as opposed to lack of anything to report.

'Is that the book you keep putting out when people are coming round? What's it called? *My Kitchen Garden* or something?'

'*My* Secret *Garden...*'

The Jones marriage seemed to have in it everything that the Webb marriage did not. Artifice, infidelity, furious rows, elaborate making-up ceremonies. When Chris and Lou were good, it was very, very good, but when they were bad, it was horrid. Mark and Caitlin kept their conjugality within more judicious limits.

'I'll lend it to you,' Lou said to Caitlin across the great divide. She was proud of her Nancy Friday knowledge. As a student, *My Secret Garden* had been an essential accessory for all thinking women.

'What is it?' Caitlin asked innocently.

'It's a book about women's fantasies. Friday was a journalist for *Cosmo* in the late 1960s, and when she asked readers to send in their erotic fantasies, she got so many replies she made a book out of them.'

'Women have fantasies?' Chris teased, sliding his hand up his wife's cashmere vest.

'Yes, we all lie in bed imagining our husbands watching us make love with other women.'

'In the mud?'

'Naturally...'

'You're very quiet,' Mark said to Caitlin, turn-

98

ing and trying to kiss the side of her cheek. He only managed a peck at the air.

'Bugger off,' she said. 'You're being horrible.'

'I'm only messing around.'

'Well, don't. I feel like I don't know you any more.'

'Rubbish. You know me too well. That's the problem.'

'You're the most secretive man I know.'

'Like how?'

'Like your entire past.'

'That's rubbish too. I tried to show you the stuff about the band on the website the other day and you walked off.'

'I had to cook the supper.'

He tried to put his arm around her but she shook it off.

'You're no fun any more,' Mark said.

'Why, because I won't join in a stupid little conversation about porn?'

If he could embarrass her, then she could him.

'Yes.'

'OK then, if that's what you want, I will. Why don't you tell us your fantasies, Mark? Come on, what do you think about when you lie next to me in bed?'

'I'm looking forward to this,' Chris said, rubbing his hands in anticipation of revelation.

'Sheep.'

'Stop hiding behind recycled jokes.'

'How do you know they're jokes?'

'You've got one more chance or I'm going to bed,' Caitlin said, the question she dared not ask right on her bumper, flashing its headlights, beeping its horn.

'Truth or dare!' Chris challenged.

'Do you think about Nina Wills?'

Mark's eyes narrowed.

'Who's Nina Wills?' Lou asked.

'The ex-girlfriend that's back in Bristol,' Caitlin said sourly.

'How do you know she's back in Bristol?' Mark asked.

'I read her notes. Lesley gave them to me and then Ali and I had lunch and she gave me a blow-by-blow account of your relationship with her...'

'Blow-by-blow, eh?'

Caitlin and Mark ignored Chris. Lou thumped him playfully.

'What, the fact that we went out for a few months and then she dumped me to go travelling? Big deal.'

'And you stopped eating.'

'That is not true!'

'Does this get any more interesting?' Lou asked. Really, she was riveted.

'According to Vanessa's rules, you can now dare Mark, Caitlin.'

'Dare away,' said Mark.

'OK. Then I dare you to email her,' Caitlin said.

Mark got up to get another beer.

'You're too late,' he smiled joylessly. 'I did that this afternoon.'

Eight

From: Mark Webb <mwebb@saltpeter.co.uk>
To: Nina Wills <nwills@hotmail.com>
Sent: 1 October, 2008, 16:55
Subject: Hi!

Would that be the Nina Wills who once told me she would 'phone me soon'?

From: Nina Wills (mailto:nwills@hotmail.com)
To: Webb, Mark
Sent: 2 October, 2008, 13:16
Subject: Re: Hi!

Is that the Mark Webb who once told me I looked like a pugnacious troll? How are you? What have you been doing all this time? I made some extremely stupid mistakes after leaving Bristol (maybe that was my first). Ten years running a hotel with a control freak in Turkey was the biggest, but I'm back now, living just around the corner from my old squat. I'm working a few hours a week in a junk shop – the one I used to buy my furniture from – Lad in Cave – remember? Haven't I come a long way? Where are you? I'd love to see you again. Nina x

From: Webb, Mark
To: Nina Wills
Sent: 5 October, 2008. 17:12
Subject: Re: Hi!

Not pugnacious troll, but 'elf in combats', which is very different. I came across the original recording the other day (OK, I was looking for it). I sound about five. I read your website notes so I know you have a daughter. How old is she? I'm embarrassed to say I've been in Bristol 'all this time' but stopped going to Lad in Cave years ago (Habitat now innit?). I'd love to see you too, but I'll have to have a hair transplant and go on the Atkins diet first.

Mark

From: Nina Wills (mailto:nwills@hotmail.com)
To: Webb, Mark
Sent: 6 October, 2008 17:23
Subject: Re: Hi!

What's the Atkins diet?

From: Webb, Mark
To: Nina Wills
Sent: 8 October, 2008 17:48
Subject: Re: Hi!

You have been out of the country for too long. Tell me more about your mistakes.

From: Nina Wills (mailto:nwills@hotmail.com)
To: Webb, Mark
Sent: 9 October, 2008 12:29
Subject: Re: Hi!

I made too many to even start. Was I a complete bitch? I'm really sorry. I'd like to apologize to your face (even if you are fat and bald). My daughter's called Chloe, and she's the best thing that ever happened to me. I have to confess I looked up 'saltpeter' and found a Salt Peter Productions in Bedminster. Is that where you work? What is it? A fireworks factory? What happened to your journalism? Love N x

From: Webb, Mark
To: Nina Wills
Sent: 10 October, 2008 18:24
Subject: Re: Hi!

It's my TV production company. (Catch the documentary about skateboarding at 7.30 on BBC 2 this Thursday.) Drink some time?

Mark x

From: Nina Wills (mailto:nwills@hotmail.com)
To: Webb, Mark
Sent: 10 October, 2008 18:10
Subject: Re: Hi!

I thought you'd never ask, but you're as cagey as ever! Your own TV production company? Wow! But are you married? Divorced? Kids? Nina xx

From: Webb, Mark
To: Nina Wills
Sent: 11 October, 2008 15:48
Subject: Re: Hi!

I had a wife of sixteen years and four boys the last time I counted.

M x

As Nina read his reply, she felt her breath leave her, as if one of Mark's myriad sons had kicked a wet leather football right through the screen into her stomach. But what was she winded by? Jealousy, shock, inadequacy, disappointment? Whatever it was, it rendered the idea of reunion too humiliating.

The bay-windowed room was empty apart from the computer. Offcuts of the newly fitted chocolate-coloured carpet lay in discarded curls on the floor, showing their paler underbellies with the same lack of inhibition as a submissive puppy. Grasping for the domestic wholeness that she now imagined everyone else in the whole world to have apart from her, Nina idly wondered if she and Chloe ought to get a dog, to pad themselves out a bit.

On top of the strewn heaps of landlord-funded

floor covering was a tangle of wires twisting messily from the socket to modem, computer and screen. Her new PC kept crashing, she hadn't yet been able to get the printer to work and there wasn't yet a desk to put it on. She thought again about the accusation made in the squat all those years ago, about her inability to experiment with a new form of living, how she hid instead in the security of recreating her old one. Maybe it was valid. Perhaps this bold up-heaval that had taken every ounce of her courage was not brave at all. Maybe her move back to Bristol was as flimsy as the decision she had once made to move to Turkey. It was conceivable that all she ever managed to do was follow men. Was that what she was doing now? Was this contact with Mark a lazy way out? Why had she come back to Bristol when she could have tried somewhere new? Why was she so emotionally attached to such a grubby little place as Lad in Cave? Why *didn't* she go to Ikea like Chloe had wanted to?

She sat among the computer leads, cross-legged in a pair of rust-coloured silk designer combats, the closest thing she had to the real thing, and tried to think of a witty enough reply. The tap-tap-tap of her nails hitting the keys echoed, making the house feel even emptier.

From: Nina Wills (mailto:nwills@hotmail.com)
To: Webb, Mark
Subject: Hi again

What time and where? Can't believe you're a father of four boys!! Have they all got the same mother?!

She tried to look at the message objectively. Maybe there were too many exclamation marks. She took them out.

From: Nina Wills (mailto:nwills@hotmail.com)
To: Webb, Mark
Subject: Hi again

What time and where? Can't believe you're a father of four boys. Have they all got the same mother?

Now it seemed there was a bitterness to it. She deleted and started again.

From: Nina Wills (mailto:nwills@hotmail.com)
To: Webb, Mark
Subject: Hi again

Four sons? I never knew you had it in you!

It was hopeless. Whatever she wrote had an echo of her former dismissiveness. She was like one of Pavlov's dogs, salivating at the ring of a bell, psychologically conditioned to undermine him, even though now he so clearly had the upper hand. He had his own TV production company. He had a wife of sixteen years (which Nina had already worked out meant that whilst

106

she had been in Greece, fondly imagining his heartbreak, he had, in fact, been falling much more significantly in love with someone else). He had four sons. Four!

She left the message unanswered and wandered upstairs to take another look at the large collection of ridiculously expensive clothes on her bed. She didn't know if the Lad would be interested in giving her something for them or not. His customers were mainly middle-class devotees of shabby chic, highly unlikely to be the kind to wear these lavishly beaded tops, leather-trimmed sweaters and suede trousers. Rauf had liked her to be showy and yet if she'd ever shown *too* much, he'd not liked it at all. The clothes reminded her of him, and despite the fact that she could not afford to replace them, she wanted them out of the house.

Besides, most of them were utterly untransferable to her new life. She picked up a wine-coloured satin bustier, wondering if it would work under a denim jacket, and walked with it towards Chloe's room. She could trust her daughter to be honest to the point of rudeness.

'Would you like wine with your meal?' a girl in a tight tee-shirt and long black apron asked.

'I'd better not,' Caitlin answered reluctantly.

'We'll have two glasses of house red,' Lesley said. 'Large, please.'

'Actually, sorry, not the Caesar salad – can I possibly change it to the goat's cheese? And some chips maybe,' Caitlin said.

107

'No problem.'

'Hold on, I think I'll stick with the Caesar salad after all, although if I can still have some ciabatta...'

'And the chips?'

'I know, scrap the ciabatta and keep the chips.'

'It's only lunch!' Lesley said with exasperation. 'It's not the last goddamn supper!'

The waitress took her fixed smile off to another table and Caitlin slumped backwards, as if ordering had taken the last ounce of effort from her.

'Did I just order chips *and* bread?'

'You really do need to get out more!'

When the wine arrived they fell on it like a pair of alcoholics. They didn't often lunch together in Muirs, the bustling restaurant next to the museum where the handwritten menu was too long, the leather sofas too comfortable and the atmosphere too Palm Court for a workday sandwich, but when they did, they made the most of it. The Côtes du Rhône tasted wonderful to Caitlin today, sliding down her tight throat.

Over the shiny green olives, they moaned about work, speculated about the date of the next general election and swapped opinions about a novel they were both reading. And then, eventually, they got on to the subject they both knew they would.

'So come on, tell me, did you show Mark those notes I gave you?' Lesley asked.

'Didn't have to – he'd already checked. But

Nina Wills seems to have taken a back seat these days. It's his old university band now. He's found his old drummer who now lives in New York...'

'No way!'

'And they've got this ridiculous plan to try and get back together for a reunion gig...'

'Why is that ridiculous?'

'You haven't heard their music.'

Lesley raised her eyebrows.

'What?' asked Caitlin defensively. 'You try living with him. For a man who always claimed the past was only for people who were dissatisfied with their present, he's doing a good job of...'

'Does it matter what he used to think?'

'He's gone from reluctance to enthusiasm a bit too quickly, that's all...'

'So he's discovered that it's fun after all...'

'The band is all he can talk about – when he isn't playing his bloody guitar...'

'I suppose it's better than playing with Nina Wills...'

'True! Anyway, I decided that if I couldn't beat him, I'd join him, so I went on the website too and had a quick look at my old university intake year.'

'I've done that but it's only ever the people you don't really remember that sign up. All the cool ones...'

'Most of the names I still knew but I did find a guy called Paul Moffat...'

'Was he cool?'

'Not exactly! I'm so stupid – of all the people I shouldn't encourage...'

Lesley lifted one side of her mouth and braced herself for disastrous news. She didn't have to wait long.

'He'd replied within an hour, and he's been emailing me three times a day ever since.'

'Oh gawd, one of those...'

'I should have known. I mean, he used to worship me to the point of incoherence.'

'You used to go out with him?'

'Not exactly. He was a strange bloke. He wore eyeliner and fake tan and he didn't have many friends. He was usually on his own...'

'And you thought it might be fun to have him back in your life?'

Caitlin laughed. 'I know! But he was sweet too. He was so shy when we first met that nothing he said to me for the first few weeks actually made any sense and then when he did eventually master the art of communication, he never bloody stopped. He used to tell me he loved me a hundred times a day.'

Lesley's face was wearing an expression of pain.

'And then I spurned him for a builder with a tattoo across his neck.'

'Someone a little more manly?'

'That wouldn't have been difficult.'

'He sounds just irresistible.'

'I'm not looking for an affair, Lesley, I just wanted to experience a little of what Mark has been experiencing, except I picked the wrong friend I think...'

'Oh well, he doesn't need to know where you are, does he? You can always go quiet on him again. You could be in Kathmandu for all he knows.'

Caitlin bit her lip. 'Ah...'

'You didn't?'

Lesley took a swig of wine, and then another one.

'He asked me where I was living.'

'Oh, Bristol is plenty big enough...'

'No, I told him the road...'

'You gave him your address?'

'He said he knew Bristol really well. He's a book rep or something and he comes here twice a week.'

'So?'

'So I said we should meet up.'

'Right! That's that then, you've found your new best friend!'

'But I've already gone off the whole idea. I only sent the first email three days ago and I'm sure it was him I saw lurking outside our house this morning.'

'You *are* joking?'

Caitlin shook her head.

'Run this past me again. You send a friendly email to someone you haven't spoken to for twenty years and he appears outside your house within a few days?'

'But if he comes to Bristol twice a week anyway, I mean, it's not like he's making a special effort or anything.'

'Caitlin...'

'The thing with Moff is that you only ever had to throw him the tiniest crumb...'

'That sounds like an understatement. What on earth were you thinking of?'

Caitlin was quiet for a moment, wrapping a paper napkin around two forefingers.

'I saw his name there on the site and I remembered how much Mum liked him, and...'

'What would he be doing outside your house? Why wouldn't he go the whole hog and actually knock on your door?'

'It might not have been him.'

'But you know it was, don't you?'

'It's in character. It was what he used to do. He spent his entire time at university waiting outside doors for me.'

'That's called stalking,' Lesley felt obliged to point out.

The waitress put their food on the table and hurried away before Caitlin noticed the ciabatta in place of the chips.

'Oh, Paul's not sinister, he's just wet. He used to tell my mum he was prepared to wait for me forever. I think she was more upset than I was about the way it ended.'

Caitlin suddenly remembered how every time one of Paul Moffat's letters – reams of plagiarized declaration on lined A4 pushed into a cheap envelope – came through the door, her mother would do everything in her power to try and get her to write back. *He doesn't love you like I do,* he'd scrawl on tear-stained paper. *Only I can love you in the way you deserve to be loved.*

'Did it end in tears then?' Lesley asked, pulling at some brie oozing from the side of her panini.

'You could say that. I tried to tell him to leave me alone but he wouldn't. He staged a week-long vigil outside my room. He used to sit there for hours on the cold tiled floor with his back against the wall...'

'That's truly spooky, Caitlin.'

'It does sound it, I'll give you that. And then once, when my builder boyfriend came up for the weekend, Paul accosted him. He asked him why he always walked in front of me, and started telling him he should walk alongside me, and let me go through the door first and all that kind of nonsense, so obviously, my boyfriend head-butted him.'

'Choice.'

'I had to wash the blood off the paintwork...'

'Excellent.'

'And by the time I'd finished, both Paul and the builder had gone. So that was it on both counts.'

'Thank God you met Mark...'

'Who never tells me he loves me.'

'You'd like to be told a hundred times a day again, would you?'

'By Mark, yes...'

Lesley, who lived alone with two cats called Delilah and Babe, absorbed the distinction. Caitlin twisted the pepper over her plate.

'Did I order chips? I thought so. But the funny

thing is, in one way, I was quite relieved to see him there this morning. At the back of my mind, I always wondered if maybe he'd gone off and done something stupid.'

'I get it! This is your residual guilt coming out.' Lesley wiped a blob of cranberry from the corner of her mouth and licked her finger. 'But I'm still trying to understand why you thought it might be a good idea to get in touch with someone who only took the hint that he wasn't wanted after he'd been head-butted.'

'I told you, Mum liked him,' Caitlin said feebly.

'And that's it? You contacted a former stalker because you were jealous of Mark, and because your mum used to like him?'

Caitlin picked up a crouton with her fingers. 'I wish they'd bring my chips.'

'You're in touch with a stalker, Caitlin.'

'He wasn't, isn't, a stalker – and anyway, his was the only name on the list that I recognized and didn't still know. You've seen the size of my address book. I'm a serial correspondent.'

It was true. Some of the entries in her battered red leather ring bound book read like the plot of a soap opera. Sue and Dave, Cheltenham (deleted), Sue and Andy, and (in different pen), Jemima, Bath (deleted), Sue, Andy, Jemima and Ben, Australia.

All these years she'd preached to Mark about the perils of neglecting one's past and then all of a sudden, there he was, resurrecting his from nothing with the click of a mouse. It wasn't fair.

'And, just tell me again, did you actually give this Paul guy your full address?' Lesley looked at Caitlin with the same measured incredulity she used for the children who ate her flakes of mummy skin.

'He's safe,' Caitlin said, waving her away. 'He used to drink orange juice and drive at forty miles an hour.'

'That doesn't sound at all safe to me.'

'Stop making me worry. I was perfectly fine before you started...'

'If that's true, why didn't you stop and say hello to him this morning?'

'I was on my bike, on my way back from cycling with Joss and Rory to school. I didn't see him until the last minute and by that time a car was behind me, and then, I don't know, something in the way he moved, or was leaning or something ... I just thought, oh, there's Moff, as if I'd seen him yesterday. He just seemed so familiar. He had this way of looking slightly hurt all the time, like a Labrador puppy.'

'So you cycled straight past him?'

'It was a last-minute decision. I turned left just before I got to him and came straight to work.'

The chips arrived.

'Oh, good.'

'I wondered why one side of your hair was at forty-five degrees to the rest. Is that jumper Mark's?'

'He's gone off it,' Caitlin admitted, fiddling with the half zip of the grey ribbed sweater. 'He says it makes him look washed out.'

'Oh, I get it! That's why you didn't stop!' Lesley clapped with delight. 'The fact that you didn't say hello hasn't got anything to do with being scared or taken by surprise, has it? You didn't stop because you didn't think you were looking your best! You still want him to adore you!'

'Rubbish!'

'I bet you a chip it's not!'

Nine

Sheila Webb didn't need telling that measuring the length of fungal growth along a window ledge was the act of a woman with too much time on her hands, but at least there was nobody around to see her.

She would hate her family to think she might be bored or, worse still, lonely. They might start behaving like the children of her friend Pam who turned up in shifts, sharing the obligation between them. At the first sniff of a duty visit, Sheila was planning to go on a world cruise.

The last week had been spent casually pretending not to notice that the Witch's Butter had crept past the middle of the central pane of glass in the garden room. If it really was a vegetal gauge of her allocation on this earth, then she was in trouble.

'Better to look your fears in the eye,' she'd said to her daughter Ali over supper yesterday evening. Ali's unannounced sleepovers were getting to the stage where Sheila would invariably cook enough for two.

'What have I got to be scared of?' Ali had snapped.

'Life on your own?'

'Huh. Living with Rob is the perfect training,' her daughter had sniffed, as saturated with self-pity as the tea towel in the kitchen windowsill that was there to soak up the autumn condensation.

Like flatmates whose menstrual cycles end up coinciding, Sheila decided that both her cottage and her daughter must be entering their high maintenance season together. She wasn't going to be much help. Old-fashioned as it might sound, what they each needed was a bit of attention from a nice strong man, although where either of them was going to get one of those from, she had no idea.

This mushroom thing, however, she could see off on her own. She took the blue plastic tape measure – or 'superior tailoring rule' as the Chinese manufacturers called it – out of the drawer of the table that ran along the back wall of the garden room and, plucking a pencil out of the tub, went over to the window.

On the eastern white wall of the south-facing conservatory was a series of pencil marks that undulated across the bumpy surface like sonic waves. The first line had been made on Kit's third birthday, the last on Rory's eighth. Sometimes, so as not to disappoint, Sheila would tilt her hand upwards as it rested on her grandsons' heads and draw above her fingers, adding an inch or so. Joss's lines were now noticeably higher than he was, but accuracy was not the chart's purpose. Measuring them was a rare fixed moment in the boys' frenetic lives, and for the two minutes it took Sheila to plot their new dimensions, they stood still just long enough for her to rejoice in them.

She bent to look at the Witch's Butter. Up close, it wasn't as pretty as she'd originally thought. Its first growth had been like the flesh of a passion fruit ripe enough to burst out of its skin under the slightest manual pressure, but lately the fungus had become gelatinous and the folds were now oozing out of the rotting wood more like pus out of a septic wound.

Holding the tape measure against the wet window, she calculated its progress. If she took two feet to represent the equivalent of seventy-one years, then one foot would be thirty-five and a half – so which section of this orange and brown freak represented, for example, her fortieth year? She found a section just over half-way, which sported a flange more photo-genic than the rest. It reminded her of the exotic mushrooms she had spent ten minutes looking at in the supermarket the other day, chanterelle, shitake, oyster. They had all invited her to buy them, but in a seventy-one-year-old frame of mind, she had picked up a ninety-nine pence tub of closed cup commercially cultivated ones instead.

She measured it, wrote the day's date in pencil on the wall underneath the sill and rolled the tape measure up. Perhaps she should have scraped the fungus off in its prime a month ago. There was a lot to be said for cutting things off in their prime.

She sat down in an old chintz-covered arm-chair, enjoying the warmth from the autumnal sun through the glass and remembering her own prime. Being forty had been such fun.

Ken always used to remember 1977 for being the year Red Rum won the Grand National for the third time. Mark would probably remember it for being the year Marc Bolan wrapped his mini round a tree. Ali would say it was the year Petra the Blue Peter dog died. But Sheila still couldn't watch Virginia Wade holding up her Wimbledon trophy or listen to Leo Sayer's 'You Make Me Feel Like Dancing' without her lips curling instinctively upwards like a Chinese for-tune fish.

The memory of that summer brought the same instant relief as the deep heat herbal remedy she sometimes rubbed into her shoulders, except that the warmth emanated from a part of her no physiotherapist would ever find. Thinking about the *spring* of 1977, however, was more like finding a cold hot water bottle in her bed.

The fact that Ken had taken his role as one of the Silver Jubilee Beacon organizers more seri-ously than she'd found attractive was, thinking about it, indicative of the staleness of their marriage at that time. It can't have been that she no longer fancied him. He was a physically prepossessing man right up to the final stages of his illness, which had chewed on his virility until it was gristle and bone. So why had she been so ripe for an affair?

What had prompted it? Was it that for 50 per cent of their marriage, 90 per cent of their family and friends had mistaken physical compatibility for love? Or had that misconception turned out to be the backbone of their partnership? It was true that if enough people tell you the same thing, you end up believing it. And in the seventies, which really had to go down in history as *the* decade for divorce, had the compliments about the perceived strength of their union fortified them both just enough to scrape by?

The decade of the 1970s wasn't just about divorce. It was also the decade for organized volunteering. Their weekends were almost always taken up with fund-raising for something or other. All over Bristol and its suburbs, they'd held up traffic with their sponsored trolley-pushes, spent over the odds on raffles and auctions, got drunk on cheap wine at barn dances.

Sheila had tried her best to join in with the volunteer army spirit. She'd rolled up her sleeves and scrubbed filthy kitchens, taken a scythe to half a mile of brambles from the back of the playing field at the back of the British

Legion, allowed Ken to push her on a hospital bed in her nightdress through the centre of town. But underneath it all, she'd found herself secretly mortified.

Ken, on the other hand, had loved every minute. He was often to be found in the local newspaper, jostling for recognition with other men all sporting the same obvious sideburns and big collars. *We did it!* the captions would read. *We made it! We got there!* There had been something unsexy in the way he had taken to his Royal Jubilee task, writing to the free press asking for the public's co-operation on the actual night, insisting on an excessive number of fire drills during May.

But good on him, all the same. The bonfire on Dundry Hill on the Mendips that he and a clutch of other volunteers had built in their own free time turned out to be the tallest in the country and when he was the one committee member picked out of the hat to strike the first match, Sheila was genuinely pleased for him. It did mean though that the evening itself was not the family affair that others remembered.

Mark was just about old enough to disappear into the dusk with his friends and not be fretted over and only thirteen months younger, Ali was the age of ersatz responsibility, and had begged to be her father's helper. This, conveniently, left Sheila in her brushed denim flares, Dr Scholl's sandals and square-necked smock top, to share her bottle of warm white wine with a group of neighbours. With a homemade banner, a sheet staple-gunned to flimsy bamboo canes, they had staked their claim on the square of dry grass and flown the words BURPS HQ with pride.

The Midland Railway, which used to loop north between Bristol and Bath through otherwise hidden villages and gentle rolling hills carrying freight for the old brick and pipe works at Warmley, had finally closed the year before. Many of Sheila and Ken's friends and neighbours nurtured fond memories of the line. As children, the train had taken them on seaside holidays to Bournemouth and Dorset's foreign coasts. As teenagers, they had kissed in its carriages, flirted on its rural platforms, played truant in its tin huts and sidings. In 1977, as adults, a mix of anger and nostalgia had stoked their determination to keep the line alive, and so the 'Bristol to Bath Railway Path Pioneers' – or BURPS – had been formed.

Sheila knew all the members of BURPS well, but one of them – a Dutchman adopted as a local for his usefulness on the cricket pitch – she ended up knowing very well indeed.

His name was Jan de Junger, a name that rolled off the tongue like a chorus line in a nonsense poem. Yan Dee Yunger, as in 'singer' with no lingering on the hard 'g'. Yan Dee Yunger. Yan Dee Yunger. Yan Dee Yunger. Sheila must have said it over and over again hundreds and hundreds of times. Jan de Junger was the name on the tip of her memory's tongue.

Not Bob or Shirley Palmer or Jackie and Eric Stock or Roger Sage, who were all there too.

122

Not them, for they were names without the power of the portal. It was Jan de Junger (like Nina Wills) who had the power.

Shirley Palmer, turquoise nylon, used to flutter her eyes at him and call him 'Yarrn'. Jackie Stock, peasant tops and slacks, always resorted to calling him 'Ian'. Roger Sage, collared tee shirts and Rod Stewart hair, called him 'Dutchy'. Sheila made none of these mistakes. His foreignness had never been a mystery to her.

'It's not my imagination, is it?' Jan de Junger dared to ask her under his breath that night as he'd poured more wine into her plastic cup.

'No,' she'd replied. And those seven words had been the evening's only covenant.

Their precious exchange had been almost immediately followed by the arrival of Jan's ex-wife Carrie, who moved through crowds with the self-importance of an emergency vehicle. Carrie had a radar in her inner ambulance, and a thermometer that could read her former husband's emotional temperature at great distance. Every time it rose to something approaching the heat of recovery, she doused him with a bucket of ice by producing their daughter, Maryse.

'She's been crying herself to sleep because of you. Who is it? Shirley? Jackie? Pam? In this country, Jan de Junger, we do not piss on our own doorsteps.'

Sheila had moved away and the hog roast she pretended to enjoy with Ken and an over-excited Ali had been cold by the time it had finished its tortuous journey from pig to bap. The apple sauce had been commercial, overly spread to disguise a lack of filling, and even colder than the meat.

'Go with Mum,' Ken coaxed their daughter. 'I've got lots to do. Your mum's all on her own.'

'I'll be fine,' Sheila told him, her permed air bouncing in clouds around her. How could he not have seen it?

When ten o'clock came, she found herself walking towards the beacon with a herd of complete strangers, watching the ground disappear under the army of feet, thinking of nothing. The dry soil of the Mendips collected at the edges of her pearly blue toenails and in the buckles of her wooden-soled shoes but she would only notice her grime in the morning, by which time, she would never want to wash again.

She sensed Jan de Junger falling in line beside her, his stature an unmistakeable presence in the darkness. She presumed Carrie and her flashing siren had gone to administer treatment elsewhere since both Carrie's first and second adulterous lovers were loose on the beacon that night too. Sheila had seen them with their forgiving partners in tow, a tense little foursome in the hog roast queue.

Without conversing, she and Jan exchanged quick smiles with a quarter turn of their heads. Bubbles from a can of cider she had just knocked back fizzed inside her, but she kept the rhythm of her pace and marched on.

There was a vantage point waiting for them, two rocks, one lower than the other, rejected by the masses for its uneven base. A space just for them. Sheila stepped up to the higher rock and pushed her hands down inside the woollen pockets of the tie belt cardigan she was glad she had brought. She looked out across the plain at the bonfire that Ken had not yet lit.

Jan took his place beside her on the lower stone, levelling their heights a little. From behind, the gap between their bodies was just enough to catch the narrowest strip of moonlight but other than that, their contract was invisible to the naked eye.

They stood together in noisy silence. People chatted around them but she heard only him, breathing through his nose, deep inhalations. The back of his right hand was one tiny swing-boat movement away from her thigh. She allowed it to be there, conveyed without speech or movement her acceptance of the intrusion into her zone. The ink on their covenant was almost dry.

They continued to watch nothing. Figures with tapers and torches hastened around the stack of donated wood. One of them was Ken, and Ali was down there too, getting in the way. Sheila said as much to Jan and he replied, but the acknowledgement of what was really happening on that rock remained unspoken.

He shifted on the boundary of his own space, she leant against the fence of her own which bulged his way. They touched.

Suddenly, a rocket screamed like a demon into the sky, exploding into a billion cadmium stars.

On the headland, her son Mark in his parka jacket cheered with his mates. Another missile howled into the night. In the dynamic dark, she and Jan both jumped out of their socially conditioned skins and shed them, like snakes, on the floor.

The fire took hold in the stomach of the stacked wood. Its fingers of flame licked and licked until its easterly face leapt into life. Jan found the hem of her cardigan. Under its cloak, he touched the back of her thigh with firm, deliberate pressure. His slow upward stroke kindled a warmth in Sheila's lower back that made her muscles tighten. Have me, her stillness said.

The petrol-soaked planks eventually burst. Orange ribbons streamed from the wood, fluttering into the evening. His hand moved across her thigh and traced the round curve of her bottom and the vertical convex stitching that divided it.

In tacit invitation, Sheila transferred her weight to her left leg. She raised her right hip slightly, the ball of her right foot still on the rock but her heel hovering above the flinty surface. On one tiptoe, the path from the back to the front of her brushed cotton jeans opened to him, and he slid his hand into it, turning his palm so the fleshy pads of his fingertips had felt the point at which the four seams of her trousers met. Around the stitching, under the soft fabric, he drew tiny circles in the plumpness.

Their eyes fixed into the far, far distance, he found every part of her. Each arch of her back, shift of balance, imperceptible swivel of the hips, asked him further in. His contact defined her shape, discovered her texture.

Another story unfolded around them. People sang, toasted the beacon, the night, each other. Combustion was all around them. Inside, Sheila crackled and sparked. Their conflagration had been lit, but it would be another month before it would actually burn.

Thirty-one years later, aged seventy-one and standing in her garden room no longer thinking about the Witch's Butter, she was wondering if somewhere in Holland, Jan de Junger still felt like tinder sometimes too. It took her no more than five minutes to write the letter.

Administration
Leiden University
2300 RA
Leiden
The Netherlands

16 October, 2008

Dear Sirs,
I am trying to make contact with an old friend, Jan de Junger, who became a lecturer in Archaeology at your university in January 1978. Before that, he lived in Bristol for six years, which was where I met him. Unfortunately, this is all the information I have. If you can help, or

*would like to pass on my forwarding address, I
would be very grateful.*
Yours,
  Sheila Webb

She sealed it in its envelope before she could
change her mind and put it in the pocket of her
coat, to post the next time she was going out.
She wouldn't make a special trip to the post
office. That would be making too much of it,
and if she made too much of it, she'd have to
play a waiting game.

Ten

Under the grey wool of his school trousers, Kit
Webb's shins were killing him. It was his mate
Sully's fault for making him lose his grip climb-
ing on to the roof of the football stand in the
park at lunchtime. The wounds were now weep-
ing a clear pale liquid that was acting like glue
against the material. Every time he pulled the
cloth free, it left a few more fibres in the form-
ing scab.

He sat gingerly on a Formica desk, resting his
size nine feet on a red plastic chair and remembering how loudly Sully had shouted as he'd
leaped to the ground – a noise designed purely
to attract the attention of others. By the time Kit

was sliding helplessly down the gritty red tiles, taking off two strips of skin from knee to ankle as he went, a small crowd had formed.

The incident had left him feeling stupid, a sensation he was only just beginning to learn to expect. Kit was used to being at the top of the pile. He was the oldest son, the biggest brother, and for most of his school life, he'd been the tallest boy in his class – advantages he had taken for granted, ones that to his credit he'd never really seemed to notice. Recently though, he seemed to be skimming down the pecking order as fast as he'd fallen through the rungs of the rotten ladder he'd climbed last week. His friends were overtaking him left, right and centre. Shaving, shagging, shooting up. Much to the amusement of his brothers, he'd started quietly working out in his bedroom to keep up.

'He hero-worships that Sully character,' his father had claimed during the last row over the park.

'Hello?' Kit had said as he sat listening to his parents discuss him at the kitchen table as if he weren't there. 'Have I suddenly become invisible?'

The thing was, he felt he had – not to his parents, he was *too* visible to them – but as far as girls went, he might as well not exist

He'd taken to lying about them to Sully, his latest whopper rewriting what had really happened between him and Vanessa in the eco-chalet. At least he'd got somewhere with her, although being Chris and Lou's daughter, she shouldn't really count. She was almost a *sister* for God's sake. And he'd had his one crack at losing his virginity to her. So who then? Sully said you *had* to do it before your sixteenth birthday or you were sad.

He could sense the girls in his class whispering about him when he walked across the playground. Occasionally, the girls and the boys (not Sully; Sully had left without a single qualification or prospect last year) would hang around together, talking. But he never managed to get any further with any of them than that. Ben Fleming had got off with Indie Jaffrey during cross-country and she had put her head in his lap at wet break yesterday. A girl's head in your lap! How the hell did you pull that one off without the obvious happening?

No. It had now got to a point with girls where Kit found it easier to give up. On a one-to-one basis with any female from thirteen to thirty, he had become entirely defenceless. He suspected it was some kind of organized female sport, hunting him for fun, tossing him around for a while and then (his fault, this bit) when he played dead, dumping him as roadside carrion.

Just at this moment, his hound was a girl called Emily Davis, sitting in the teacher's swivel chair in the otherwise empty classroom. It was after four o'clock and they were waiting to show prospective Year Ten pupils around the school. He and Emily Davis were always picked for this kind of thing. Polite and friendly, his report always said. Hers probably did too. They

130

were just the sort of pupils who reflected well on the school. Was she a virgin too, he wondered?

He liked being in school after four o'clock. It was as if the building got out of its uniform, put on a hoodie and hung its legs over the sofa to watch TV. None of the daytime rules stuck. So why couldn't he loosen up too?

He *so* didn't want to feel like this about girls. Sully moved through crowds like a hungry shark, comely plankton swimming voluntarily into his open jaw. But Kit saw only predators.

He pulled again at his trouser legs, waving the loose material to let the air circulate around the grazes. Then he held his limbs out straight, the cloth pinched between his fingers and thumbs. To do this, he had to hunch his shoulders and lean forward.

Emily Davis tossed him a brief but not unfriendly glance.

'Sorry,' he said.

'What for?'

'Oh, my legs...'

It was typical of his timing that Mr Knight's head and shoulders then appeared round the door, his back foot off the ground, his hand pressing down on the handle.

'You two know what you're doing, yeah? Start with the Sports Hall, go on to Modern Languages, that way round. If you need back-up, go to 9K's classroom.'

'Uh huh.' Emily Davis nodded.

'Kit, what are you doing?'

'I ... er ... just...'

'Well, don't, mate all right?' Mr Knight said. 'It looks odd.'

Kit nodded too but decided not to speak. His voice had more or less stopped doing that high one minute, low the next thing – these days, his Adam's apple stood prominently above the open collar of his white shirt – but he still ran the risk of squeaking when the pressure was on.

Mr Knight shut the door again.

Kit looked at Emily Davis.

'My legs are sticking to my trousers...'

She looked back at him briefly, like a vegetarian passing a butcher's shop.

'I ... the skin is all ... I fell off this...' he said.

'You're making me feel sick.'

'Sorry,' he mumbled hopelessly.

He hadn't realized he actually *wanted* to make an impression on Emily Davis until a few minutes ago. She had been in the same class as him for three and a half years and he'd hardly noticed her. It was the way she was sitting at the teacher's desk, using her hips to swivel the chair in a gentle arc, her toes pointing inward, her hands tucked back to back between her thighs.

He wondered if she and her friends did it on purpose. Did they all meet up in the girls' loos at break and discuss how best to sit next? Did they all agree to put their elbows on the backs of their chairs so that their shirts gaped open? Did they know when they crossed their legs that they showed so much leg? 'Do bears piss in the woods?' he could hear Sully asking him.

Damn! Now he needed to adjust his trouser

material somewhere else as well. He put his hands in his pockets and pinched some soft thigh skin as hard as he could. Life was like a constant arm wrestle – just as he felt on the edge of taking control, something stronger would rise up and overpower him. He tried not to think of his disastrous grope with Vanessa, which had been like trying to read Braille without the code. His hands had fumbled over her raised dots, her dips, her curves, her angles. He'd cupped her small breasts and touched his tongue with hers but he was still none the wiser. Sex confused him more now than ever. Sully said he should just shag Kayla down the park like everyone else did, but Kit didn't want it to be like that.

Emily Davis stopped swivelling on the teacher's chair.

'Are we going to do it together or what?'

He hated himself for blushing. 'Do what together?'

'Show people round. What did you think I meant?'

Kit opened his mouth to say yes, that would be good, but just as he was gaping like the gormless tropical fish at the Chinese restaurant his parents took him to, the treat that was supposed to make him feel grown-up but in fact did the opposite, the door swung wide and Mr Knight walked back in. Following him was a girl who made Emily Davis and her seat swivelling seem as interesting as a kid on a swing.

Emily Davis noticed the bright coral scar running the length of the tall girl's otherwise threateningly perfect, olive-skinned face, but Kit saw only the pout. It was the most beautiful mouth he had ever seen.

'On your feet, Kit, this is Chloe Wills. If she likes what she sees, she's joining us next Monday, so make it good, will you?'

He'd have fallen to his knees if Mr Knight had asked him to.

Whether Kit would mind a parent coming to meet him at the school gates, Mark wasn't sure, but he was prepared to take the risk. His urge to walk the uninspiring mile through suburbia had a lot to do with what his partner Chris Jones had just told him about his own son Olly.

'His feet are a size bigger than mine now,' Chris had boasted proudly in the tobacco factory bar. 'He must have grown more in the last two months than the last two years put together. But what am I telling you for? Kit and Dylan must be the same.'

But Mark didn't know what size shoe any of his boys wore. Their wardrobe requirements were Caitlin's department. So was their dental care, their hair, their school timetables. He simply hadn't kept up with their development in the way he'd intended to. He'd started out so well, studying their growth charts, counting their teeth, charting their fine motor skills, but somewhere along the line, he and Caitlin had fallen into more traditional parenting roles. She sorted the boys out and he paid the bills.

It was the specific reference to shoe size that

had got to him. All afternoon, he'd been staring at images of Kit's feet. Kit's toes wriggling in a cot. Kit's foot in his mouth. Kit's corduroy bootie. Kit's first sandals. The digi-tapes that Stan had delivered from the telecine firm were still scattered all over his desk.

The first tape he had put into the machine was the one he remembered best. Taken fifteen years ago, it showed his eldest son's first moments in the world, ET in swaddling clothes. Seeing the newborn Kit bloody and squirming in his mother's arms had made Mark want to kiss his fat little tummy again, to smell that infant eczema cream, to put him on his shoulders, hold the saddle of his bicycle while he wobbled down the pavement, move over for him in the middle of the night. His lovely fourth son Rory was still available for the last privilege but it wasn't the circumstance he mourned, it was the child.

When Chris had mentioned his own son Olly's huge feet, all Mark had been able to see was Kit, tottering awkwardly across a lawn in a pair of navy blue Start-rites. The weird thing was, he knew exactly where to find the very same pair of shoes. He'd seen them on top of a box in the loft when he'd been looking for his guitar. Brittle and dusty, they'd been curled up like two old dog chews fit for the bin.

Mark cut a quick path through the late-after-noon shoppers, promising himself he would take advantage of the opportunities his youngest two still offered him, and then hating himself for his almost immediate apathy. It wasn't that he loved

Kit more than the others, just that he was beginning to regret more. Kit had grown up without warning. None of the parenting books on the shelf in the study had said that would happen.

Walking down the gently sloping high street, it seemed as if his whole world had changed when he'd been looking the other way. Take the second-hand clothes shop Caitlin was always asking him to take stuff to, for example. It had turned, Cinderella like, into a deli overnight. Its neighbour, the mini-cab firm with its oily vinyl bench and fog of cigarette smoke, was now a wine store.

He could hardly walk 50 yards without a victim of refurbishment shining back at him. Where, for instance, did all these old ladies pushing canvas shopping bags go for their tinned peaches and pork chops now? He looked into one or two of their faces to see if they minded the hi-jacking of their vicinity, but they seemed not to even notice it, in the same way he supposed he hadn't noticed Kit's increasing shoe size.

He crossed the road an inconsiderate six feet away from a pedestrian crossing and thought more about the drip-feed effect of time passing. When had Kit stopped being the Kit he was used to? How long would it be before Dylan crossed the threshold? Was there any other wood he couldn't see for the trees?

If someone had asked him at breakfast how much he and Caitlin had changed physically since their twenties, he most probably would have answered 'not much'. But with Stan's digibeta delivery, the reality was staring him in the face. At the click of a mouse, he could create a gallery of 'before' and 'after' shots to send shivers down their spines. Where, if he wasn't by any means bald, had his hair gone? How, if he didn't consider himself to be at all fat, had he somehow doubled in size? At what age had Caitlin swapped the light-hearted look for the level-headed one? When had their individual styles merged to become one interchangeable wardrobe of black and grey?

As he weaved between the shoppers, he began to reconsider the idea of presenting his wife with a birthday film after all. Home truths were hardly what you needed on your fortieth. As an editor, he could rearrange and tweak the details as much as he liked until they suited his purpose, but that was the celluloid equivalent of a toupee and bum tuck. It all aged you in the end.

He turned left off the high street along a residential road dotted with wheelie bins and started to think about a section of film he had yet to rediscover. It lasted two minutes at the most and dated back to the early days when he and Caitlin were rarely out of bed. It had been the way her legs had made a tent with the bedclothes that had made him go and get the camera.

The thing he liked so much about it was the arty concern with the space between her heels and her buttocks. It never failed to rouse him, the way the lens panned in and roamed around the triangle of thin white cotton. The voyeurism is short-lived because then she notices him and the camera moves up too quickly so that her face and hair become a blur. There is an edge of his hand, an indistinct frame of flesh and twisted cotton, and then she stands up, the camera capturing her full length. She is wrapped in a sheet which is tight around her breasts and tummy, bunched at the back like a bustle, trailing on the floor behind her like a train. 'Marry me,' his disembodied voice says, and her face erupts into an expression not unlike a high shutter speed shot of a rosebud bursting into flower.

Crossing the tarmac apron of Kit's school coach park, he nodded, head down, in confirmation at the revived potential of his retrospective. No wonder then that Mark Webb – on his way to meet his fifteen-year-old son Kit – and Nina Wills – on her way back from meeting her fifteen-year-old daughter Chloe – had no idea they had just passed, even though they were both so much at the edge of each other's minds.

Eleven

Ali Webb sat in the armchair, with her feet curled neatly beneath her. Hugging a large brightly spotted mug, she looked as though she were sharing secrets with a girlfriend rather than paying the going rate for a professional ear.

Erica Muller had tried hard to create that precise atmosphere in the front room of her terraced Georgian house. Single women in their thirties were a niche market, Erica's German dentist husband reckoned. They had money and baggage in equal proportions.

Erica's young and perceptive receptionist worked from a waiting room that might once have been a drawing room. At the weekend, it doubled up as the Muller children's playroom but during the week, the toys were cleared and the cupboard shut.

'You only want coffee table books in your treatment room,' Erica's husband had advised from behind his frameless glasses. 'No magazines full of self-help articles. Leave those to me and my surgery.'

On the china blue wall over the Victorian-tiled fireplace hung a huge canvas of clouds and sea, flanked on the cream walls either side by a series of framed prints of mermaids on rocks, sea monsters, and jellyfish drifting along. Art that soothed, Ali thought.

Erica, who wore black, heavy-framed glasses so as not to match her husband, always offered fresh coffee, herbal or Earl Grey tea, or hot chocolate in colourful non-matching mugs. Today, her third time, Ali had gone for the hot chocolate.

Erica was cross-legged in her chair, her flat leather pumps sitting neatly under the book-stacked glass table. In the fire grate was a white orb of light – a low energy bulb inside a frosted globe that glowed optimistically all the working day.

'So this was when?' Erica asked, sipping at a glass of sparkling water.

'1977, the year of the Queen's Silver Jubilee,' Ali told her. 'I was wearing a pair of flared jeans, a blue towelling top and a blue and white headscarf tied at the back of my neck.'

'Very specific. It's actually quite common after a shock to remember precise details like that.'

'Thank you for saying that. It *was* a shock.'

'And it's important to you that other people recognize that, that they don't make light of it.'

'But I can't remember *her*. She is just a blur, a shadow...'

'Maybe she isn't important.'

Ali shrugged.

'Tell me, which parent would you say you were closer to at that time?'

140

'My father. I worshipped him in a way I never did with Mum. If there was an opportunity to spend time with him, I'd always take it.'

Ali paused and picked at a manicured finger. Erica nodded for continuity, in the style of a television interviewer.

'Dad was a planning officer but he was always doing voluntary work too. His free time always seemed to be spent clearing footpaths, or building the beacon bonfire for the jubilee celebrations, or painting a village hall or something. And I used to go along. I liked being with him whereas my brother Mark didn't. He used to say Dad embarrassed him. He liked being important, you know? He liked the health and safety stuff, he'd arrange meetings with police officers to talk to youth clubs about vandalism in the park – stuff like that. He was a bit ... a bit up himself, I suppose you'd say.'

'But you chose him above your friends?'

Ali let the hot chocolate touch her lips. 'He made me feel special.' She ran a finger along her perfectly plucked eyebrow and circled the skin at the end as if she had a headache. 'He liked to show me off. He used to introduce me to people, produce me from the back of the car with a flourish, as if I were this great surprise, as if me being there meant it was going to be much more fun for everyone than if I'd stayed at home. It sounds very princessy but I used to think of my presence at these grown up events as a sort of treat for people. He made me feel as if I really were the loveliest thing in the world.'

Erica nodded some more.

'And now...' Ali said self-pityingly.

'No one makes you feel special any more?'

'It's worse than that. I'm like the bad fairy turning up at the...'

'You feel like the jealous old witch at the new baby's naming ceremony?'

'I think that's how I'm seen...'

'As someone who sabotages other people's happiness?'

'I ... well ... I don't ... I mean...'

'How's your relationship with your mum?'

Ali took her fingers away from massaging her head and released one of her legs from under her in the leather chair.

'I know she loves me. It's not that. It's just that she doesn't need constant reassurance like I do. She's good at being happy. She does it more or less without anyone else's help. Mark's the same. He just plods on, being him. I'm different. I need to be told.'

'Who do you tell?'

'What do you mean?'

'Who do you tell you love?'

'Rob?'

'Anyone else?'

'I don't ... I mean, my family's not like that...'

'If your mum was so good at being happy without help, would you say your father wasn't so good? Did you feel he needed a little bit of help?'

'I used to think that was the case, until I saw him doing...' Ali hesitated. Erica kept entirely

142

quiet.

'Until I saw him with his hand up another woman's skirt. I saw his hand in her knickers.'

'That must have been a shock.'

'It was.'

Ali looked at the chocolatey sludge at the bottom of her cup for a long time, thinking about the kind of jealousy she seethed with over Rob and his bloody squash obsession, about her anger that he could choose to spend two hours on a sweaty court with a man he'd worked with all day rather than have an evening meal with her. Was it that simple? Was it just that her father chose someone else over her?

'I wasn't jealous, if that's what you're thinking,' she said at last. 'I mean, I felt really stupid for having bought the myth, for believing he was the perfect husband, the perfect father. And now I'm angry because...'

Erica waited while Ali repositioned her mug.

'Because I can't believe in loyalty like everyone else. My family all point to Mum and Dad as being the perfect example of a long-term, successful marriage and I know it's rubbish. I *know*. That's the problem. Everyone else is playing a game that I just can't join in with.'

'And you want to?'

'I don't know. I'm just sick of pretending to go along with it. Take Mark and Caitlin for example.'

'Your brother and his wife?'

'They're throwing this huge party for their joint fortieth birthday, inviting God knows who, and we'll all put on a great show of celebrating our togetherness whereas in reality, they're barely speaking to each other.'

'Because of his contact with the ex-girl-friend?'

'Mostly.'

'And you're feeling guilty because you were the one who made the contact happen in the first place?'

Ali reddened.

'Oh ... er, no ... that wasn't what...'

'And you're frightened of turning up like the bad fairy again?'

'Am I?'

'OK,' Erica Muller said, looking at the clock. 'I'm afraid we're going to have to stop there for today.'

'But...'

'Good work, Ali. I'll see you the same time tomorrow.'

And with that, the receptionist knocked on the door to tell her boss the next client was waiting.

'Blue or black?' Nina heard her daughter ask from behind her bedroom door.

'I don't know – black?' came the voice of the boy Chloe had brought back from school, who seemed to hang on to her every command.

'Look up. Don't blink. Keep still, I haven't finished,' Chloe said as Nina walked in, carrying a smoothie in each hand. As she caught the wicked glint of power in Chloe's face and a look of mortification on the boy's, she wished she'd left the drinks outside.

The boy glanced up, his long lashes like spiders against the dusting of blue eyeshadow that shimmered beneath his brows. His skin, smattered with the usual teenage blemishes an hour ago, was now porcelain smooth. His cheekbones gave him the sort of androgynous hardness that reminded her of the vinyl album covers of the 1980s that she used to line her bedroom walls with. He was beautiful in his cosmetic humiliation, which made her daughter's domination all the more unpleasant.

'What do you think, Mum?' Chloe asked, waving a mascara wand. 'Pretty, isn't he?'

'You've got better bone structure than I have,' Nina told the boy, struggling to ignore his embarrassment.

Chloe grabbed her mobile phone off the bedside cabinet and held it to the boy's face.

'Smile, Kitty-kitty!'

'You don't have to let her do this to you,' Nina told the boy crossly, grabbing a nearby bottle of make-up remover and throwing it on to the bed. 'She's showing off.'

'No, Kit! Don't take it off!' her daughter squealed. 'I want to take a photo!'

'Chloe, stop it,' her mother said.

'Mum, you smell of old furniture.'

'I doubt it, I haven't been at work today.'

'Then it's seeping into your bones.'

'Delightful, isn't she?' Nina said to Kit.

'She is,' Kit said, glad to be agreeing with Chloe's mum.

'I was wondering if you two could give me a hand with the mattresses when they arrive.'

'Of course,' Kit said.

'Speak for yourself,' Chloe shouted as she flounced out of the room.

Twenty minutes later, Kit was beginning to feel hopelessly awkward. Chloe had been gone for double the amount of time she said it would take to go and buy two packets of crisps from the corner shop. How much longer did she expect him to sit here on her bed like a painted clown? He knew he ought to take it off but every time he reached for the bottle of white cream her mum had tossed him, his hand froze. Was keeping the make-up on some sort of proof to her of his love? Was it a passport to something else?

He sat there a while longer, fiddling with her iPod and waiting for the sound of her feet on the newly carpeted stairs. Then he smelled her pillow. He found a tee shirt underneath it and smelled that too. He got up, opened her wardrobe and shut it again. Her room was the only one in the house that had a full quota of furniture, most of which he recognized from the Ikea catalogue he'd found on her bedside table.

He couldn't work out how the metallic panels had been fixed to the lime green wall, nor could he decide if they were supposed to reflect the halogen spots on the wire running from her bed to her sink or whether they just did so by chance. Some of the panels were convex, some were rippled, some had a pattern that reminded him of the quilt on the bed he stayed in at Sheila's. On the opposite deep blue wall, the silver floor to ceiling shelves had curvy supports so the whole thing waved in the shape he might make with his hands if he were describing her beautiful body to Sully. Well, not Sully, Sully had seen her for himself, and for once, Kit had felt like the shark, not the crow.

He pulled his phone out of the side pocket of his jeans and sent him a text message.

R U gng 2 prk 2nite?
Kit
16/10/08 16.47

Already hr dickbrain. Get Chloe 2 cum
Sully
16/10/08 16.49

She's mine u bstrd
Kit
16/10/08 16.50

not 4 long mate. She wnts a real man
Sully
16/10/08 16.51

Am in hr bdrm ... don't c u here...
Kit
16/10/08 16.52

wot the fk RU doin txtng me thn?
Sully
16/10/08 16.53

She's gn 2 gt drink
Kit
16/10/08 16.55

tell hr to gt sme 4 me 2
Sully
16/10/08 16.56

tell hr yrslf
Kit
16/10/08 16.57

Kit sat, his fingers poised for further exchange, but neither Chloe's footsteps nor Sully's reply came. Only the engine noise of a large van coming to a stop outside the terraced house managed to yank him out of his stupor. When he heard the doorbell, he grabbed the bottle of white liquid, squeezed it on to the cotton wool and began smearing it over his face. Black mascara streaked his cheeks and the cleanser dripped on to the neck of his dark hoodie. The cotton wool was useless and he put his fingers into his cuffs and started using the ribbed material as a scourer. At the sound of voices, he pressed harder, looking in horror at the orange, the pink, the blue and the black that was coming off his face. In the mirror above Chloe's sink, spotlit like an actor's dressing room, his face – a melted drag queen – stared desperately back at him. He took some soap from a steel dish and began to scrub it directly on to his cheek, as hard as his mother used to work the skin on his knees or the biro on the back of his hands. The top of a spot came off and began to bleed. The raw chin that he had experimentally taken a razor to the day before flared up in a rash. He dried his face, leaving dark smudges on a soft lilac satin-edged towel, and then stood there like an idiot until he heard the sound of something heavy being dragged in through the front door.

'Oh, you're back!' Chloe's mum said when he came down the stairs. 'I didn't hear you come in.'

'I, er, I didn't go out,' Kit said stupidly.

'You didn't?' Nina's face turned the same purple as her hair.

'No.'

'Chloe went to the park on her own?'

'She didn't go to the park. She went to the corner shop to get some crisps.'

'I don't think so,' said Nina, the text her daughter had just sent her flashing from the pocket of her trousers. 'You know what? I really wouldn't bother with her...'

'What d'you mean?'

'She's not worth it.'

Kit didn't understand. He couldn't think of what to say next so he stood there feeling like an idiot.

'I think maybe you should go home,' Nina said. 'Don't wait for her here – she won't thank you for it.'

'You think she's gone to the park?'

'I know she has.'

'Oh, right.'

'I'm sorry, love. I had no idea you were still up there. You were so quiet.'

'I don't want her to be in any trouble with you.'

'I'll tell her you left no more than a minute after she did.'

'Thanks, Mrs Wills. Do you want some help with the mattresses?'

'No, they can stay down here for a while. Chloe can help me.'

'Don't say anything to her, will you?' Kit mumbled through his embarrassment. 'Please don't give her any grief.'

'I'll try not to. Goodnight, Kit.'

'G'night.'

He walked the long way home to avoid the park. He'd been told the other day that he was heading for a string of As in his GCSEs but he wasn't exactly being the brightest star in the galaxy tonight. His preoccupied brain failed to register the significance of his new friend's name – he was only able to make one connection that evening. Chloe Wills was at the park with Sully.

Twelve

As dawn broke through the gap in the curtains, Caitlin rolled from her left to her right side so that she faced her husband. Mark was still asleep on his back, his brow slightly furrowed as always. Her waking body shifted in this way every morning. It was the mirror image of the movement she made at night as she turned her back to Mark for sleep. Her semi-conscious stirrings had become as biologically programmed as a baby turning its head in the birth canal.

This morning, she swung her left leg a little further across the mattress than usual and it brushed across her husband's warm body. It surprised her how good it felt so she left it there, pinning his furry thigh with the softer skin of her own until the sensation of early morning arousal permeated his consciousness too.

The alarm, set for seven, had not yet gone off, but they were both now awake. They didn't speak, but their lips found each other's necks and shoulder blades. Caitlin kissed the strip of skin where Mark's arms joined his upper body. She ran her tongue along it to feel its smoothness, and then, against the side of her mouth, she felt the coarser texture of his chest hair. They

151

both smelled of sleep. He found her buttocks, squeezed them gently and made a soft groaning noise as she pushed herself up in a quick agile movement, technique number two from their repertoire of around ten.

Later, as Caitlin straightened their duvet before leaving for work, she smiled. They couldn't be all that disaffected if they could still manage to make love before breakfast.

As always after unexpected sex, she felt more alive. The ghost of him would be inside her all day, affecting the way she laughed, the clothes she chose to wear, the things she said to people. Sex refreshed their marriage like a plunge in a pool on a hot day.

But when would the two of them learn? They should know by now that what usually lay at the back of marital indifference was a prolonged period without making love. One week without sex was neither here nor there. Two weeks and the distance began creeping in. Three weeks and they were strangers. And all it ever took to put right was an accidental brushing of flesh.

She cycled to work with the memory of their lovemaking still dancing around her mouth. The museum was in a street that reminded her of London. It had a diversity about it, with all the different nationalities teeming up and down, darting between the traffic or waiting patiently in sensible packs at the pedestrian lights. Every face she looked at was different to the last – bearded, pierced, dreadlocked, shaven. It made her feel entirely invisible. It was where she shed one role in readiness for the other, domestic goddess for working woman. But for a few precious moments before she entered the building, she was neither.

A bus was perilously close to her on her right side, so rather than pedal harder, she braked and pulled into the kerb to allow it past. Then she got off her bike, bounced it on to the pavement and pushed it for the last few yards through the crowds. A group of Oriental students were milling around the entrance to the narrow alley that led to the museum's bicycle lock-up and she nudged her front wheel through them. As they divided, Caitlin caught a glimpse of a man in black leaning against the iron railings holding something in his arms. A puppy, or a kitten perhaps? Then she realized what she was seeing and she lost the ability to swallow.

It was Paul Moffat again! Was it? Was she seeing things? Was that a good thing? A bad thing? A scary thing? A safe thing? Had he not received her email then? The one in which she asked him for plenty of advance warning if he had further plans to turn up on her doorstep? Yes, yes, of course he had because he'd replied saying, 'You saw me then!' and she'd launched into a three paragraph apology about why she hadn't stopped, and he'd said it was OK, he would forgive her and ... and ... and...

Her co-ordination was five per cent off accuracy as she tried to steer the handlebars through the double wooden entrance at the same time as groping in her bag for the swipe card she would need for the airlock door once inside.

The lock-up was left permanently open, doubling as access for the fire brigade in the event of an emergency. Anyone could follow her in. Had he seen her? Was it him?

Her heart was thumping but it wasn't a straightforward fear. She was thrilled too, bursting to shriek out loud like a schoolgirl pounced on by a friend in the dark.

Inside the lock-up, with the wooden doors still swinging, she phoned Lesley's mobile.

'Look out of the office window,' she hissed urgently into its voicemail. 'If you see a man in black leaning against the railings, that's him!'

As she lifted her bike on to one of the free wall cages and fumbled hopelessly with the padlock combination, her imagination took over. What if the wooden fire door suddenly burst open and he sauntered in? Was he still harmless? Still sweet?

Her fingers bungled the undoing of her cycle helmet, and she dropped the swipe card. A surveillance camera broadcast her clumsiness on an upstairs monitor where the receptionist in the Great Hall sharpened a pencil and filled in the seventh clue of a crossword.

Caitlin cursed as she ran the card through the slot a second time. At the same time, the receptionist saw her on the monitor and pressed the button to let her through, but she dropped her rucksack a couple of inches too short of the point at which she could let the door swing shut and had to pull it forward with her foot. At last, the heavy door closed behind her.

The basement was quiet. Very, very quiet. Just a drip here and a scratching there. She took the three floors of wide stairs like an athlete, her black linen wide-leg trousers still in her bicycle clips, her small loose breasts flapping frantically under her grey-flecked, hooded cardigan.

As she ran, she realized what he had been holding. Not a puppy or a kitten, but her old teddy bear, the one Paul had found it amusing to make such a fuss of, taking it to lectures, giving it birthdays; the one her mother had made a cap and gown for when Caitlin had left for college. 'He's come to give it back,' she thought, trying to calm down. 'That's all. He's come to give it back.'

She was breathless by the time she burst through the door of the open-plan office on the third floor that the education officers shared with the design team.

'Lesley! Is Lesley here? When did she go? Do you know when she's coming back? She barged through the maze of tables and swivel chairs and storage units and room dividers to get to her own desk. A bruise from a corner of furniture began to develop on her thigh as she snatched the phone to dial reception.

'Hi, it's Caitlin Webb. Has anyone asked for me at the front desk? A man with a teddy bear? You're sure? OK, thanks.'

She sat down and moved paper restlessly around for a while. She and Mark had an unspoken rule to keep non-urgent phone calls at work to a minimum. Yesterday, it wouldn't have occurred to her to call him just because she thought she had seen someone she once knew. Today, because of their refreshed footing, it seemed the most natural thing in the world. She called his work number.

Jenny, his girl Friday, picked up almost immediately. 'Salt Peter Productions, Jenny speaking, how may I help you?'

God, how many times did she have to be told not to answer like that?

'Jenny, it's Caitlin.'

'Hi, Caitlin, how are you?'

'I'm fine. Is Mark there?'

'Mark who?'

'Ha ha, no, really Jenny, is he there?'

'Well, he's not *all* there, obviously...'

'Can I have a quick word?'

'You can't even have a slow one. He's gone to get his hair cut,' Jenny said with a snigger. 'Just the one hair, I presume. He said he wouldn't be back till after lunch.'

'After lunch?'

'He said he was going shopping for some new clothes. Are you going somewhere nice?'

'Not as far as I know,' Caitlin said, new blood rising in her cheeks. So what happened to him being too busy to take the cat to the vet's today because of the heap of editing waiting for him in the office? 'Thanks Jenny. Bye.'

She called his mobile.

'Welcome to Orange answerphone. I'm sorry but the person you've called is not available.

Please leave your message after the tone. If you want to re-record your message, press one at any time.'

A wave of disappointment sloshed around her insides. The intimacy of their early morning lovemaking had gone and she was back to resenting him again. She felt weaker in her post-shock state, like she did after the drama of child injury – the distant scream, the older brother running to find someone, the limp child, the blood, the tears. Then the arnica, and the rescue remedy, and the boiled sweet. Mark was supposed to have been her boiled sweet.

She cupped her palm over her cordless mouse and wiggled it for the sake of something routine to do. Her computer flashed into life and she checked her emails. There was one from Paul, saying he was in Bristol today, delivering, would she believe it, to a shop in the same road as the museum, and would it be convenient to call in? She leaned back in her chair and laughed out loud. Here by appointment! Sort of anyway. But hardly a stalker! If only there was someone on hand to share the joke. And then, as if her wish were its command, the instant messaging box in the right-hand corner popped up.

'Ali says hello!' it said.

In the absence of Lesley and Mark, Ali would do. Caitlin clicked to enlarge it.

To: Ali.Webb81@btconnect.com
Never give out your password or credit card number in an instant message conversation.

Caitlin says: Hi, Ali. You're at it early today.

Ali says: Nothing better to do! I hear my darling brother is in email contact with the traveller again, then!

Caitlin says: Yes, he did finally tell me he'd sent her one.

Ali says: That's not the same as giving her one, is it?

Caitlin says: Better not be.

Ali says: How do you feel about tomorrow?

Caitlin says: ???

Ali says: Oh God, don't tell me you don't know!

Caitlin says: Remind me...

Ali says: Mark is having lunch with Nina Wills.

Caitlin says: That's news to me.

Ali says: You mean he hasn't he told you?

Caitlin says: No.

Ali says: Oops.

Caitlin says: I wouldn't worry about it. I'm not.

Caitlin signed off and with the bicycle clips still gripping her black trousers to her ankles, she got up from her desk, pushed her way back through the office and ran down the stairs at an even more neck-breaking speed than she had come up them.

'Bloody lying bloody bastard,' she muttered as she swung around the curve of the banister and shouldered open a fire door that led on to the public gallery. Past Minerals and Fossils, past Ceramics and Glass, past wooden statues, stone busts and a wall of Far Eastern Art. Like a post-modern Cinderella she fled down the central staircase into the Great Hall and through the front door on to the pavement outside.

'Paul?' she shouted at the figure in black who was walking away towards the university tower, beginning to merge with the crowds. It was the slope of his shoulders, the way his thigh-length black jacket hung as if it were two sizes too big, that convinced her.

'Moff?' she called again. 'Moff, it's Caitlin!'

Paul Moffat span round on his pointed-toe ankle boots that gave him more height than he actually had. He used to wear his fringe falling across one eye, but Caitlin saw his hair was now closely shaven. He still had that femininity about his face though, and it lit up like a child's at Christmas.

'Caitlin!'

'It *is* you!'

'I saw you arrive, I was going to call you but then I got cold feet – I thought you were avoiding me!'

'I didn't see you...'

'You looked like you had...'

'What on earth are you doing with *that*?' she said with a laugh, pointing at the bear, its little mortar board and gown still intact. She felt hot and self-conscious, as if she were under a full set of stage lights.

'Big Ted? I'm returning him. I took him from your room before I left Uni...'

'I know you did. I was furious.'

'And he's been sitting on my bed making me feel guilty ever since.'

Caitlin took the bear from him.

'It's good to see both of you,' she said, suddenly shy.

'And you.' Paul smiled, holding out his arms. 'You haven't changed a bit.'

'That's such a lie!'

'I've tried to contact you a few times but I guess your parents must have moved. How are they?'

It was a long time since Caitlin had had to deal with such an enquiry and to her surprise, she was grateful for it.

'Oh God, Paul, you don't know, do you?'

In the coffee bar, Caitlin squeezed her teddy bear under the table as she recounted the awful tale. Wonderful holiday, time of their lives, delayed flight, they'd phoned her from the airport, safe but exhausted, arranged lunch on Sunday, amazing stories, dark night, bad visibility, long-distance juggernaut driver also killed.

'No,' Paul kept saying. 'No, I can't believe it, I can't believe it. When? Where? How? Where had they been? Where are they buried? What about you? How old were you? What did you do next?'

Far from finding it painful, Caitlin was comforted by his shock, tempted to indulge herself in his grief all day. It had been for ever since she'd talked about her parents in such intricate detail, because she had surrounded herself with people who'd never known them. Had she done this on purpose? Paul asked. No, Caitlin said, she didn't think so. But it was very soon afterwards that you met Mark? She had to admit it was. Not exactly on the rebound but certainly in a precarious state, he said. I suppose so, she agreed. But before they knew it, they were back to the accident again, the last phone call from the airport, the juggernaut no more than an hour later, the chance for them both to agree John and Erin wouldn't have known anything about it.

'Sorry, do you mind me asking?' Paul checked every now and again.

'No, I like it,' Caitlin confessed.

The more Paul demanded particulars, the closer Erin and John Rees came back to her – their expressions, their language, the hair on the back of her father's hands, the freckled, moisturized skin of her mother's.

'Their friends survived but they're in wheelchairs, or were. They've both died in the last few years, too.'

'Of complications?'

'No, of old age.'

Paul's eyes filled with tears. 'Erin was bloody marvellous to me,' he finally said.

Caitlin wanted to hug him. Those few friends who *did* remember Erin and John had also, quite rightly, all but forgotten them at the same time. But Paul's sorrow was as fresh as her own.

'I'm sorry,' he said, wiping his eyes with the back of his hand. 'I went to see Erin when I left university, did you know that?'

'No, I had no idea.'

'Well, you wouldn't, because I asked her not to tell you. It's typical of her that she never told you. I couldn't go straight home, I was in too much of a mess, and I couldn't think of where else to go. Erin seemed such an obvious choice, which makes no sense when you think she was the mother of the girl I was running away from.'

'I was such a bitch. What must she have thought? I'm so sorry.'

'She ended up looking after me for days. She made me have stitches in the cut, called the college, everything – your dad must have thought it really odd.'

'Did she know how you got the cut? I never told her anything about it.'

'She didn't ask.'

'Do you think she knew it was something to do with me?'

'Why else would she have been so kind?'

'Because she liked you?'

162

'We did have a real friendship,' Paul said, his tears reforming and his chin developing tiny dents. 'We had lunch every time she came to London. She became so important to me, I actually don't know what I would have done without her.'

'You know, Mum always secretly hoped the two of us would...'

'I think she soon realized she was barking up the wrong tree there,' Paul added hurriedly.

Caitlin looked up from fiddling with her wedding ring and saw he was embarrassed.

'I'm sorry, I was too young. I didn't know a good thing when I saw it.'

'I didn't know what I wanted then either ... but your mum...' He flicked a tear away and wiped his finger on a tissue napkin. 'Anyway, when she went quiet on me, I put her sudden silence down to you finding out, perhaps you asking her not to see me any more...'

'When in fact she'd gone silent on us all...'

'God alive,' Paul sighed.

He sat across the table from Caitlin, stirring his coffee, too wrapped up in his own memories to offer any further sympathy.

'And what about me then?' she asked coyly. 'Do you still love me too?'

He put his hands across the Formica and found hers.

'Course I do,' he said consolingly, in a different tone to the one she was after, 'we go back such a long way, how could I not?'

* * *

163

It was only later, when Paul Moffat was on his own in a bedroom that wasn't his, that he really let go. Erin Rees had changed his life and she had died without him even sensing it. By accepting him as he really was, if not actually identifying it for him, she had given him the confidence and the strength to be himself. So last year, when Andrew had finally left, he had craved her advice all over again. His dismal attempts to trace her had left him feeling emptier than ever, not convinced enough that she wanted to be found by him. And then Caitlin's email had popped up on to his screen and it seemed as if his prayers had been answered, if a little too late.

He would definitely take Caitlin up on her offer to visit the grave together. From what she'd hinted, it would comfort her to have someone with her who could actually picture Erin, who had loved her properly too. He lay on the bed in the immaculate guest house he always stayed in when he was in Bristol and tried to remember that last conversation more than twenty years ago.

Sometimes I wonder if I'm gay, he'd told Erin in Selfridge's over a salt beef sandwich, as if the builder's head-butt had finally knocked some sense into him. She hadn't batted an eyelid. She was neither shocked, nor curious, nor any of the other things he had feared a woman of sixty might be. Sometimes I wonder if you are too, she'd replied, and together they had explored the possibility and ended up laughing until they were nearly sick.

So why hadn't he told Caitlin what she hadn't guessed, what her mother clearly hadn't told her? Why had he found it so easy to tell her he was a sales rep for a B-list publishing firm of contemporary women's fiction and that he lived in Slough, but not (surely the most acceptable fact of the three) that he was homosexual? He had seen her face searching for something from him that he knew he couldn't give, hunting for a reminder of his desire. She'd looked as sweet as ever, the gap between her teeth and her freckles still making her look vulnerable, without artifice. But how could he tell her he'd only been in love with her sexlessness? That in his young adult confusion, she had been neither girl nor boy to him? Today, in the café, she was clearly all woman: a mother, a wife, a sexual being and while he could love her for that, he couldn't desire her, which was what he vaguely suspected she had contacted him for in the first place.

He felt lonely and wished that Maxine and Steve, the couple who ran the guest house, were available for a chat, but they were full tonight and had locked themselves away in their private flat. When he was their only guest, they would invite him to join them for supper in their neatly tiled kitchen – he would always come with wine in his suitcase for them just in case and they would drink it while he sipped Diet Coke and argued about whether Midge Ure from Ultravox had been the true pioneer of the thin sideburns or not.

Maxine and Steve had been real friends to him during the traumatic break-up with his boyfriend Andrew a year ago. He was too young for you, they'd told him. He's never even heard of Spandau Ballet. You can't live with someone who's never heard of Spandau Ballet.

Caitlin had heard of Spandau Ballet though. She'd even been to one of their concerts with him. Maybe they could talk about that next time. With that thought in his head, Paul got off the bed, spruced himself up and headed for a club to spend yet another night with strangers.

Thirteen

October 17

Caitlin woke up wishing that October 17 was already over. She steeled herself to get out of bed the way she used to in pregnancy, not wanting to put the procedure into play, knowing that the moment her feet hit the floor, she had twelve exhausting hours to get through before she could seek refuge again.

Nineteen years' worth of October 17s had taught her that the minutes on this day lasted as long as two on any other day of the year. She had also worked out the strategy to fill this double time. She had to keep busy, she shouldn't be alone. Most particularly, she shouldn't expect anyone else to remember, and when they didn't remember (which they wouldn't) she shouldn't mind. And then she remembered. This year she had Paul Moffat.

She washed and dressed herself like an invalid, a gentle flannel here, a cursory wipe there. What she needed was for this October 17 to go like clockwork, to require no effort and present no difficulties.

What she got instead was a minefield, right outside her bedroom door. Mark was about to get in the shower. Kit wanted to be in the shower. Dylan had just had a shower and the hot water had been turned off.

'Shower in the apothecary,' Kit was suggesting dismissively to his father, but not even Caitlin chose to shower in there. The apothecary was for slow bathing. It barely had enough pressure to warrant the word shower. Drizzle was more like it, or light rain. Besides, it was Caitlin's space.

'Can't you have one tonight?' Caitlin asked her usually reasonable husband who was standing defiantly in the middle of the family bathroom with a towel round his waist. She noticed a few more grey chest hairs below his neck and despite herself, she wanted to kiss them. 'Kit had rugby last night, he's filthy.'

At least Kit should have had rugby, but when she'd checked his bag, instead of mud on his shirt she'd noticed traces of foundation around the neck.

'That's his look-out,' Mark said. 'He should have showered at school.'

'It was an away match,' Kit lied.

'Then you should have showered at home.'

'I had homework to do.'

'Mark, do you really have to have a shower this morning?' Caitlin asked wearily. 'You had one yesterday morning.'

'No, I don't really have to have one, but I really want one.' Mark leaned into the clear glass cubicle and turned the stainless steel dial towards the wall. The water surged out and all but drowned her next question.

'Why?'

'You know why.'

October 17 always made her feel as if she had swallowed her own heart. All day, it would lie like a lump of indigestible offal in her stomach.

'I don't know why.'

'Oh I get it, you're having lunch with that woman today,' Kit said. The build developing under the faded blue tee shirt and boxer shorts he wore to bed was beginning to put Mark's shape to shame.

'What do you mean, *that* woman?' Mark laughed defensively as he stuck his arm under the spray to test the temperature. 'She's not *that* woman.'

Caitlin nearly brought the lump up on the black non-slip bathroom mat. 'On October 17?' she wanted to shout. 'You are going to meet an ex-girlfriend on the anniversary of my parents' deaths?' But she didn't shout anything at all, she

168

simply reminded herself that there was always Paul Moffat.

As she made her way through the noisy protest and down the stairs, Kit threw his towel on the floor and started filling the sink.

'I need a shower, Dad.'

'You need to look in the mirror, son.'

'Why?'

'What's with the make-up?'

'Oh, that was someone ... she was just having a laugh...' Kit said, rubbing his lids with his fingers and making matters worse.

'Yeah, well, we all need to have a laugh now and again.'

'Why can't you take Mum to lunch instead?'

'I'll take your mother to lunch tomorrow, OK?'

'She's working tomorrow.'

'So Saturday then.'

'I've got a rugby match in Plymouth on Saturday.'

'So Sunday.'

'Dylan is playing hockey in Bath.'

'You see what we're up against then, do you?' Mark snapped. 'Anyway, you started it. You were the one who subscribed me, remember?' and he dropped his towel to walk into the thundering water.

Downstairs in the kitchen, Rory Webb helped himself to another bowl of cereal. He picked up the full, large plastic container of milk and, steadying it with one small hand on the bottom and another on the top, he tipped it at an angle appropriate for a nearly empty ketchup bottle. Caitlin watched helplessly as the lake of milk spread across the table, over the edge like a waterfall, and into his grey flannel lap.

'No use crying over spilt milk,' Joss said, jumping up and pulling Rory off his chair.

'I'm not crying,' Rory shouted.

'There's nothing wrong with crying,' Caitlin told them automatically, turning her back and holding on to the sink.

Mark knew College Green – the grassy lawns in front of Bristol's fine medieval cathedral – almost as well as he knew his own long and narrow back garden. It featured heavily in the story of his life. It was a space he often filmed in, where he'd taught his boys to ride their bikes, or where he often ate a sandwich on the hoof. And it was also the place where he had first met Nina Wills, which was why he had chosen it for their tryst today.

In his mind, the iron and wood municipal bench under the tree opposite the cathedral's main entrance had always belonged to him and Nina. It might as well have been carved with their names and a date, like the one he'd had commissioned for the picnic spot on Dundry Hill for his father which said, 'In memory of Ken Webb, 1929–1991.'

He was feeling every bit as nervous as he had that first time, every bit as desperate to make a good impression. He crossed his legs, uncrossed them, got out his phone, put it away again.

A group of boys about Kit's age played politely on their skateboards on the paved circle next to him; pupils from the nearby Cathedral School, he guessed. They held his attention for a minute, but then he was surveying the walkways again, scanning every woman he saw for elfin familiarity.

The air became damp and heavy and the boys skated off. He got up and began to head for shelter too but before he could make it to the north door of the cathedral, rain started splashing from the sky with the sort of pressure that the shower in the apothecary could only dream of.

At least there were some compensations for having thinner hair, he thought inside the cathedral porch, rubbing his hand through his close cut and flicking off the spray. A steward nodded at him disinterestedly, bored with the sight of wet strangers seeking refuge.

He was still ten minutes early for their assignation, so he pushed open the door to the great pillared hall – the only one of its kind in England he remembered – and walked into the hush. Nineteen years ago, he would have still been out there on the bench getting soaked, too keen by half. No wonder Nina had so often verbally slapped his earnest face, which he then used to turn to offer her the other cheek. Where had that ardent young man gone? Maybe she had squeezed him into her traveller's rucksack and dumped him over the side of the cross-channel ferry, because the obsession that had been such

171

a feature of his love for Nina had never been a quality in his courtship of Caitlin.

A nostalgia for his young freckled wife hit him like the hail that had started to ricochet off the mobile hoarding on the green advertising the Hippodrome's Christmas pantomime.

Caitlin had been so sweet in her early twenties. After Nina had dismantled, brick by brick, what little confidence he'd had, Caitlin had come along and picked up his pieces. Stone by stone, she had rebuilt him, cementing his rocky moments with constant reassurance. He had been her strength, holding her together in her newly orphaned state. But that girl had disappeared without trace too. Somewhere in the past, there must be a huge flock of unsophisticated souls wandering around looking for their middle-aged bodies.

He checked his watch and the date finally registered, sending a heat through his bones. Shit, it was October 17, the worst day on Caitlin's calendar. Remembering the way she fled the bathroom that morning, as if she couldn't get away from him fast enough, he pulled out his phone. *I've just realized what day it is,* he typed. *Don't forget I love you.* He pressed send three times but the signal inside the thick walls was non-existent.

So how would he describe Caitlin to Nina? The phrase 'a good mother' always got in the way of everything else, but she was other things too. Serious about her family, loyal to her friends, conscientious at work. Caitlin was as solid as the cathedral itself. She hung on in there, bringing up children, holding down a job, loving her husband as best she could.

Mark ran his hand down one of the pillars, thinking about the structure of his own life. At the four corners of their marriage were their sons, shoring it up. In ten years' time, when the last of the boys walked away to begin constructing their own permanence, would the marital walls remain standing? He liked to think so and yet here he was, on October 17, getting excited about a girl he knew damn well had an instinct for undoing.

The wind whipped through the church portals and caused a pedestal topped with a flower arrangement to rock on its four wooden feet. Still the hail bounced on the pavements outside, like popcorn kernels hitting the heat.

He picked his phone back out of the pocket of his black nubuck jacket and tried to resend the text message but the signal was still too weak.

Through the locked glass and iron doors at the end of the nave, he could see a tower of scaffolding and green tarpaulin marring an office block's top half, with workmen picking their way across the vertiginous platforms. If one of them dropped something, the velocity of the object could cause injury or death. If they spat, would a direct hit be distinguishable from the sting of the hail?

These were truly his thoughts as Nina Wills stepped out of a taxi on to College Green. Mark Webb had stopped thinking about what he looked like, whether he had aged, how he would measure up. Such things were a female's concerns, and Nina's in particular as she put up her umbrella and picked her way around a puddle.

The bench under the tree was empty, so she used her initiative and headed for the cathedral. Inside the lobby, the steward nodded another tired acknowledgement as she shook her brolly and fluffed up her purplish hair.

Her flat leather boots made a slight squeak on the vast tiled floor as she crept cautiously inside. A trickle of rain ran down her hairline and her make-up began to tickle. She regretted wearing it. She regretted wearing Chloe's bulky waterproof jacket, she regretted the denim mid-calf skirt that hardly allowed her enough room to walk, she regretted the skimpy red sweater over the even skimpier white cami, the chunky silver bracelet. She regretted trying so hard.

The inferiority boomerang that she thought she had thrown away when she had left Rauf came hurtling back, and the speed at which it clocked her around the head knocked every last shred of confidence out of her. This was it. She could no longer hide behind the witty turns of email phrases but she would have to look him in the face. Or rather, she would have to let him look into hers.

Suddenly, she had no idea how much the years had changed her, and she turned quickly to go back out, to dive into her handbag and check her face in a mirror just one more time. But she was just that split second too late.

'Nina?'

She span on her heels and saw a broad-shouldered man walking towards her. Mark walked through a small group of grey-haired ladies to approach her with big confident steps. Oh hell, I fancy him, she thought.

In the two seconds Mark took to reach her, he took in her increased size – no longer exactly an elf – the added lines around her eyes and lips, the consequences on her skin of living in the sun, the more conservative clothes.

I don't feel a thing, he thought with relief, but despite that, he held her close for a second too long.

'Good trip, was it?' he asked.

'A bit longer than I intended,' she laughed into the oily black leather of the jacket that protected the soft blue linen of what was very definitely not any kind of descendant of the polo shirt.

As they walked out of the cathedral, down the riven paving steps alongside the cathedral school, over a main road, across the cobbled leisure complex and towards the dockside restaurant, Nina answered his question more fully. She fast-forwarded almost immediately to Chloe's birth.

'So I'm in Greece, leaving the maternity hospital with a ten-day-old daughter – not exactly the plan I had in mind – and an old woman comes up to me, grabs my hand and tells me I'll have two more children – dark-haired boys apparently – before I'm forty...'

'How old are you?'

'Thirty-seven.'

'Better watch out then...'

They walked over the old weighbridge, past a building that looked, with its long low walls and arched windows, like a railway station but was in fact a tourist information centre. Nina's boots were soaking. Her hair stuck to her head, and her mascara had run in little rivers down her cheek, leaving a trail in her foundation.

'Do I look ridiculous?'

'No, you look wet.'

They crossed the bridge over the river with the steel funnels sprouting from its structure, past the houseboats and over the road into a leafy square.

'I had two rooms above the taverna to myself, and Chloe used to play in the sand on the floor counting the cigarette ends...'

'Camel?'

'You've been there!'

'Little place on the waterfront, tables outside, octopus hanging on lines to dry?'

'That's the one! It was perfect, until a man walked in one day, promised me the earth, and I mistook him for the father of my two unborn sons. Not good.'

'Oh, dear. But do you mind me asking who the father of your daughter is?' he dared to ask.

'Well, he's one of two possibilities, neither of which is you!'

'No, I didn't mean ... I didn't think for one...'

'You think I wouldn't have told you?'

'No, no, just curious!'

Mark opened the restaurant door and stood back to let Nina through. She walked under his arm, the top of her head barely wiping his leather jacket sleeve. Somehow, now she looked a mess, Mark began to feel the stirrings of something.

As they ate by the window, looking out into the murky grey water of the dock and the bow of an abandoned coaster, their flirtatious laughter attracted attention. It felt to Mark like lying in the sun, probably not good for you in the long run, but suddenly, after so long, too nice to seek the shade. Nina was doing all the talking.

'My biggest regret is that Chloe has been at boarding school since she was eight. Eight! He just had to have me to himself. He was so jealous...'

She told Mark everything, including the night Rauf Abaz had hit Chloe, how the stone in his gold ring had caught her daughter's cheek and ripped into her skin, how she, Nina had packed their bags and driven to Izmir the next day, how their lives had changed overnight.

Mark listened, relief coming in great puffs out of him, dissipating into the air. It was all under control.

Eventually, Nina stopped talking. She took some more wine and looked at him.

'God, that's enough about me! What about you?'

'Me?' Mark put his fork back into his risotto and leaned back on his chair. 'Oh, not much. Too much work and no play makes Jack a dull bastard and all that...'

'Sounds like I got here just in time.'

A mile away, Sheila put her arms around her daughter-in-law Caitlin where they felt appreciated, which made up for the pointlessness of her morning. The shoulders of her blue canvas fisherman's smock were smudged with mascara where her daughter Ali had, in rather overblown tragedy, fallen in through the door and sobbed against her three hours ago. Sheila had put aside her usual trip to a farmer's market to listen, but Ali was still sitting at the kitchen table sniffing indulgently into her untouched coffee.

'Are you all right?' Sheila whispered into Caitlin's ear. 'I realize what date it is.'

'I'm fine,' Caitlin murmured back. 'Oh, Ali, what's wrong?'

She said it with more warmth than she felt. October 17 was *her* problem. Only people whose parents had been killed in car crashes were allowed to indulge in self-pity on October 17.

'It's OK, no one died,' Sheila said, fully aware of the comment's resonance. 'Rob's going to Spain for a squash tournament.'

She rolled her eyes as she said it. She was relaxed about her frustration with Ali. She didn't view her daughter's unhappiness as her own maternal failure. She just accepted it as the way Ali was.

Her little kitchen smelt of baking. Sponge layer cake, a tray of muffins, gingerbread –

offerings of comfort. This lunchtime, the warmth had a lemony flavour to it.

Caitlin's own domestic hub had a permanently savoury aroma, which had the effect of making her think there were things to do. Meals to get on the table, a dishwasher to pack and unpack, uneaten leftovers to scrape into the compost bin. For some reason, sugar and flour and eggs had an altogether less busy smell than tomatoes and onions.

'Over my birthday,' Ali sniffed. Ali was a Scorpio, which according to a specific astrological reading she'd once had done made her 'virtually impenetrable emotionally'. The phrase had become a family joke.

'Oh, that's a bit of a blow,' Caitlin said.

'I think he's done it on purpose.'

'What? Persuaded the Spanish Squash Association to stage their tournament during your birthday week just so he can miss...' Sheila stopped, and gave a frustrated laugh.

'Can you not go with him?' Caitlin asked.

'He hasn't asked,' Ali answered miserably.

'Men, eh?' said Sheila mischievously. 'Who'd have them? Speaking of which, how's my dear son's mid-life crisis coming along?'

'Ask me again tonight. He's having lunch with Nina Wills,' Caitlin said, cutting herself a tiny slice of lemon drizzle cake to make up for the breakfast she had been unable to eat.

'The girl that "broke his heart",' Sheila said, wiggling two fingers in each hand in the air to emphasize the inverted commas.

Ali pulled herself up out of the gloop of self-pity.

'Are you quoting me?' she asked her mother sharply.

'Isn't that what you called her?'

'She *did* break his heart.'

'Hardly. He brought Caitlin home almost immediately!'

'And we barely knew anything about you until he'd married you – he's so bloody secretive,' Ali spat.

Caitlin leaned against the old cream Rayburn, picking lemony crumbs off her sweater and wondering which one of them was closer to the truth.

'He's a man of few words,' Sheila said. 'He loves quietly.'

'What in hell's name does that mean?' asked Ali.

'Some men treat their children and their wives like trophies, but Mark's not like that. He gets on with it quietly.'

Yes, Caitlin thought, so quietly, we can hardly hear him. She realized then how noisily her parents had loved her. How many photographs of the same person did a mantelpiece need?

'I suppose I was a trophy child,' she said.

'And do you wish you were a trophy wife?' Sheila asked.

'Sometimes,' Caitlin replied, honestly.

'You're married to the wrong man then,' Ali said.

'I don't think so,' Caitlin said. 'He'll do me.'

'And Rob will do me.'

'I wish you'd settle for something more,' Sheila said to her daughter. 'Rob has got such a lot of growing up to do. He's still a boy. In some cultures, you'd be old enough to be his mother.'

'You'd never talk to Mark like this! I came here to be comforted, not criticized,' Ali said bitterly. She wondered about her therapist's advice not to talk about what she was working through, but it would make her feel *so* much better just to come out with it. Dad had an affair! she could shout. The marriage that everyone in this family holds up as being so bloody perfect was in fact a travesty! That would shut them all up.

'I *have* comforted you, and I'm not criticizing,' Sheila said. 'I'm trying to get you to see sense. Rob is not making you happy.'

'Yes, he is.' Ali sniffed. She could so easily come out with it. You think you had such a good marriage, do you, Mum? Well, let me tell you something.

'Looks like it.'

'Stop being horrible to me.'

'Stop feeling sorry for yourself.'

Ali's throat welled with the saccharine taste of self-pity again. It was a sickly taste, like the third chocolate from the box that leads you to think you might as well have a fourth. The kitchen fell silent.

'Have you any idea how lucky you two are to still have each other?' Caitlin eventually said curtly.

'Yeah, well...' said Ali. The syrup of misery was warming up and running looser now, allowing her spoon to stir a little more easily. 'Before you go I ought just to tell you ... I mean, you probably already know, but...'

'It hasn't escaped anyone's notice that every time you and Rob have a row, you try and make trouble elsewhere,' Sheila warned.

'Why are you so defensive of Caitlin and so critical of me? Just because her husband is having lunch with an ex-girlfriend, she gets special treatment. What about me? My boyfriend is going to Spain with his mates for my birthday and he didn't even have the decency to ask me before he booked it.'

'What did you want to tell me?' Caitlin asked impolitely. It was October 17. Nothing mattered much.

'I'll get that jacket of Mark's,' Sheila said, walking out of the kitchen and making a point of shutting the door firmly and loudly behind her.

Ali made a face after her.

'It's probably insignificant, but do you know that when Nina left to go travelling, Mark thought she might be pregnant?'

Caitlin gagged on a cake crumb. Lemon flavoured spit collected in her mouth.

'How do you know that?'

'I remembered last night that just before she disappeared, he wanted to know my views on abortion, and when I asked why, he told me.'

Caitlin made a noise that bore a strong resemblance to a laugh. It was October 17 and her

182

husband may or may not have another child by the woman he was having lunch with.

'Thanks for telling me, Ali. You have a good day now!' And she walked out of the cottage without bothering to close the door behind her.

Fourteen

The row, when it came, was over mice. Or at least initially it was. It was going to have to be over something, and Caitlin was as sure as hell it wasn't going to be over Nina Wills, so when a parcel from a pest control company with *'From mouse to house!'* stamped all over it arrived by Parcel Force, she thought to herself, that'll do.

'There are two issues at stake here,' she practised on Kit who wanted to open it before Mark was home from work. 'One is that your father is becoming obsessed with internet shopping and the other...'

'Is that he went to lunch with—'

'It's got nothing to do with that. The other is that...' She shuffled the rest of the post into a pile on the hall table. 'Well, there are ways of dealing with mice that are cruel and there are ways that...'

But Kit walked off, and as she went through the teatime ritual of emptying lunch boxes and odorous sports bags, her brain continued to mutter with the monologue. Mark had turned into an online junkie. Hardly a week went by when something or other didn't arrive at their door as a result of some late-night whim, but pest control? He'd asked her what she thought of mousetraps the other day and she'd told him she didn't like them. Hadn't he listened? What was the point of asking if he wasn't going to listen?

In the kitchen, the table – or at least the 6 inches of its surface area that was visible – was scattered with matches.

'Rory!' she shouted up the stairs. 'Bring the matchbox here this minute and then put all these bloody matches back in it!'

Cross with everyone and everything, Caitlin crashed and banged her way through the house, snarling at anyone who came within range. She was like a paper bag made too heavy with damp potatoes, about to give.

'Go and have a bath, Mum,' her third son Joss suggested after Rory had tripped over the bowl of fresh milk she had just put down for the cat.

'Do I look like I've got time for a bath?'

Mark should have spotted the clues as soon as he walked in. The supper ingredients were being slammed in line on the work surface. Half a family jar of Bolognese sauce that had been in the fridge for five days, a tin of tomatoes, a pack of Swedish meatballs not yet defrosted – and two opened packets of different sorts of pasta. Grudge cookery.

'Dad, have you got a matchbox I can have?'

Rory asked. 'I want to see if worms hibernate.'

'There's a parcel for you in the hall,' Caitlin said.

'Excellent!' Mark said, emptying the box of matches Rory had just refilled, tossing the matchsticks in a bowl on the dresser and handing the box to his youngest son. Mark came back with the parcel, pulling out its contents and reading the labels as if it were a Christmas hamper.

'Ten sachets of rodenticide, six cardboard mouse boxes, four open bait trays, one Nipper Break-back Mouse Trap, one pair of gloves, and ten disposal bags...'

'Could I have one of the cardboard mouse boxes?' Rory asked.

'You're not putting poison down in the house,' Caitlin snapped.

'I thought you wanted me to get rid of them,' said Mark.

'I don't want you to *kill* them.'

'Oh, you want me to ask them to leave?'

'But why am I wasting my breath? You always do what you want, whether it affects me or not.'

'Don't argue,' Joss said. 'You never argue.'

After a further twenty minutes of silent tension, Caitlin dished up five portions of the whatever it was, and flung four in the vague direction of each child. Her husband's stayed where it was, next to the empty ovenproof dish.

'What about you?' Rory asked.

'You can have mine,' Joss said, with a rising panic. 'Mum, have mine.'

'Shut up,' said Dylan.

Mark stared at Caitlin and Caitlin stared back at Mark, facing each other like two stubborn cars on a narrow country lane. You reverse. No, you.

'OK,' said Mark at last, using his legs to push his chair backwards, 'if you want a row, we'll have one.'

'I don't want a row,' Caitlin said calmly, 'I just want some communication. You know, that's when one person says something, and then the other replies, and then, based on that reply, the first person says something else...'

'So what is it you'd like to say then?'

'She's just told you,' Joss said, without looking up. 'She doesn't want you to put poison...'

'Shut it, Joss,' said Dylan.

'I don't think we'll do this now,' Caitlin said with a tight smile, throwing a tea towel in the sink.

'Make up your mind,' Mark said.

Neither of them knew how long they would have continued to draw the vicious circle if the doorknocker hadn't sounded just then, but the rat-a-tat-tat brought the bickering to a close. Although the voice that carried along the tiled hall and seeped its way into the kitchen was little more than an alto murmur, Caitlin recognized it immediately. She grabbed the tea towel back out of the sink, wishing she'd had a bath when Joss had suggested it.

'What about pudding?' Rory asked hopefully.

'Have some fruit and then you can have a

biscuit. In fact you can have the whole packet.'

She started busily picking some bruised pears out from under a heap of fresh apples, chatting randomly at her children, manically eliminating the bad atmosphere.

'Who wants a pear? They'll be fine peeled. Or a kiwi? There are two kiwis. Eat the old stuff first.'

Paul Moffat was standing in the brick archway of her kitchen, tilting his head and smiling at the domestic scene the way old ladies do when they look into prams.

'Hiya,' he said, holding out both his hands.

The boys stared at him as if he were a nutter on a bus. His thigh-length coat of soft black felt was fastened down the left-hand side. The first few buttons were undone and the material fell in a triangular fold backwards. It could even have been the same New Romantic inspired coat he'd worn at college, except it was immaculate. The last twenty-five years appeared not to have shaped his sense of fashion in the slightest, and he looked to Caitlin like a cartoon overlaid on film. He's gay, Kit thought disinterestedly.

'This is Paul. Paul, these are three of my boys. The one that so rudely disappeared is Dylan. This is Kit, Joss and Rory.'

'Hi guys,' Paul said.

'Hello,' Kit, Joss and Rory replied.

'I'm sorry, I should have phoned. I'm interrupting family time. I just wanted, you know, with it being the anniversary and everything, to...'

'What anniversary?' asked Rory.

'Well, it's lovely to see you. Have a coffee. Or wine? A beer? Kit, have we got any beer?'

Since when had Kit been the one to ask if they had any beer? It was only that she couldn't look Mark in the face.

'Can I cut this up?' Rory asked, leaving the contents of a cereal box in its white bag on the side.

Paul turned to Caitlin. 'Isn't he just the spit of Erin?'

'Who's Erin?' Joss asked.

Rory started cutting the cereal box in two.

'Paul, will you excuse me?' Mark asked politely. 'I was just on my way out.'

'Me too,' said Kit quickly.

'Where to?' Caitlin asked. 'Not the park.'

'No, not the park.'

Kit was happy to promise that, to stop the interrogation. He disappeared after his father.

Mark slammed the door. This, thought Caitlin, from the man who told me I should report Paul Moffat to the police as a stalker. So it would serve him right if he returned to find her throat slit. When she turned back around, Paul was hunting in his shoulder bag. He handed her a dog-eared wallet of photographs with 'Your Colour Prints Are Inside' written on the front.

'I thought you might like these.'

Caitlin lifted the flap and pulled the first one out, expecting to see herself in a baggy jumper and pixie boots lying on her bed at university. Instead, she saw a grainy snap of her mother, in

188

a grey felt-brimmed hat. Behind Erin was a copse of tall trees, their leaves just beginning to turn colour. She'd never seen the picture before, and the effect of its unfamiliarity was incredible.

'There are more.'

Caitlin pulled out a second picture of Erin in what she used to call her autumn blouse, sitting in a restaurant with a glass of wine lifted to the camera.

'Oh, Paul, they're lovely,' she said, terrified she was going to cry in front of the boys.

'Good subject matter,' Paul said. 'Very beautiful lady. I loved the way Joss didn't know who I meant when I said Erin. I suppose she's always been Granny or something, has she, Joss?'

Caitlin jumped towards him quickly. 'Off you go, boys, go and get your homework done. Hey, you, give me a hug,' she said to Paul, putting her arms round his waist briefly and then, when it wasn't returned, letting her touch fall away.

Mark's car took him on automatic pilot in the direction of his office. There was always something legitimate to do there and God knows he'd managed to waste enough time lately, but as he slowed to pull into the tobacco factory's compact car park, he could see the lights in Chris's third floor office were on, and Lou's car was tucked into a corner.

He wasn't in the mood for company so he pulled up a little further down the road to think. Had he actually said, 'I'm going to the office?' No. He put the car back into first and released the handbrake. He knew where he wanted to go. He'd known since leaving the house. He just didn't quite know how to admit it to himself.

'Hello, it's me,' he said into his mobile fifteen minutes later with a surprising lack of guilt. His overriding concern was getting the story right. What should he tell Nina? What would he tell Caitlin?

'I thought I'd come and see you,' he said. 'But you'll have to direct me.'

As he drove through one of those common fringes of gentrification that so often border more destitute areas, he refused to question himself. Home tonight was not where he wanted to be, October 17 or not. Caitlin had picked the fight, not him. Paul Moffat, with his attentive nostalgia, seemed to be much more what she needed.

The detached Georgian houses and the tree-lined streets ended abruptly at an arterial road. For a few hundred yards on the other side, the houses hung on to aspiration, but then gradually the front gardens stopped showcasing urns and turned into places that grew only dustbins and self-seeded buddleia.

If Nina had been a bloke, no one would have batted an eyelid, he argued to himself. If for example, Gibb – Vortex's pale-faced drummer – lived in Bristol and not New York, it would be quite likely that he, Mark, would go and see him on a whim like this. Reunion made you hungry for each other. His behaviour was not so out of place.

He noticed the first of the metal security sheets at the windows as she had said he would. Nina's street, with its graffiti-riddled sign, was poor in the way he'd forgotten streets could be. Windows all along the quiet terrace were smashed, boarded up or hung with filthy rags. He could see bare light bulbs lighting up even barer rooms. Knackered cars with flat tyres took up what would be precious parking space anywhere else.

Dotted in small groups along its length were tribes of children younger than Rory, who had yet to be allowed to walk to the shop on his own. Out of his car, he was forced to walk through a particularly savage-looking bunch. A kid with a shaved head shouted, 'Fuck you, mister' after him.

Even with all these clues, the outside of Nina's house shocked him. She had tried to place it on the social scale for him but he'd supposed she was being harsh, that ten years of hotel opulence had spoilt her natural assessment of things. As it turned out, she'd been almost generous.

He knocked on the new gloss of the wooden door, more nervous of his BMW's immediate future than anything else. Inside, he heard a female voice shouting, then irregular footsteps, something heavy being shifted, a crepitation of plastic wrapping. The door opened, and to his pleasure and relief, there she was.

Nina was wearing a pair of loose denim drawstring trousers and Mark could see the straps of her bra between her collarbone and the neck of her loose black sweater. Her purple hair was tied back in a stumpy ponytail and she wore no shoes or make-up. Her toenails were purple too. Through lack of effort, she looked ten years younger than she'd done seven hours earlier.

Behind her, blocking the stairs, were two new mattresses still in their cellophane wrap.

'Come in,' she said with a smile, wiping her hair with the back of her hand. The blush of exertion crept around her neck and up her cheeks. 'I was just thinking I could do with a man.'

Upstairs in the lime-green bedroom with the halogen lights, Kit was offering himself to Chloe less effectively. He had a letter in his hand that he had written at lunchtime.

She was lying on her bed with her feet up the wall, her hair falling over the edge of her bed towards the floor. Even upside down, Kit thought she looked beautiful.

'Why won't you read it?'

'Because if I read it, I'll have to write back and I hate writing letters. When I was at boarding school I had to...'

'It says I'd like you to be my girlfriend,' Kit said quickly. 'Properly. So people know.'

Chloe's legs brushed the wall and she tipped herself upright.

'I don't really want a boyfriend at the moment.' Her hair hid her face.

'But if you did, would it...?'

'You can't ask me that!'

'OK, just tell me it wouldn't be Sully then.'

Kit was the only boy in their class who knew how she had got her scar and he carried her trust around with him like an amulet. It made him bigger, luckier, more important. But when Sully was sniffing around, he felt the amulet's power trickling away from him. His secret was to charge it up as often as he could. The more Chloe told him about Rauf, the more the amulet would flicker. Kit was ashamed to admit it, but he liked to hear her voice wobble, to see her eyes flash with tears. Then he could comfort her, put his arm around her, tell her she was safe now.

Chloe laughed. 'You're so weird about Sully. You worship him and you hate him.'

'No I don't. Is it because of Rauf you don't want a boyfriend?'

'I wish he were dead.'

'I'll kill him for you if you want.'

'Oh, yeah? And how would you do that? Smile at him until he cracks up and shoots himself? Actually, forget death, humiliation is better ... have him wet himself in a public place or something...'

Well you won't need my help with that then, Kit thought unhappily. He was trying not to think of Sully's triumphant smirk at the park the other day. Two weeks it took me to have her, Sully had whispered behind Chloe's back. Kit should have punched him there and then, so what had made him put his left hand in the crook of his right elbow to raise a fist in celebration instead then?

When the doorbell had gone ten minutes ago and Chloe had flown down the stairs, he'd been terrified it was going to be Sully.

'So who was it then?' he asked. 'At the door?'

Chloe rolled back on the bed, showing the stud in her navel. Her tummy was smooth and brown.

'I think my mum's got a man,' she said in a low voice.

'What's he like?'

Chloe shrugged.

'Ordinary.'

Together, Nina and Mark had heaved the bigger mattress to the top of the stairs where it now lay against the wall outside Chloe's bedroom door.

'She's got a boy in there,' Nina puffed quietly, standing so close to Mark she could feel the heat coming from under his shirt.

Her own bedroom was only a few feet away and Mark had already seen the crumpled crimson duvet, the red sweater he'd seen her in earlier draped over a long free-standing mirror, a pair of discarded knickers on the floor. He raised his eyebrows, but before he could say anything else, a door flew open and a tall olive-skinned girl stood in front of them. Behind the girl, he caught a glimpse of male legs and big feet sticking out from the bed.

'We were just wondering what all the grunting was about,' Chloe said wickedly.

'You try humping a mattress up a flight of...'

Chloe sniggered.

'You must be Chloe,' Mark said. He moved away from Nina and put a hand on the mattress as if to say, I'm here to help, that's all.

As Mark's voice filtered around the bedroom door, Kit flinched and sat up. His mind flicked through scenarios like a search engine trying to find the right website. His father had come to find him because something had happened at home? His father had followed him? It wasn't his father at all?

'Hi. I'm Mark.'

Kit got up slowly and came to the door to stand behind Chloe.

'Dad?' he heard himself say, his voice finding all extremes.

For a second, Mark forgot where he was. Time and motion froze. When they melted again, the flood was overwhelming.

'This is your dad?' Chloe spluttered.

'You're not *that* Kit?' Nina managed to say.

But Kit's expression didn't even change. He looked through Mark, right to the other side, and even though his thoughts were barely formed, his father knew exactly what he was thinking.

'Kit,' Mark said quickly, grabbing his son's upper arm. The boy shrugged him off angrily and pushed past, beginning to take the stairs two at a time. 'Kit! Come here ... this is Nina! You know? From the website?' Mark called hopelessly after him.

But Kit did not need to be reminded of how this catastrophe had begun. He did not want to

195

remember how he had subscribed with his father's credit card for a laugh, how he had pushed his dad back into his past. He did not want any part of it.

His mother was at home with a man who knew what to do on October 17, and his dad was supposed to be at the office. He thought of his brothers, then of Sheila. It was Sheila he would go to. Sheila would know what to do next.

The central heating had gone off long ago and the wood in the multi-burner had turned to ash but the temperature of the sitting room seemed appropriate to Caitlin as she pulled a throw off the back of her chair and wrapped herself in it.

'I'll go and get him,' Mark said suddenly, rising from his uncomfortable perch on the sofa arm and digging in his pocket for his keys. 'I don't want him to get the wrong end of the...'

'Is there a right one?' his wife asked coldly.

'I could see in his face that he thought I was...'

Caitlin glared at him. 'Are you bloody surprised? You told us you were going to work. Some heavy editing, I think you usually say. Is that what you're doing now? Editing your story for me and for your son, who saw it with his own...'

'He didn't see anything. There was nothing to see.'

'So why did you go?' Caitlin asked loudly.

Mark rubbed the bridge of his nose with a finger.

'I've told you.'

His mouth tightened. There was a long pause. She knew his expressions well enough to know a truth was coming.

'I just want some fun,' he said eventually.

Really? Caitlin thought. Bully for you. Bully for fucking you. But she said nothing, and just rocked slightly in her wrap. Her silence annoyed him, despite the thin ice he was skating on.

'Because, let's face it, it's not much fun here any more, is it?'

That was it. She got up too then, letting the throw fall back into the chair.

'Come with me,' she said wearily. 'I'd like to remind you of something.'

Rory and Joss slept with a side light on. Under the covers they looked like twins with their thick tufts of hair, the orange glow from the wall socket diffusing the difference between Joss's freckles and Rory's more sun-friendly complexion.

Caitlin walked into the middle of the room – the biggest in the house – and stood between the two beds whilst Mark hovered unsurely by the doorway. She didn't bother to keep her voice down, knowing her youngest two would sleep through a thunderstorm.

'Rory had a dentist appointment at lunchtime today so Lesley took the last half an hour of the workshop for me.'

Mark nodded. He supposed he deserved whatever was coming.

'And Joss needed new shoes, which we got

after school.'

'No need to wake them,' he whispered.

'But the first shop didn't have the ones he liked in his size,' she carried on, still at the same volume. Caitlin knew what woke them and what didn't. Her voice in the middle of the night never did. 'We had to cross town. At five o'clock. Which, as you know, isn't the best time.'

At the foot of each bed on top of two identical painted wooden toy-boxes were two folded piles of clean clothes for the morning.

'Did you know Rory is going to a party on Saturday? The present is downstairs, wrapped, next to a permission slip he needs to take to school.'

She turned around and opened the tall door to the airing cupboard. The top shelf was full of sheets, duvets and pillowcases, the second shelf was for towels. The third was for unseasonal clothes, sweaters in the summer, shorts in the winter. She pulled out two towels.

'Swimming tomorrow for them both,' she said, flinging them over her shoulder.

On the wide, uncarpeted landing, the ironing board was up, with the iron still plugged in. A red washing basket full of paired socks was on the floor and two white school shirts hung on wire coat-hangers from the board's edge.

Across the landing, Dylan's room was a mess. His bare legs, still smooth but chunkier than they used to be, were hanging out either side of the blue-and-white quilt. There was a smell of

burgeoning adolescence in the air. Caitlin handed the warm towels to Mark and bent over to
pick up the clothes on the floor, pushing tee
shirts, more socks and boxer shorts into a laundry sack on the back of the door, folding jeans,
tidying trainers. On her way out, she pinched
two dirty coffee cups with one hand.

'You see?' she said outside the door. 'You see
why it's hard to be the life and soul?'

'I see,' Mark said, 'now can we please go to
bed?'

'Oh, it's not over yet,' Caitlin said. 'This is
only the start.'

Fifteen

An intermittently warm sun and an azure sky
made it feel more like September than October
as Kit and Dylan unhooked the bikes from the
back of Caitlin's seven-seater car. Sheila tried to
get the others down from the roof rack but her
right shoulder gave a muffled scream as she
reached up.

'We'll do it, Granny,' Kit said.

No Shee that time, Sheila registered.

Her two youngest grandsons Joss and Rory
had been unusually quiet on the journey here but
the eldest two were doing their best to cover the
silences. All four of them should have been at

the optician but the last twelve hours had simply been too much for everyone.

Their parents had looked scratchy-eyed and crumpled this morning, like dishevelled holidaymakers stranded at an airport during a baggage handlers' strike. They'd been over-grateful to Shelia for coming to their rescue and she'd been glad to get away.

Theirs was the only car in the car park, so her worries about parking the monster of a car turned out to be no problem at all.

'Do you think Mummy and Daddy will still have the party?' Rory asked.

'Don't worry about it,' Dylan told his littlest brother.

'What if they get divorced? They can't have a party if they get divorced?'

'Shut up, Rory,' said Joss.

'No one's getting divorced. Everyone's parents argue from time to time, it wouldn't be normal if they didn't,' Sheila said cheerfully. Kit glanced quickly at her and she nodded reassuringly.

The wooden, slatted waiting room on the old railway station was locked, its blackboard shutters closed with a fading message in green chalk – *Closed for the season. See you all at Easter!*

Unpeopled, the platform had a dreamlike quality about it. As she fitted Rory's shiny blue helmet under his chin, she tried to place herself there not as a granny on childcare duty but as a mum in a smock, with sunglasses pushing back her dark blonde hair.

She glanced at the railway sleepers that formed the nearby rectangular flower bed. They had been positioned there by her own husband nearly thirty years previously, using chains and a hired digger. She could almost hear the chug of the engine.

The Bristol to Bath Railway Path, the old trackbed of the former Midland Railway, was now a 3-yard wide, tarmacked off-road tourist route. Like so much else, its history had been recycled, its past put to another, less industrial, use. Warehouses were art galleries, tobacco factories were bars, and a defunct train line was a cycle path. That was Bristol for you.

Complete strangers beetled all over it with no clue about the sweat that had been poured into it, but at least the track still had a purpose. As long as feet still moved over and through and along it, it lived. And as long as *her* feet still trod on (or pedalled over, depending on her mood) it, then so did she, although she hadn't gone as far as Bitton, which was where she was taking the boys today, for years.

The Webb boys were more familiar with the urban stretch of the path, where schoolchildren and postmen and commuting cyclists wove in and out on their way into the city, fighting for the supremacy they would need when they got there. They showed no curiosity for the magic that lay beyond the tunnel at Staple Hill where the modern world fell away, and everything became greener, quieter, emptier.

But this was the stretch that she had been

involved with. Inextricably linked to, if she was being honest.

She sometimes bumped into Bob Palmer (not Shirley any more, as she had died of breast cancer six years ago) and Jackie Stock (who no longer wore peasant tops but had stuck rigidly to her slacks) in town. Invariably, they still talked about the Herculean effort that had gone in to hacking out a new identity for their section of the path.

She often saw notices in the local press of Bob's talks, complete with slides about the founding of BURPS, for which he charged sixty pounds. She had even been to one a year or two ago, when her Gardening Society had invited him to their AGM. One of his photographs had showed both Ken and Jan de Junger in fitted cotton shirts and flared trousers with a rather busty Sheila between them, wearing a thin rugby-style shirt and a choker of wooden beads. ('Yan Dee Yunger, actually,' Sheila had whispered to the woman next to her, after Bob had made such a botch of his beautiful Dutch name.)

Next year, largely thanks to Bob's unceasing work, the only part of the track that was still dust, the few miles between Mangotsfield and Warmley, should get its new surface. And yet Bob, and Jackie, and the tens of others who had given up years of free time to organize firework nights in the sidings, live music in the goods shed and meetings in the old booking office at Bitton station, who had learnt to drive mini-diggers and handle industrial strimmers, to work in teams of four to move 200-weight of wooden sleepers and make lunch for twenty in a truck in the cattle dock, all these good, energetic, determined people never seemed to be able to bring themselves to actually *use* it. They talked about it, they raised money for it, but they never actually *used* it.

This puzzled Sheila. When she was asked to have the boys, she'd known immediately what she could do with them. It was her perfect excuse to go as far as Bitton.

Perhaps the memory of so much hard work made it impossible for the more active members of BURPS to enjoy. Perhaps Bob and Jackie and Roger and the rest of the faces she never saw along the way took one look at the neat wide level road and thought only of the time they organized a fund-raising trip to the Leicester Transport Museum on a minibus and spent four hours at a motorway service station somewhere near Birmingham waiting for the AA, or the freezing night of the 'Magic Lantern Show' in the goods shed when everyone filed out afterwards, desperate for an open fire or a warm bed, only to find their cars under a blanket of snow and the roads impassable. Perhaps it all seemed too much like hard work. Perhaps it belonged to their youth.

They wouldn't, like she could, think of lazy picnics in wildflower meadows or the fun of sheltering from summer storms in derelict waiting rooms. They wouldn't remember what it was like to find a hundred ladybirds on your

203

naked body, or the art of swapping mouthfuls of chilled cider with a man who was not your husband, nor would they know the sound of consummate peace, because they weren't her. They were people who led proper, straightforward, uncomplicated lives, which bore scrutiny and trumpeted honesty. She and Jan had been alone in their selfish joy. 'We must enjoy it while we can,' he used to say.

'Is it two and a half miles there, and two and a half miles back?' Rory asked nervously.

'It's all level. There are no hills.'

'What if when we get there, we're too tired to get back?'

'We'll eat our energy bars,' Dylan reassured him.

They always pull together in a crisis, Sheila thought.

'Are you sure you'll be all right on that, Granny?' Joss asked as they mounted their bikes on the grass verge. He was the worrier of Mark and Caitlin's brood, the checker of facts, the one who wanted everyone always to be happy. The abnormality of today was probably hitting him the hardest.

Her large, thin-wheeled silver ladies bicycle looked like a museum piece compared with her grandsons' mountain bikes. Its skeleton-shaking suspension made the stiffness in her joints protest even before she felt the rigid white plastic seat between her legs. She could have borrowed Ali's chrome-framed alloy-wheeled Marin, which had been sitting in her shed gathering dust for the last year, but she wanted to ride *her* bike, in the same way that she wanted her picnic to be bread, cheese and cider. 'I'll be fine. Don't wait for me, just keep me in sight.'

As the boys pushed off, standing on their pedals, their hips rocking up and down in a rhythm like early industrial pistons, she took a long draught of the autumnal air. As she exhaled, she said his name.

'Oh, Yaaaaaaan.'

Her days with Jan de Junger had been playing on a continuous loop in her head ever since she had posted the letter to Leiden University a week ago. The act of slotting it into the box, releasing her thumb and forefinger and letting the envelope go, had set in motion something she now had to leave to fate. The outcome was beyond her control.

Over the years, she had cooked up quite a life for him. In her imagination (for she had nothing else to go on) he lived in a suburb near Amsterdam in a simple house he had designed and built himself. Lately, she had pinched a few details from Caitlin's account of the eco-chalet Lou Jones had taken them to, so now Jan's home had a glass roof and thick concrete walls. He was in the process of winding down his commitment to Leiden University's Faculty of Archaeology – she knew it still had one, she had seen mention of it in the *Observer* – and he was spending more time cycling, gardening and reading. She wavered between him having a partner (when she couldn't bear to think of him lonely) and living alone (when she couldn't bear to think of a contender to her throne).

She had so nearly started her search for him in 2002, when the Queen had celebrated her Golden Jubilee. All that red, white and blue everywhere, just as it had been for the Silver. And she was glad she hadn't, because by now, she would know the upshot. She would know if he was a grandfather of millions, in love with one of his students, or just a fuddy old man. It was the not knowing that was giving her the sort of energy she needed to cycle five miles on an old boneshaker.

The ladybirds had over-bred that year, she remembered. Every leaf, wall, stone and trunk had crawled with miniature red armies, like tiny enamel clockwork toys.

'It's a feminist revolution,' Jan had once said as he lay in a field and watched a battalion take over his bare foot.

'Not all ladybirds are ladies,' she'd pointed out.

'And not all ladies are women either,' he'd replied, kissing her tanned summer skin. If she walked over to that stile now and looked left, would she see him lying in the meadow in his cream canvas jeans, bare-chested, his collared white cheesecloth short sleeved shirt hanging on a low twig jutting out from the hedge? Would she hear the sighs that peppered his talk and expressed so eloquently their hopeless desire to stop the world and get off?

The brown towelling bikini that she used to

wear underneath her clothes on these secret trysts was still kept safely in a drawer in a pine chest in the spare bedroom at home. With its wide sides, its circular gold buckle and incongruous white piping along the seams, it didn't know whether it wanted to be sporty, practical or chic. It was a fashion disaster but every time she had a clear-out, it escaped the cull. It would provide a laugh for someone one day; Ali sorting out her belongings, holding the item up to Caitlin, the two of them having a tender snigger at her expense. She couldn't throw it out – it wouldn't be fair to deny them the opportunity.

The bikini represented the confident middle bit of their affair, but the very first time she and Jan had met along the path, she had worn tights under her cotton skirt and a halter-neck top over a conventional bra – a suit of armour to ward against temptation. Except it hadn't worked.

'I don't understand. What are you wearing?' Jan had whispered once they had jumped across the physical abyss to their first kiss. His hands were trying to sort out the straps and layers, which made no sense. And suddenly, it had made no sense to her either. She'd walked back to her bicycle with her breasts loose under the sun top, the flimsy material of her skirt swishing against her bare legs, waving a stalk of cow parsley like a wand all the way home.

But it was autumn now and flakes of red, russet, brown and ochre swirled in her grandsons' wake. Sheila forged happily through the backwash, the debris scrunching under her wheels and dancing in the watery beams of sunlight that filtered through the increasing gaps between the oaks, ash and beech.

Every now and again, the boys turned and cycled back to her to ask or tell her something.

'How did Grandad lift up the track?'

'He must have been very strong.'

'Were you proud of him?'

'Oh, very, very proud.'

In truth though, she had fought not to prostrate herself like a suffragette on the sleepers and beg Ken to leave them be, so that the world she and Jan had so covertly inhabited the year before could remain as it was, a shrine to their romance.

At last, Bitton station came into sight and the prospect of it made them all put on a final spurt. Kit won of course, but instead of the gleaming steam engine she had promised, there was only an elderly gardener, turning over the soil in the brick-walled planter that no longer spelled 'Welcome to Bitton' in begonias.

Sheila noticed his air of neglect: a misshapen beige V-neck over a beer tummy, the worn collar of a moss green, striped shirt teamed with a red polyester tie. There could be no woman in *his* life, she was surprised to find herself thinking.

The five of them sat on the cold iron platform bench, disembowelling their lunch boxes and telling her about tricks they could do with a skateboard. Their idle chatter was a real treat and the interruption was an intrusion.

'Sheila?'

The shabbily dressed gardener had one hand on his hip as if to ease a pain in his back.

'Is it Sheila Webb?'

She got up and looked at him more carefully, then she recognized the West Country burr, the bubble of a joke that always formed a froth on the surface of his talk.

'Is that Roger?' she called back.

The same Roger Sage that bought more rounds at the bar than anyone else was clambering clumsily down from the northbound platform and making his way across to the southbound. She remembered his gate vaults twenty-five years earlier, his hip-swivelling disco dancing.

'Well, blow me!' he said, smiling all over his unshaven face. 'And Dutchy was only talking about you the other day.'

'You look awful,' Lesley told Caitlin as they stood a few feet away from a security guard, one flight of stairs up from the museum's hauling way. Twenty valuable paintings – including sketches by Van Gogh and Raul Dufy – were about to arrive by Securicor on loan from the Royal Academy for a touring exhibition entitled 'Harvest', due to open on Saturday. Soon, the place would be crawling with art handlers, conservators, curators, press.

'I can't talk about it right now.'

The entire museum staff was hanging around the stairwell. What anyone hoped to glimpse through the crocodile of large, brown, wrapped parcels no one knew, but it was better than working. Only the select few would be invited to the special preview once the exhibition was hung, but after that, it would be Bristol's for a fortnight.

'Oh.' Lesley looked disappointed.

'Up all night dealing with a marriage crisis, like we didn't see one coming.'

Two cleaners in light blue, short-sleeved shirts and matching trousers looked at her.

'Not about the band and all that?'

'Nina bloody Wills, actually.'

'Not serious though, is it?'

'There's no room in a marriage for separate lives, is there? I've asked him to introduce me to her, to have it all out in the open, but he won't.'

There was no time for Lesley to respond. The security guard called across the echoing stair-well – 'They're here!' – and she swiped her card through the lock. The door opened and in front of the paintings walked a small procession of staff from the Royal Academy. They arrived nodding and pointing, visibly impressed with the lighting, happy with the light, the air, the temperature. Behind them, muscle-bound men carried the paintings like huge presents being presented to a queen in a storybook. And then, behind the paintings, somehow diminished, walked Mark.

Caitlin didn't see him. She had been dragged into the edge of a discussion about the exhibition layout. A thematic hanging of the paintings had been agreed on, but now there was a suggestion that it could be combined with a chronological one. She was fascinated by the potential for error and was almost annoyed when he arrived at her side with flowers.

'What are you doing here?'

'I brought you these.'

'Why?'

'I needed to see you. I want another go at explaining.'

'You told me you were going to work. Heavy editing, remember?'

'That was my intention. But we've gone over this.'

'And we will be going over it again and again until...'

'Hey, you two, come and see this,' Lesley said.

Mark thrust the roses at Caitlin.

'What am I supposed to do with those?' she asked him coldly.

Lesley took them.

'They're just what our boring old office needs, thank you,' she said. 'Have you seen this fabulous little sketch? It's based on the famous Potato Harvest.'

Mark peered at the random pencil sweeps and identified with the figures' tiredness. As he drifted towards the next one, Lesley hissed in Caitlin's ear.

'Take the afternoon off.'

'I can't. The Education Department needs educating, apparently. One of the exhibition organizers from the RA is coming in to talk to us about teachers' evenings.'

'Sod teachers' evenings, this is your marriage.'

'One is more appealing than the other at the moment.'

'Then go out tonight, just the two of you.'

'I'm too tired.'

'Oh, I'm beginning to see where he's coming from,' Lesley said.

Mark wandered back. 'Can we nip out for a coffee?' he asked as if it was something they were in the habit of doing, when in fact the suggestion had all the hallmarks of a communication breakdown.

'No.'

'What about in an hour?'

'No.'

'When then? I'd like to do it before the boys get back.'

Caitlin thought of him in Nina's house again, her own version of the mattress scene, the stairs, Kit coming out. Oddly, she had it uncannily right, even to the detail of the glimpse of a crumpled bed across the landing.

'You think it's that easily fixed?'

'I haven't done anything to break it.'

Caitlin locked her eyes on his. 'Do you promise me you're not having an affair with her?'

She had asked so many versions of the same question already. How far would you have gone? No distance. And there was never any pregnancy? No baby. And you're not still in love with her? Not still in love with her.

'I am not.'

'And you don't want to.'

'I don't want to.'

But Caitlin heard the clause before he even said it. She bit her lip.

'Although I do want a friendship with her.'

'A friendship that doesn't necessarily include me?' she asked.

'A friendship that doesn't necessarily include you, yes.'

Sixteen

When Caitlin, feeling as if her boots were filled with lead, turned to rejoin her colleagues, the atmosphere in the gallery had changed to something approaching a drinks party. And boy did she need a drink. A trestle table covered by a starched white cloth had miraculously appeared. On it, a tray of glasses caught the light and a cluster of green wine bottles were showing a promising film of moisture. The London art handlers, identifiable in their uniform of black designer jeans, had finished their work and were clearly expecting to be welcomed socially.

Caitlin formed a quick plan to knock back a glass and then go home to take advantage of an empty house, but a woman with a mass of red curls piled haphazardly on her head was already introducing herself. Her name failed to permeate.

'Am I the only one tired of post-Impression-ism?'

'Do we really have to actually point out the pointillist influences in his work?'

'Wouldn't you prefer a Gauguin if you could choose?'

All the time the woman talked, Caitlin thought of Mark and his impossible demands. What was it he really wanted? An open marriage? No marriage at all, perhaps? What did Nina want? Were her sights set on the ultimate goal?

'He really is quite something,' the woman was saying.

Caitlin had lost the thread of the conversation. Who was quite something? Gauguin?

'You'll either love him or you'll hate him. Like Marmite! He's an acquired taste.'

'All artists are when it comes down to it,' Caitlin said, hazarding a guess.

'Oh, Bill's not an artist. Who told you he was an artist?'

Bill? Who was Bill? Caitlin pretended to remember where she'd heard the rumour from.

'I must be muddling him with someone else...'

'Bill's not normally someone you'd confuse with anyone else!'

Caitlin wondered if this woman with the red curls was in love with Bill, whoever Bill was, but the speculation wasn't enough to distract her from her new insecurity with Mark. She forced herself to stop thinking of him by trying to work out how her assailant had tied her pashmina. She could never get her own quite right. Maybe it

214

was the size that made the difference.

'He sounds...'

'Oh, he's amazing, an exhibition organizer second to none. I've known him since he started curating shows at the RA back in 1998. There's nothing he doesn't know. It'll be a fascinating talk. It always is, and I've heard him talk more times than I've had—'

'Hot dinners?' Caitlin finished for her. Marmite, hot dinners, this woman didn't have an original thought in her head.

'It's just that he so knows how to work an audience...'

When people said that, it usually turned out to be the opposite.

'I'll listen carefully,' Caitlin said. Maybe it was the actual knot of the pashmina. It was unconventional, she had worked that much out. But what did Mark mean exactly when he said he wanted a friendship that didn't include her?

Her glass was empty already, so she went over to the table and poured herself another. Thankfully no one else came to quiz her, and for a few glorious moments, she blanked off entirely, forgetting Mark, Nina, work, the boys, how she was going to get home if she'd had too much to drink, what they would eat for supper and when. She absorbed the surrounding words here and there, letting the wine muddle her slightly. The name Bill Winfrey swirled around her like a Chinese whisper. He said this to me the other day, he showed me that, he phoned me, he took me to dinner, he gave me this job, that. Just as

Caitlin was thinking that for a man who was talked about as much as Bill Winfrey, it was bloody rude to be late for his own lecture, she realized he was already there. What happened next she would always remember in slow motion.

In the first frame, he hovered momentarily on the edge of a messy clutch of London people, gesturing apologetically, pulling a hand over his high forehead. In the second, he stepped away, pushing his spectacles further on to the bridge of his nose. In the third, putting one laced soft-soled shoe in front of the other, he came towards her. Towards *her*. The fourth had him flicking out a lick of wavy greying hair that curled under the collar of his loose blue suit and in the fifth, he was taking a full glass of wine off the table, tipping it to his lips and downing it almost in one.

'I only do that when I'm late,' he said to her, widening his eyes slightly as the alcohol hit his system.

'Best not to be late too often then,' she replied.

So he was the 'acquired taste', was he? Caitlin assessed her first impression of him and she decided, like Marmite, that in the right mood, she would like him. Having agreed that with herself, she hardly listened to a word of his talk. Instead, as his good-natured educated tones fill-ed the room, she tried to imagine life without Mark. She envisaged the two of them in the kitchen telling the boys they were getting a divorce, Joss crying. She saw herself waving her four sons goodbye from her doorstep, watching them get into Mark's new car, with Nina Wills sitting discreetly in the passenger seat. She even got as far as trying to work out the financial viability of staying in Dryhouse Lane, and it was only in contemplating the process of moving out that she came to her senses.

Study the speaker she told herself. Count his wrinkles, the creases in his suit, the number of times he says 'exciting', anything to stop this ridiculous train of thought.

Bill Winfrey's face had some serious lines. There were two grooves from his nose to the corners of his mouth, three ripples across his high forehead that creased when he made a certain sort of point, and a horizontal slash on his chin.

'The order in which works are displayed can shape an argument,' he said as she studied the way in which he was displaying himself. On closer examination, his blue suit wasn't a blue suit at all. It was a pair of light cotton navy trousers and a heavier black jacket, maybe moleskin. The top button of his chambray short was undone and the purple silk tie was tied low, as if he'd started off with good intentions and then given up. His shoes were brown suede lace-ups. Not vain then.

'For example, if we want to show works as a complex historical survey, then a chronological approach is best, but this one would probably not work in that way.'

She twisted her wedding ring and found

herself wondering whether the woman with the red curls and the pashmina had anything to do with him. When she looked up, he was staring right at her. Intentionally, she felt, which made her blush.

There was a tinge of hero worship in the Londoners' clapping. He walked away from his space and was given a second glass of wine. She thought about leaving, and then, 'You were putting me off,' he said in her left ear.

'Me?' Caitlin said, looking around to see who else he could mean. 'What was I doing?'

'You weren't listening to me.'

'I'm sorry.'

'I forgive you. Actually, I don't think I was on form.'

'I'm sure you were. I was miles away, trying to sort out a silly ... my husband has just ... my sons are ... I've got so many things to do that I...'

'I understand,' he said warmly.

'From that?'

'In a way.'

The woman with the pashmina was suddenly at Bill's side. 'Brilliant as always,' she purred.

'This member of the audience didn't think so...'

'Oh, I did!'

'I'm sorry, I don't know your name...'

'Caitlin.'

'Well, I'm sorry to say that whilst I was scintillating the rest of you with my finely honed speech, Caitlin here was writing a mental shopping list...'

'More fool her,' said the red curls.

Bill Winfrey laughed gently and said he was only teasing. The woman pushed her hair off her face and shot Caitlin a warning look. Caitlin blushed again. Bill leaned forward, away from the fringes of the pashmina that were doing their best to make contact with his jacket.

'What was on that shopping list, then?' he enquired.

'Marmite,' Caitlin answered cryptically, not caring whether he understood her or not but somehow knowing he didn't care either.

Mark left the museum in a hot fury. Caitlin was going to make him suffer for something he hadn't even done. He felt cheated and misunderstood and undervalued – three perfectly good reasons to retrospectively justify his actions. Before he had even reached his car, he had – like an addict merely going through the motions of recovery – reached straight for his next fix.

Half an hour after his wife had given him short shrift, he was sitting next to Nina Wills on the College Green bench, a half-inch gap between their thighs. *Is evrythng ok?* her well-timed text message had asked, with its chirpy little clarion call as he'd thundered away from his wife. But he hadn't been the first to contact her. That was the important thing.

'Did I get you into trouble the other night?' she wanted to know.

'No. I managed to do that without your help.'

'So it's OK to see each other?'

Nina had brought two tortilla wraps with roasted vegetables, marinated in the Turkish way. Bits of oily green pepper and chargrilled zucchini were falling out all on to their laps.

'Why not?'

'Your wife might not like it?'

'I've just told her I want a friendship with you that doesn't necessarily include her,' Mark said, doing a better job with his food than she was, simply by taking much bigger mouthfuls. There was something uncharacteristically uncouth about his manners which he recognized, but which also felt right.

Nina laughed a little too loudly. 'You did what?'

'I told her I want a friendship with you that doesn't necessarily include her,' Mark repeated. His delivery was to the point, no messing.

'You can't go round saying things like that.'

'Why not?'

'Well, you're at least going to have to be more explicit, then,' she said.

Mark knew that further explanation would be the kind thing but he hadn't got a clue. It had been easy to promise Caitlin total fidelity just now. He loved her. He didn't want to do anything to hurt her. But, but, but...

His lips were shiny from the olive oil. Nina tried to remind herself that he was a married man with four children.

'Have you ever been unfaithful?' she asked, pulling a circle of courgette out of her wrap and popping it carefully into her mouth.

'No.'

'Have you ever wanted to be?'

Mark concentrated for a moment. It was a dangerous thing to say, but he was going to say it all the same.

'Not until now.'

The gap between their thighs closed to nothing.

'If I were a better person, I'd tell you that there was no chance,' Nina said.

He took one of her hands in both of his.

'It's me that's bad,' he said. 'You're not the one trying to stay faithful.'

'Have an apricot,' she said quickly, opening a lid on a square plastic tub.

'I think I'd rather have a kiss,' he said urgently.

'Have an apricot.'

'Kiss me.'

'If we do, Mark, we're doomed.'

'We might be doomed anyway.'

Nina put the top back on the apricots. 'Not here then,' was all she said.

Paul Moffat took the slip road off the motorway to the services between Bristol and Slough at the very last minute. He was feeling tired and sick and in need of a drink – a consequence of his spending far too many nights clubbing lately – but they were not the reasons he broke his journey.

All that showy grief he'd displayed in the café with Caitlin when she'd told him about Erin's

221

accident had so far amounted to nothing. The solemn promises he'd made to himself about the role he felt he could play in Caitlin's life were fast becoming hollow. If he shirked his new responsibility much longer, he might as well never contact her again. He called her mobile but after a telling three rings, she must have switched it to voicemail. A text would do.

Sorry – did I call you at an inconvenient time? Feeling a bit delicate today – spent a night in the Queen Charlotte! – Caitlin would surely know the QC was a gay bar and although it was a cowardly way to drop a hint, he had to get around to having that conversation with her sometime – *Just wondering, when are you free to visit Erin and John's* – what should he call it? Grave? Resting place? – *special place? I would very much like to do that. We could make a day of it, have lunch somewhere nice, my treat. I'll get that photo you like framed asap too. So good to be back in touch, take care sweetie, Paul xxxx*

His phone told him his message was too long to send as a standard SMS and did he want to send it as two? He read it again to see where he could edit it. The second sentence wasn't crucial. In fact, mentioning the Queen Charlotte didn't sound right next to Erin's name, and then there was the fact that married women – or married men come to that – didn't generally understand promiscuity. He deleted the reference and pressed send before writing another text of an altogether different nature.

* * *

222

Back at Nina's, Mark slipped out of his heavy leather jacket, and as it hit the floor, he heard his keys jangle. Keys that opened his own front door, his back door, his garden shed door that was full of boys' bikes and footballs, keys that Caitlin had copies of on her own leather fob.

Nina leaned against the wallpaper that she had started to strip. She pulled her hair off her face and held it back so that her elbows made triangles with her head. He ran his hands along either side of her jawline and across her ears until his fingers joined hers. Then he slid his touch down the back of her arms to her ribs. Under her long-sleeved tee shirt he felt her oddly toned muscles. An image of her in a hotel gym came to him and he couldn't help comparing her contours to Caitlin's.

When he moved his hands to the curve of her waist, a thumb pressed against a hip bone and brushed the beginning of her tummy. His hand crept around the corner and found the thin strip of a thong along her back. The lacy material dug slightly into her flesh and he put a finger under it.

All sorts of thoughts were coming at him. The comfortableness of Caitlin's altogether softer shape, his own lack of definition, Nina's skinny ribs. His chest sagged, his stomach hung over the top of his trousers – could he do this *and* keep his clothes on?

'You can kiss me now,' she said.

There was no first gear, no suggestion of holding back. He didn't know how to stop it.

'Are you ready to be doomed?' she whispered, her lips level with the neck of his shirt.

Mark let his forehead crash against the wall behind her.

Nina stayed completely still, his body pinning her in position.

'You're not, are you?' she said at last.

The strange thing was it seemed entirely natural to Caitlin and Bill to be the last two left in the exhibition hall. They'd been locked in almost rudely exclusive conversation by the drinks table long enough for the rest of the group to feel uncomfortable about butting in. One by one, their friends and colleagues had drifted off. She had told him about naming the crouched burial 'Fred' and he had told her about the first time he'd seen a preserved corpse on a visit to the British Museum in 1955. She had asked him if he thought the mummies minded and he had asked her if she would mind if she were a mummy. She had said she would, and he'd agreed. She had told him about being offered the chance to see her parents' dead bodies and how glad she was that she'd declined and he'd described to her the awful twenty minutes he'd once spent waiting for help on a mountain with a stranger's warm body at his feet. Death had never been so fascinating, he'd said. And slowly, as they'd talked, Caitlin had found herself arriving at a new understanding. 'But I do want a friendship with Nina Wills,' Mark had said, 'and I want one that doesn't necessarily include you.'

Neither Caitlin nor Bill Winfrey had much noticed the clearing of the hall. Lesley had hovered for a while but even the woman with the pashmina had eventually given up her vigilance and gone with the others to Muirs, the restaurant next door, to sit on leather sofas and play I Know More About Art Than You Do.

'I don't want to keep you,' Bill said at the first hint of overstretching the situation.

Caitlin, usually prone to feelings of inadequacy, didn't hear it as his bid to escape.

'From what?'

'All those things you were thinking you had to do...'

'Not so much things to do as things to decide,' she confessed, 'but the longer I stand here drinking and talking to you, the less I feel inclined to do even that.'

'Decisions are often better made stone-cold sober,' Bill said.

'And I'm definitely not that.'

'That makes two of us.'

'I didn't have lunch and I'm supposed to be cycling home but...'

'Let me take you to dinner.'

It was said in such a wonderful rush of conviction.

'I've got children.'

'Of course...'

'But their father...'

Already, Caitlin was talking about Mark as something once removed.

'You're on good terms?'

Her shrug of the shoulders was neither truthful nor untruthful.

'I'll text him,' she said. 'The boys are with their grandmother but I ought to see how the land lies.'

Caitlin took her phone from behind the unmanned security desk. The message from Paul about her parents' grave didn't even make her blink.

Instead of going straight home after dropping Kit, Dylan, Joss and Rory, Sheila drove to Bitton. It was the longest she had driven in the dark for years, so she had to concentrate, squinting at the oncoming headlights, leaning forward, gripping the wheel so hard she nearly missed the final turning, swinging left at the last minute, slewing on to the wrong side.

There was no moving traffic in Station Road, just locked cars parked neatly outside semi-detached houses. Four, six, eight on the left-hand side, three, five, seven on the right. She barely had her foot on the accelerator and when she got to the end of the even numbers, she turned around without looking. Forty-nine, forty-seven, forty-five.

Forty-three. She'd written the number down on the back of her hand. Her heart thumped so loudly, she feared for it. Was this it? Did Jan have a blue door, a hedge, a parking space outside it? She pulled into the kerb, not knowing what on earth she was going to do next. There was a light shining from the rectangular pane of glass above the door but the windows were black holes, the curtains were open.

She sat there, with the engine running, frightening herself. Jan lived here. *Here.* In this house. Inside were his things. His collection of Delft tiles, his signed first edition of *The Quiet American* by Graham Greene, things he treasured, that she had once been privy to. But what else was in there? A wife's wardrobe? Photographs of grandchildren? The trappings of disability, illness? What had Roger Sage meant when he'd said Jan was lucky to be alive? Was he in there too, quietly dying?

The last question pulled her up sharply. What was she doing here, spying on a man she had known for four months, twenty-five years ago? What gave her the right to do this after all she had said to the younger generation lately? What made it OK to tell Caitlin to be wary of the man who used to camp outside her door, to tell Mark he was playing with fire, to tell Ali that Rob was not worth it? She cupped her cold bare hands and blew into them, ready to set off for home.

Just then, out of the darkness, emerged the tall slightly stooped figure of a man. Big feet, rangy legs, walking! Alive! Jan! Let it be Jan!

A burst of emotion flowered across her face in the darkness. Her eyes scanned the figure, searching for something that would convince her, but he was hidden by the night. A hat covered his head and a scarf covered his mouth. She closed her eyes. It *was* him, she could feel it.

She sat there, clutching the gearstick with one hand and the steering wheel with the other, drinking up every last drop of him until, much too soon, he reached his door and disappeared.

Her body started shaking violently and though she knew it was nothing to do with being cold, she pulled on her coat. It was a few more minutes until she felt safe to drive home.

Unlocking her own front door, she went to Ken's old toolbox that she kept behind a curtain under the kitchen sink and took out a screwdriver. In the garden room, the Witch's Butter along the windowsill yielded immediately to the pressure of the sharp metal and the fungus fell away in lumps over her fingers and on to the floor. She scraped hard at the viscous folds, taking shards of decaying wood out of the frame as she went. Then, when it was all gone, she got a dustpan and brush, swept up the mess and tipped it with one decisive movement into the bin. Life suddenly was well worth the living.

Seventeen

The house in Dryhouse Lane at six-fifteen in the evening was abnormally quiet. All four boys were in the sitting room watching *The Simpsons*, waiting for the roast chicken their father had put in the oven half an hour ago. It was odd, Mark thought, savouring the peace with a beer in the study, how an all-male household very often meant companionable silence. He wondered if Caitlin ever realized how her female presence disrupted the order of things. He wasn't sure if he wanted her to or not.

She was at another late meeting again, talking to a curator at the Royal Academy about the Harvest exhibition. When she'd called at lunch-time, she'd asked him, rather over-cautiously, if he minded her having supper with Paul Moffat on the way back. As if you need permission after the way I've behaved lately, Mark had said, remembering her peculiarly tense reply as he sat now at his cluttered desk waiting for Outlook Express to finish receiving mail.

His computer pinged with its own harvest. Three new messages from Coxy, Gibb and Lurch – bass, drummer and keyboard, the essen-tial Vortex line-up. The ex-band members had even arrived through cyber-space in the order he always thought of them in! Only their rhythm guitarist was missing, but that was nothing new – Joey Bertoli used to make such a habit of turning up halfway through a gig, people started thinking it was part of the act.

As he pushed aside a calculator, an empty crisp packet and a packet of batteries to make space for his cordless keyboard, Mark stopped thinking about Caitlin and wondered if maybe Gibb, the drummer, was having a laugh at his expense. Maybe he'd created fictional addresses for the other two for a joke, to get him going. Gibb could dine out on the number of times he'd wound Mark up.

Twenty years ago, Gibb had been one of those waxy-skinned kids whose light thin hair had hung in curtains around his skeletal face so his huge personality had always been surprising. At the same time as being the joker, Gibb had also been the cynic, and the laziest friend you could imagine. He'd been the first to lose touch after graduation which was why his real name – Alex Gordon – on the reunion website had been so easily overlooked the first time round. Or was it because six weeks ago, Gibb had been the mere cotton to Nina Wills' cashmere? Either way, he was the very last person Mark would have expected to see on there, which is why it had been such a thrill.

Like everyone else, Gibb had changed, with perhaps more reason than most. *Webbo!* his first email had read. *Can't believe you're on that fucking sad website too! I put myself on there after 9/11. I worked in the North Tower but I was late that day and was in a coffee shop trying to charge up my cellphone when the buildings collapsed. I'll tell you the rest another time but what's your excuse?*

Mark, who had lived his whole life in Bristol, had immediately understood everything that Gibb (short for Gibbon because of the way he danced) wanted from him. He clicked on Gibb's latest.

Right, we're on! Coxy's going to contact you. He reckons Joey's in Italy, running a café with his ex-girlfriend's grandmother (is he having me on?) and he's still in touch with Lurch. I tell you what, if we can get even four out of the five of us together, I'll stop being such a nervy wanker and get on a plane. I've got to come home and see my mum soon anyway. Cheers, Gibb.

Four out of five of them, just like that? Mark shivered with delight. Vortex At Forty! He could see the flyers around the students' union now. If he announced it on the website, would that girl who gave him the silk scarf turn up?

Who next then? Lurch or Coxy? He couldn't decide so he sat and enjoyed them in their un-opened state a little longer, feeling like a contestant on a TV programme in the days when people really did walk away with nothing if they made the wrong choice. 'Take the money! No! Open the box!'

Eventually, his mouse clicked on Lurch, the keyboard player. Lurch, whose real name was

Pete Smith, was six foot four. He used to stand around with his tongue lolling out of his mouth, which was the only facial expression he seemed able to achieve. Just like the faithful manservant in the Addams Family after whom he was named, Lurch used to be a man of very few words. He'd had the last laugh though. He was the only one of the five of them to have picked up a first-class degree and he'd walked straight into a job as researcher to the then Labour leader Neil Kinnock. The last thing Mark had heard, which was admittedly fifteen or so years ago, Lurch had written the definitive political biopsy of the 1987 election disaster, broken away from the party and – clearly finding speech fluency at last – had briefly become a rising star on news analyses programmes whose producers couldn't get enough of him.

Is Coxy pulling my leg about a Vortex reunion? Do you still play? I'm in a band with an aggregate age of 247 called 'Dads Dancing'. Other than that, I'm a political editor for the Independent – *what about you? Pete. PS l don't normally go in for all this stuff.*

Nor do I, Mark wrote back, *but I can't start calling you Pete at my age. Dads Dancing? Christ Lurch, and I thought Vortex was bad. Are you up for it then? Cheers, Mark.*

As he pressed send, it struck him how easy it was to reply to these guys compared to the anxieties over contacting Nina. All those deleted words, all that rereading, all that expectation. Women were exhausting.

He took a swig from his bottle of beer. He'd known exactly who he was when he'd been in the band – a pretentious English and politics student who fancied himself as Ritchie Blackmore. The others had known – and still knew – exactly who he was too, as he knew them. There was no point in pretending otherwise. No need to force-feed them clues about Salt Peter Productions or having four sons and a divorce-free past. No point even. Vortex At Forty, he wrote idly in jerky script on a piece of scrap paper.

'How old are you?' his sister Ali had asked him earlier, when he'd told her what he and Gibb were trying to set up. She'd popped round in Caitlin's absence to see if there was anything she could do, and he'd said, 'Yes, next time I perform on stage, you could get one of your young friends to rush up to me on stage and give me a scarf during the last number,' and she'd actually laughed out loud – an almost forgotten sound.

Now Coxy. Much to the rest of the band's amusement, Coxy had sold out for a while in the final year of college and grown his sideburns in a stupid stripe from his ear to the middle of his cheek and then shaved them off during the next gig for a laugh. 'Who needs a smoke machine when a band has this kind of stage presence?' the union mag review had asked.

Mark wiggled the mouse and brought up

David Cox's email. He tried to picture Coxy at forty. Did he still have a halo of bubbly brown hair? Was he still with his wife – the girl Coxy had married at the age of nineteen? Were they both still teaching?

Mark, you bastard! (as I said to my one-year-old grandson the other day). How are you doing? A Vortex reunion? You sad old git! Where and when?

Be good to see you, Dave

Coxy was a granddad! Mark leaned back in his chair and opened his mouth but the revelation was only funny for the length of time it took him to laugh out loud. *Coxy was a grandad?* How the hell had that happened?

Caitlin walked towards Bristol Temple Meads station, wondering if she looked normal. She didn't feel it. She was wearing the black flat boots and charcoal grey moleskin skirt she wore at least twice a week in the winter, but she felt less like herself than ever. More like somebody she might notice across the street perhaps. Her physical confidence usually hovered somewhere around the non-existent mark but in the un-precedented madness of the last week, she had received a positive kick from catching her own reflection. Seeing herself as Bill saw her per-haps?

'I'm not doing anything too awful, am I?'

she'd asked Paul Moffat in his pristine car that lunchtime as he'd handed over a stack of party invitations that he'd had printed up for next to nothing through his work. IT'S NEARLY ALL OVER! COME AND HELP MARK AND CAITLIN DROWN THEIR SORROWS!

'The wording isn't quite so funny any more, is it?'

'Irony is a healthy thing,' he'd said.

'Do you think I'm being stupid? It's not like it's a physical thing.'

'Nothing more than a few trysts.'

'Three, without so much as a kiss.'

'No kissing? Are you telling me the truth, the whole truth and...'

'Nothing but the truth.'

'I wouldn't mind having three trysts in six days.'

'But you'd want the kisses, right?'

'Don't you?'

'Don't ask me that, I'd rather not hear my answer.'

'So what's it all about then?'

'I just feel so drawn to him.'

'So,' Paul had challenged as he'd rubbed at a tiny smudge on the windscreen, 'if Mark had said that to you about Nina, what would you have thought?'

She'd managed to look sufficiently contrite then.

'I'm only trying to say the things your mum might have said,' he'd said. 'But, hey, come on, you deserve a bit of fun, and you'll know when to stop.'

'You're sure about that, are you?'

Paul Moffat had become Caitlin's pocket psychiatrist. So far, she had restricted her sessions to daylight hours only.

'Paul?' she puffed urgently into her phone as she almost walked into the path of a taxi. 'I've got another favour to ask.'

'More invitations?' Paul Moffat asked, adjusting the microphone attached to the lapel of his jacket as he drove towards Reading.

'No, I'm sure a hundred will be ample.' Or even a hundred too many she thought. 'I was going to ask if you'd mind me using you as a cover.'

On the other end of the line, Paul took a breath. *Do I mind, Erin? Should I mind being used as a cover? What would Erin say?*

'Bill is coming down,' Caitlin said, squeezing between parked cars to avoid a bus. The noise of its engine drowned her out.

'But he's only just gone back.'

'I know.'

Even his colleagues were saying that he'd never been this hands-on with a touring exhibition in the whole fifteen years he'd been curating at the Royal Academy. 'Is there something in Bristol you've got your eye on?' they were asking him. 'What is it this time? A pre-dynastic flint blade? A pink jasper scarab? A loaf of bread from the First Intermediate Period?'

Caitlin had been going over and over and over the same phrase – 'Is there something in Bristol

236

you've got your eye on?' – ever since.

'I've told Mark I've got a late meeting and might pop out for a drink with you on the way home. It's not a big deal. I just need back up that's all.'

'Do you have to lie?' Paul asked, but he heard Caitlin's emphatic 'Yes' even above the swishing of cars overtaking him in the middle lane. 'As you told me, it's not a physical thing.'

'But that just makes it all the more difficult to explain.'

She repeated her request a second time as a swarm of people with suitcases, briefcases, rucksacks came towards her.

'Oh, go on then,' he said. 'As long as you promise to take me to Erin's special place as soon as you can.'

Caitlin was shocked to find herself laughing.

'That's ... how can I say ... very tweely put!'

'I was just trying to be sensitive.'

'Of course I'll take you, but I'll have to call it a grave, OK?'

'Grave it is.'

As she crossed the platform bridge, she felt oddly detached, as if it might be possible to see her sons walk towards her and not know who they were. She heard a train pull in beneath her. Was Bill on it, about to alight? Had he been awake for most of the night too, trying to find some perspective?

'We'll have to sort something out,' he'd said to Caitlin when they'd said goodbye at the same station three days ago, having spent no more

237

than a total of nine hours in each other's company. Two hours after the lecture, another three the following day, four more the day after that. The counting thing again.

But Bill Winfrey's train was not beneath her feet. She heard its delay announced and imagined him looking out on to a section of track alongside boggy marshland studying the thinning clump of trees and acknowledging the fact that he had seen the same clump before. He had used the London to Bristol route so often lately, she guessed he might even be able to anticipate the names on the industrial units that, in a few minutes, would signal the end of the countryside. He had been back to oversee the Harvest exhibition twice already, and had agreed to every talk the Bristol curators had suggested. Apparently, his assistant Meena was overwhelmingly grateful to him for letting her keep on top of the flow of ideas in London. In a fortnight, there would be no excuse left.

Another train pulled in and Caitlin scanned the spilling crowd. She saw him immediately. From above, she noticed the small circle of tanned skin on his crown. He was wearing his glasses, and he had on a scarf tied high around his neck, a plain one that he could only have chosen for warmth. He looked at least his age: an unremarkable, travel-weary academic; but for her – and she still had no idea why – he stood out like a rare first edition in a library of paperbacks. As she put her foot on the first step down from the bridge, the ground seemed to come up to greet her and she grabbed the handrail. Bill walked steadily along the platform towards her, suppressing a smile. When he reached her, he took hold of each end of her scarf and stabilized her. There they stood, joined together by the inadequacy of wool, until the station had emptied and they had overcome the overwhelming desire to put their arms around each other and never let go.

At home, Mark carved the chicken for his boys and told them the plan that had just come to him in a flash of inspiration.

'It'll save us a fortune,' he said.

'But are you any good?' Dylan asked nervously.

'We used to be. Ask Nina.'

'Nina?' said Kit. It was the first time he'd mentioned her name in front of his father since the evening they'd all met on the landing.

'She used to come and listen to us every week.'

'Nina Wills wouldn't know. Look at what she does to her hair. Anyone who thinks purple is a good colour for hair isn't going to be the best judge of...' Dylan said.

'Is it true she smells of old beds and woodworm and rust?' Rory asked. 'That's what Kit said.'

Mark understood what his sons were doing – they were their mother's best defenders – but he wished he could tell them there was no need. Nina's hair was ridiculous, he could see that now.

'You haven't played together for twenty years, Dad. You might be rubbish.'

'We'll rehearse. There are rehearsing lock-ups in St Paul's. The Electric Mill, it's called. I've just found it on the web.'

'You'd better get another band lined up as well,' Dylan said, heaping chips on to his plate. 'No offence like, but just in case.'

'It's Mum's birthday party, too,' said Joss. 'Not being rude, but she might not want your band at her...'

'It's not just Mum's party, it's all of ours, a family party. You guys could invite a few of your own friends.'

'Where's it going to be?'

'The tobacco factory bar.'

'I don't want to be difficult,' Joss said, picking the skin off his meat, 'but I don't think we should have a party at all.'

'Why not?'

'You and Mum, you're not exactly in the party mood, are you?'

'We'll be all right. I've apologized for going to see Nina without telling her. Nothing's going on, I told you.'

'Does she believe you?'

'Where is Mum, anyway?'

'Working late,' Mark said.

'That's what they all say,' murmured Kit.

'Will people bring presents?' Rory asked. 'Or just stuff for you and Mum?'

'Oh, Mum and I have got everything we need,'

Mark said, looking at the four dirty-blond heads around the table, 'and I think she'd be the first to agree.'

Eighteen

Sheila had asked both her daughter Ali and her friend Pam, in that order, to come with her to Bitton for a lunchtime drink. Each of them had declined.

'Bitton?' Pam had sneered. 'If we want a day out, I'm sure we can come up with somewhere more exciting than Bitton!'

Ali's reaction had been even more emphatic. 'Asking me to accept you had an affair with a man whilst you were still married to Dad is one thing but thinking I might like to meet him is another altogether.'

But Sheila could see their night of mutual revelation had changed something in her daughter all the same. Ali admitted it had. So much in fact that she had phoned her therapist Erica and cancelled her next appointment.

'Telling your mother you saw your father kissing another woman is not usually seen as a positive thing,' she'd said, 'but then nor is hearing an adulterous confession from your mother.'

Getting ready to go was a nightmare. Sheila knew it was daft to worry about what she looked like to a man who knew her inside out but she tried on the entire contents of her wardrobe anyway. Her usual style, if it was anything, was vaguely arty. She relied on scarves and fisherman's smocks and wide-legged trousers but those staples seemed wrong today.

She eventually went to her favourite chocolate brown straight skirt with a kick pleat at the back, which she always fell back on when she wasn't sure. The only things she ever wore with the skirt were a pair of flat, tan leather ankle boots and an old but much loved cream sweater with orange and brown stripes around the polo neck, cuffs and hem.

Before putting them on, she walked into the garden room in her bra and slip and got a roll of Sellotape out of the drawer. As she sat in the boys' favourite armchair, pulling bobbles of lambswool off with the tape, she admired the fungus-free windowsill. Then she walked back into the kitchen, used a butterfly clip to pull enough hair off her face not to look like an old witch, and left. No handbag as usual. Handbags, as she'd once told Jan, were for the Queen.

She still had no answers to the questions that had come repeatedly upon her in the last few weeks. Why was he lucky to be alive? How long had Jan been living on her doorstep? Who, if anyone, shared his life? Only one persistent doubt spoiled things. If he'd wanted to see her again, why hadn't he got in touch?

Sheila couldn't remember the last time she had walked into a pub on her own, if indeed, there had been any time at all. Even this very pub, in which she had once collected for a raffle dressed as Hiawatha, made her feel nervous. She took a deep breath and turned the knob on the white door inside the tiny lobby but as soon as her feet touched the red fleur-de-lis patterned carpet, she knew she had made a stupid mistake. She had walked into the lounge bar.

A few retired couples were already eating. Plaice, chips and peas. Chicken, chips and peas. Steak chips and peas. Damn! Jan and Roger were public bar drinkers – the only time they ever used the lounge was if they were in evening dress, having a quick pint before heading for the more glamorous lights of Bristol. Not knowing what else to do to remedy her mistake, she headed for the long polished wooden counter that ran along the inside wall of the L-shaped room. It looked through to the other bar; the bar she wanted to be in.

She smoothed a beer towel on the glossy wooden surface, cursing her mis-step and trying not to peer too hard through the gap. Her window into the public bar was 3 feet wide at the most. Two pints of half-consumed beer sat on a rectangular brass drip tray, and two unconnected and not very youthful male hands reached for them in perfect synchronization. Mounted on the back wall behind this framed snapshot of rural England was a public payphone, a relic from the days before the ubiquitous mobile. Men like Roger Sage used to call their wives from it and tell them to put their dinners back.

'I'm meeting a friend here for lunch,' she lied to the neat, middle-aged barman as he greeted her in a sentence of such bland hospitality she wondered how many hundreds of times he must have said it before. 'She doesn't seem to be here yet.'

'What's the name, please?'

She raised her voice in the hope it might filter past the till, across the optics and over the steel beer barrels into the ear of someone who might recognize it.

'Sheila Webb,' she said confidently, but neither hand through the gap seemed to twitch at the sound of it.

The barman – a different kettle of fish to his roly-poly predecessor – smoothed his tie with the horses' heads on it against his checked brushed cotton shirt and ran his finger down an open page of a thin burgundy leather book.

'Webb? No, sorry, there's nothing here. Is it in your friend's name perhaps?'

Friend's name? She hadn't thought that far. She couldn't use Pam – all sorts of people in Bitton knew Pam.

'Nina Wills?' she ventured, leaning over to pretend to study the upside-down page.

'No Wills here...'

'I'm beginning to wonder if I have the right day. Perhaps I could phone her?'

To her surprise, her artifice worked.

'There's a phone in the public bar,' the barman said, disappearing for a second and popping up almost immediately next to her. He showed her through a low white door with a black iron latch and into a smaller simpler room with a slate floor and whitewashed walls.

A game of table skittles – nine wooden pins set in a diamond shape on a wooden block and a vertical pole for a wooden ball on the end of a string – took up a good part of the space, not that anyone on this weekday lunchtime was playing on it. Sheila wouldn't have expected them to be. Saturday and Sunday evenings were table skittles nights.

She remembered balancing on a high vinyl-covered stool in this very room, shoulder to shoulder with other cricket wives on other stools, breathing in their vending machine cigarette smoke and gamely mustering the spirit to enjoy yet more hours of spectator sport in support of their husbands.

'Flopper!' the cry would go when all nine pins fell at one swing.

'Spare!' they'd shout when just one pin was left standing.

'Twenty-seven!' someone would cheer at the notch-up of a top score.

The drinkers whose hands she had seen reaching for their pints from the lounge were the public bar's only customers. Farmers, she guessed. One wore a navy blue all-in-one overall and hobnail boots, the other was in a quilted shirt and sleeveless green jacket. The man facing her, the one in the overall, smiled briefly and with it, her hope finally disappeared below its own horizon. Coming over dull and cold and feeling ridiculous, she concentrated on finding a coin for the phone.

The farmers had fallen into a comfortable silence, which didn't help. All she had to do was play the charade through and then she could take her stupidity and her self-consciousness home where she would do her best to try and laugh it off.

As she dialled her own number, intending to leave a message on her own answering service, another lunchtime drinker walked in through a different door to her right, which used to lead to the beer garden where she and Ken would some-times leave Mark and Ali with a packet of crisps and a bottle of Coca Cola.

The sound of the latch was surprisingly familiar. She used to hear its click and hope it was Jan, but this time, a large, cleanly shaven man in corduroys and a crew neck came in and boomed a hello at the farmers. The door shut behind him. Then, almost immediately, another man followed. She was aware of the new-comer's height because she could sense he had ducked on entry, but nothing else. She had her back to the bar but still, her neck strained to look, as if it were being pushed by a strong hand.

Both the farmers and the cleanly shaven man greeted the new customer warmly, but the tall man did not reply. Her tension subsided. If it had been Jan, he would have said something back. She always used to think his well-mannered courtesy was something to do with his nationality, a feeling perhaps that he needed to be friendlier than everyone else to warrant his inclusion.

She pushed the money into the slot and heard her own out-of-body instructions telling her she wasn't in, but if she would like to leave a message, she'd call her back.

To her relief, the conversation at the bar started up again.

'Er ... hello,' she said preposterously to herself into the mouthpiece, but then another voice so unexpected and so out of place resonated across the stone floor and made her lose her thread entirely. It reminded her of a loudhailer the boys had been given last Christmas that had turned them all into robots.

'I-owe-you-for-yesterday,' the somehow electronic voice said.

Maybe it was a joke, but if it was, no one laughed. She continued to ramble absurdly to her own phone, knowing her time was all but up. Eventually, reluctantly, she said goodbye to herself.

'Sagey settled up for you,' the barman said. 'You've drawn him on Sunday, first round of the Christmas Turkey Trot.'

'That-is-not-the-draw-I-wanted.'

The voice was inhuman and it came to her that maybe, it was the speech of a person lucky to be alive. Rattling her car keys in her pocket for reassurance, she half turned, and as she did, the door to the beer garden opened again and Roger Sage walked in.

'Well, I'll be ... nothing for years and then

twice in fortnight!' he said.

From the corner of her right eye, she sensed the three men at the bar watching them. The tall one, the one who must have produced the electronic voice, got off his high stool and stood up. She felt a realization waft her way.

'I'm supposed to be meeting a friend, but she's ... her car has broken down ... I was just on my...'

Her heart thumped as the lope of the man came into view. He was thin – much, much thinner than Jan – and his shoulders were wrong. All this she gleaned from a sideways glance. The tall man took his place beside Roger and out of courtesy she turned to acknowledge him. As he nodded his head, a rocket exploded into a billion cadmium stars inside her and on a headland somewhere long ago, her son Mark in his parka cheered.

'Jan?'

He took hold of a device, the machine that must have produced his speech – a small flat-ended tube with two buttons along its side, like a tiny electric shaver – and pointed it to a place under his chin. He gulped and a noise that sounded like Shee-la came from the contraption.

'Dutchy's little box of tricks!' Roger said proudly.

'Oh, he won't need it with me,' Sheila said. 'We speak sign language! Perhaps, now that I'm here, I can buy you two gentlemen a drink?'

Jan put up a thumb.

'Oh, that kind of sign language!' Roger laughed. 'For a minute there I thought you were talking about something the rest of us wouldn't understand!'

'Aren't you talking to me any more?' Chloe taunted Kit at the top of the steps with the chipped white metal railings that led down to the school canteen. Her posse of new friends formed an adoring little cluster around her, whereas his old ones just carried on running, leaving him high and dry.

Kit tried to pretend he hadn't heard her. He hadn't so much as caught her eye since the mattress debacle, which, thanks to Chloe, was now all over the school. At first, he'd tried to put the record straight – 'So the man Chloe thought was her mum's bloke turned out to be your dad?'

'She only thought that, he wasn't actually...'

'Your old man is shagging Chloe's mum?'

'No, they used to go out when...' but no one wanted to listen. Anyway, the story was yesterday's news now and he wasn't about to give Chloe the chance to re-kindle it.

She grabbed his lower arm and despite everything, he didn't know how to resist. The words he knew he should use to reply were circling in a fog in his brain. There was a clever retort in there somewhere, a beautiful little arrangement of words that would both impress her and shut her up simultaneously. But they weren't the ones that came out.

'What do you want me to say?'

'Tell me what you had for breakfast.'

Her friends sniggered.

'Toast,' he said stupidly.

Sully's triumphal smirk, his boasting at the park – 'been there, done that' – refused to go away. It was at the front of his every reaction to her, ahead of the mattress even.

'Butter?'

'Can you let me go, please?'

Chloe put her hands to her head and grabbed a fistful of hair from either side of her face. The movement revealed her scar – now a soft baby pink. Soon it would be gone completely, he thought.

'You're doing my head in, Kit,' she said.

'So now you know how it feels.'

He thought he could see shadows under her eyes.

'What have I ever done to you?' she asked, playing to the crowd.

'Ask Sully. He'll tell you. He's told everyone else.'

'What do you mean?'

As her complexion changed to a faint olive green, Kit felt a hitherto unknown power.

'It's all around the park. Everyone knows.'

Chloe pressed her fingers against her lips, biting their tips. It made her look vulnerable when he suspected she was really indestructible. She dismissed her posse with a wave of her arms.

'I'll catch you lot later, yeah? Kit and me, we've got...'

'No, we haven't. I'm going to lunch.'

'Correct. With me.'

She took his hand and pulled him towards the school gates.

He still wanted to please her. He wanted to be special.

'Piss off, Chloe,' he said, yanking himself away.

'Kit...'

'I said piss off.'

To his horror, Chloe started to cry.

'I don't mean it,' he told her, his hands hovering over her, frightened to touch, as if she were made of ice, 'I just said it to ... I do want lunch with you ... It's just...'

'Prove it,' she sniffed.

'How?'

'You could tell Sully he's out of order.'

'For what?'

'Putting stories round about me.'

'So it's not true? You didn't let him?'

'Do what?'

'The things he told me you did.'

'Believe what you want,' she huffed, her tears gone now.

He could feel her slipping away.

'OK, I will. I'll tell Sully he's out of order if that's what you want me to do.'

'Do you want to do it, though?'

'If it makes you happier, yes.'

'You'd do that for me?'

'I'd do anything for you.'

Chloe's features softened. 'Come on then.

We've got enough time.'

'What?'

'The park. Let's go and find him.'

'We can't just walk out of school.'

'Yes, we can, watch me.'

Nina was at the top of a ladder scraping the last of the ancient wallpaper off the landing walls listening to her radio when the phone rang. *Fifteen per cent of Britain's adult population has registered with a reunion website which now boasts nine times more active members than the Church of England. No contest when you accept that the hunt for old school friends is about nothing more than those two old chestnuts, sex and showing off.*

Her tinted hair, now without the sheen, like an aubergine past its prime, was decorated with flakes of gluey woodchip. She was wearing a pair of filthy old tracksuit bottoms with Rauf's hotel logo on the bum pocket. The sleeves of her long-sleeved grey tee shirt were feathered with scraps of brown lining paper and her nails were filled with the blue emulsion she had painted the kitchen with last night.

So what is the website's appeal? Is it like sneaking a look in the teacher's mark book to see who has done better or worse than you? Or perhaps a last chance to raise the Titanic of your past loves before the barnacles set in?

She came down from the ladder to answer the phone half expecting it to be Mark. But it wasn't Mark, it was his mother, Sheila Webb, telling her she had Chloe, Kit and a policeman at her house.

Caitlin was in the bath in the apothecary using her feet to pull the plug chain and drain the tepid water that surrounded her. She couldn't remember the last time she'd had a bath at lunchtime. Once upon a time it would have seemed an indulgence too far, but put now against her other selfishness, it was nothing.

She lay there as the water gurgled around her, until only the bubbles clung to the side of the tub. Then she got out, wrapped herself in one of the white fluffy towels, and lay on her bed to enjoy the feeling of being both clean and calm. After that, she moisturized, blow-dried her hair, put on a little make-up and dressed in a grey cami, a new white cotton blouse and pistachio green linen trousers. She found a necklace with a silver hoop on a black leather thong, and slipped on a pair of flat charcoal pumps. There was no reason on earth to make the effort but she was pleased she had. *If only Bill was here to see me looking this good*, she couldn't help thinking. *Or at least somebody.* She didn't have to wait long because next to her, the phone rang.

'No need to panic, love,' said Sheila, 'but I've got Kit and a friend here. It's not so much the truancy issue as the fight in the park. They were brought here by a policeman.'

'Oh God, has Sully beaten him up?'

'Not exactly,' came the careful reply.

* * *

253

A remarkable two hours later, Sheila and Jan sat on her late husband Ken's memorial bench on Dundry Hill at the foot of the Mendips and looked out across the gigantic stone backslash that they no longer had the energy to climb.

'I hope Caitlin's not going to be cross with me,' she said. 'I just thought it was about time she and Nina met.'

A river of dark terracotta flood water was running down the slope behind the bench, taking with it little clumps of rusty rubble.

'Perhaps I should have given her some warning, but difficult meetings like that are sometimes better when they happen out of the blue...'

Whenever Sheila brought her grandsons here, the knees of their trousers turned a rich orange which Caitlin never entirely managed to wash out. Even on a grey wintery day like today, you could feel the warm glow of the hills.

'It's not a common occurrence, my grandson being brought home by a policemen, you know. I don't know what you must have thought. And I'm sorry Kit was so rude. He wasn't himself at all.'

'No-offence-taken.'

'You're going to think I'm making excuses, but he's putty in that girl's hands.'

Jan patted his shoulder and turned his palm up towards her as if to say 'I know the feeling'.

'No, but really,' she said, 'she's her mother's daughter all right. Years back, before he was married, my son Mark used to go out with Chloe's mother. The ability to manipulate the male Webb line must run in their genes.'

'You-never-wore-jeans. Only-skirts-I-recall.'

'Caitlin looked lovely just now, didn't she? She's a very pretty girl when she makes an effort. She looked so much more attractive than Nina, didn't you think? How anyone could think Mark would prefer the skinny brashness of ... oh, sorry, I'm gabbling.'

Sheila took Jan's hand, enjoying having him beside her on the hill again. They had stopped to catch their breath many times on the way up, sometimes on the flat sandstone rocks that had helped build so many of the villages beneath them, sometimes on the rough grass that grew between them. And they still knew how to stand there, listening to each other's breathing, watching nothing.

There was no need for words anyway. After lunch in the pub, Sheila had all the answers now. Jan *had* been in Holland all these years, moving from the university to private practice in Amsterdam after his second marriage to a fellow lecturer had failed. His cancer had been caused by his smoking, which had made her want to throw away the battered oblong tin with the ghost of a Dutch windmill on the lid. She already knew it would no longer smell of wild-flower meadows or picnics when she opened it.

Jan had had his operation five months ago, in Bristol. He hadn't contacted her, he'd said, because he hadn't had a voice. You could have written, she'd teased him on the way from the pub to her cottage, where they had arrived to find the police car parked outside.

By the time they'd reached Ken's bench, they'd established that they'd both been on holiday in Scotland in May 1988; that Jan's grandson Robbie was only a month younger than Sheila's grandson Joss; that Jan's marriage had split up in the same year that Ken had died.

'Have we been stupid?' she asked. 'Have we missed out on the best years of our lives?'

She stopped talking abruptly. Jan's breathing had changed. He seemed to be struggling to fill his lungs, concentrating on taking in air. His fingers were hunting around his throat.

'Jan? Are you all right? We've walked too far. You've overdone it.'

She noticed his box of tricks lying on the bench next to him, and she picked it up to give it to him. He shook his head and carried on fumbling under his scarf for his neck, for the place of his operation.

'Jan?'

And then, suddenly, out there in the vast space, she heard his real voice, not his artificial electronic efforts but his real voice, his old warm beautiful voice. It was the sound of meadows and cider, the tickle of a ladybird on her foot.

'We must enjoy it while we can,' he said.

Nineteen

From: Mark Webb <mwebb@saltpeter.co.uk>
To: Nina Wills<nwills@hotmail.com>
Sent: 10 November, 2008 13:53
Subject: apologies

Hi Nina, thanks for all your messages. Apologies for my lack of contact. I've made an almighty mess of things and it's been difficult at home but thankfully nothing terminal. Sorry for running off like that and then going to ground – it has just occurred to me you might think it was payback for all those years ago but it's not, it's merely a male inability to cope as usual. Love, Mark

From: Nina Wills (mailto:nwills@hotmail.com)
To: Webb, Mark
Sent: 10 November, 2008 16:36
Subject: Re: apologies

Hello stranger. I was going to say no need to say sorry but we've both made a hash of our reunion so I'm sorry too. You'll be pleased to hear that I've come a long way in the last few days. Finally meeting Caitlin (under unusual circumstances it has to be said!) changed my perspective, although she did keep me at arm's length, which is fair enough. I looked a bloody wreck for a start. Anyway, it hit home that you are a married man and I absolutely get that now. But I wonder where we go from here? N x

PS As you say, shame about the ASBO even if Chloe does think Kit is now the coolest kid on the block.

From: Webb, Mark
To: Nina Wills
Sent: 11 November, 2008 11:10
Subject: Re: apologies

I was hoping we could all be friends? Our children seem to be managing it. How is Chloe coping with being grounded? It's actually really good to have Kit back in the fold and not disappearing to the park every five minutes. I think he's secretly enjoying it too. Caitlin is working long hours for an exhibition at the moment but when it eases off and we're back being a family again, maybe you and Chloe should come round for supper or something? Mark x

From: Nina Wills (mailto:nwills@hotmail.com)
To: Webb, Mark
Sent: 11 November, 2008 15:20
Subject: Re: apologies

Are you serious? I don't think that's such a good

idea – Caitlin and I found it uncomfortable enough just being in your mum's kitchen for ten minutes, and that was with a man in uniform to distract us! I'm not going to be around much in the next month anyway. I've just booked a flight to Turkey to sort out some unfinished business. Nina x

From: Webb, Mark
To: Nina Wills
Sent: 12 November, 2008 10:12
Subject: Re: apologies

With your ex? Is this a wise idea?

From: Nina Wills (mailto:nwills@hotmail.com)
To: Webb, Mark
Sent: 12 November, 2008 14:44
Subject: Re: apologies

You of all people should know what unresolved endings feel like.

From: Webb, Mark
To: Nina Wills
Sent: 13 November, 2008 09:36
Subject: Re: apologies

Fair point. Is Chloe going with you? Kit will be gutted.

From: Nina Wills (mailto:nwills@hotmail.com)
To: Webb, Mark

Sent: 13 November, 2008 18:10
Subject: Re: apologies

Not at the moment. She's refusing, and given her history with Rauf, I can't and won't make her so I'll have to work something out. Any room in your house for a paying lodger? N x

From: Webb, Mark
To: Nina Wills
Sent: 13 November, 2008 18:55
Subject: Re: apologies

My turn to ask if you're serious? One more teenager around the place won't make any difference. I rather like the idea but I'll have to see how Caitlin feels about it. It would make more sense of our 'reunion' as you so quaintly put it, and Caitlin is always complaining how the house lacks a gender balance. We'd have to ban bedroom hopping though. Got to go – I'm chief cook and bottle-washer again tonight. Cheers, Mark

Mark logged off and went into the kitchen to check on the progress of the twenty sausages, five potatoes and three tins of baked beans he'd put on. On his way, he poked his head around the sitting room door. Kit was on the sofa, putting some distance between himself and the usual horseplay. Dylan was sitting on a prostrate Joss. Rory was standing on the arm of a chair. All seemed well.

Kit didn't notice his father. He was too busy considering how different exploring Chloe's body was to exploring Vanessa's. But exploring wasn't quite the right verb. It was more like discovering with Chloe, whereas that night in the eco-chalet with Vanessa had been more like tussling. In the chalet, he'd been more concerned with not making a fool of himself than anything else but it just wasn't like that with Chloe. He still knew next to nothing about where best to put his hands but to his surprise, Chloe didn't have much of a clue where to put hers either. Not that they'd had much of an opportunity to practise since they'd declared themselves an item, being grounded and all that. Now that he knew Chloe was still a virgin too, it seemed a precious state. One worth cherishing even. What he had come to realize was that it wasn't the *speed* with which they lost their virginity that mattered, it was the *way* they lost it. Together and legal, with a bit of luck.

His three brothers were throwing cushions at each other in what he considered a woefully juvenile display of excess energy. The heat their bodies were creating warranted the opening of a window even on this cold November night, but Kit pulled a throw around himself for the hug factor. He took out his mobile phone to send his girlfriend – his girlfriend! – a text but there was already one there waiting for him.

Hey boyf! missin u xxx
Chloe
13/11/08 19.02

Missin u 2. Was just finkin of u. glad u told me
wot u did xxxxx
Kit
13/11/08 19.03

Glad u glad! Used to fink it sad but now fink it
good. xxxxx
Chloe
13/11/08 19.04

We take it slow, yeah? xxxxx
Kit
13/11/08 19.05

U 16 in few weeks, me 16 in few months. U
can't break law 2wice!
Chloe
13/11/08 19.06

Don't want 2 do it jus coz we can. Want 2 do it
coz its rite
Kit
13/11/08 19.07

Me 2 luv u xxxxxxxxxx
Chloe
13/11/08 19.08

Luv u 2 xxxxxxxxxxxx

Kit
13/11/08 19.09

Kit put his phone back in his pocket. His brothers wanted to know why he was looking like the cat that got the cream. He wouldn't tell them so Dylan threw a bolster at him and knocked an empty mug from a table to the floor. Its handle fell off on impact.

'You clumsy prick,' Kit said, but even then he couldn't keep the joy out of his voice.

Bill Winfrey wasn't a clumsy man so when he dropped his knife in Muirs, the restaurant next to the museum that was currently enjoying increased takings thanks to the Van Gogh exhibition, his colleagues – especially the woman with the red curls and the pashmina – noticed it. Caitlin noticed her noticing, and it gave her a thrill to see Bill's famous charisma in action. Everyone wanted a piece of him but unbelievably, he wanted a piece of her. What piece, she wasn't yet sure. It can't have been her mind, because at least half the females around the table had initials after their names. It certainly wasn't her body, so what then? The gap between her teeth?

'Get a grip, Bill,' a younger but balder man said from across the long full table in a bid for a crumb of his mentor's attention. Caitlin found him irritating, like a wasp continually buzzing around an otherwise perfect al fresco meal. He was something to do with the exhibition's pub-

263

licity department – he'd told her the design of the leaflets and posters was his, and that the yellow colour of the wording was 'all wrong'.

'It's my age,' Bill said, ducking beneath the white linen cloth. Sitting next to him, to her complete shock, Caitlin felt his fingers curl around her ankle. It was a touch that well and truly crossed the boundary she thought they had created for themselves and as such it sent the most fantastic shiver up her leg. She congratulated herself on wearing her pumps and not her knee-high flat leather boots as she so nearly had.

Seamlessly continuing a conversation about Bristol's art scene with a man the spitting image of Danny DeVito, Caitlin's left foot found Bill's right one. He acknowledged the move by pushing his calf her way a little, the extra pressure their private conspiracy. Both of them did well to carry on the charade of being fully engaged with the above-table anecdotes when their real story was going on below. They were like that old cliché of the BBC journalist who once read the news in jacket, tie and suspenders.

'We've got the Watershed, the Arnolfini, the...'

'But do ordinary people go to these places? The harbourside seems to me to be populated entirely by the middle classes.'

'Are you saying the middle classes are *extra*ordinary?'

'You know what I mean.'

'I don't actually.'

Bill's shoe slid up her leg.

'Oh!' she exclaimed, her voice a little squeakier than she'd intended, 'there's Paul!'

That she didn't automatically assume Paul Moffat had come as the messenger of bad news said something about the moral distance she'd travelled recently. He was wearing a tailored shirt and jeans that made his heeled boots look more like a statement than a necessity and was with a man whose entire demeanour let the world know he was proud to be gay. If she hadn't been inextricably linked to Bill she would have jumped up to say hello. Or would she?

Paul and his – what? Partner? Friend? Business associate? – disappeared into a part of the bar she couldn't see and her attentions returned to the table.

'Are you expecting a call?' the woman with the curls and the pashmina asked Bill, picking up his phone from the white tablecloth.

'My daughter,' he told her firmly, taking it back. 'She texts me goodnight before she goes to sleep.'

'Every day?'

'Every day.'

'How old is she?'

Caitlin felt a glow of superiority. She knew Lizzie Winfrey's age, her school year, her habits, her fears, her food preferences. Bill talked about Lizzie a lot. Much more than Caitlin talked about her boys, but there were four of them and therefore there wasn't time to present them as much more than an amalgam. Rather than do them that injustice, she'd decided to leave it until he asked. Which so far he hadn't.

On cue, Bill's phone pinged. As he momentarily cut himself off from the group, so Paul Moffat came back into view. She saw him touch the other man's arm.

'Of course,' she said, finally realizing what she'd known all along. She turned to Bill to share the observation but he was busy pressing buttons and anyway, what did Paul Moffat mean to him? In recognition of the gaps in the knowledge they had of each other, she moved and with a barely perceptible shift of limbs, his foot was no longer entwined with hers.

With four separate screens on the go, the sitting room was a very blokey scene, even Mark could see that. The television was on, despite the fact that neither he nor Kit and Dylan were watching it, something generally not allowed. He had his glorious MacBook open on iPhoto, which as applications on this little beauty went, was currently running neck and neck with iTunes. Dylan had purloined the family Sony laptop and was instant-messaging Olly Jones who was apparently on 'report' at his boarding house in Somerset for nicking some raffle wine from a teacher's drawer and Kit was playing with Mark's new iPhone. Caitlin would have hated it. She would have been slamming around in the kitchen checking lunchboxes for banana skins and peeling muddy rugby socks from the bottom of games bags, somehow letting them all know her disapproval.

It occurred to him what a luxury of a thought that was. With the knowledge that his wife was now on her way home, where she would dump her satchel, plonk down the inevitable food shop, throw her coat on the hall bench and most likely announce that she was bursting for the loo, he could afford to enjoy her absence. Her imminent return allowed him to observe that sometimes, the household was easier without her. Lazier too, and undoubtedly unhealthier in the long term, but in the short, it was to be enjoyed. But what if she hadn't been coming home? What if this laddish community was the norm? Would the atmosphere still be as chilled? Would Rory and Joss be sleeping in their own beds as they were now, or huddled together in his? Would Kit and Dylan choose to be in the same room as their father – who may in this parallel scenario have betrayed them – or would they be skulking in their own private spaces, seething with resentment and hurt? He knew the answers, which was why, when he heard the familiar sound of Caitlin's key turning in their front door, he jumped to his feet, flicked off the TV and issued heavy instructions to his sons about going to bed.

Twenty

November 17

Twenty hours, Caitlin worked out as she stepped off the train into the early evening darkness at the small South London station – the sum total of private time she and Bill had managed to clock up together in the last four weeks. Not even enough for a return flight to Las Vegas. Less than the amount of time she had marinated a leg of lamb for. Four hours short of the time it would have taken Gene Pitney to reach Tulsa. So, how on earth did it feel like fifteen lifetimes? And why did she not feel guilty?

Deceit wasn't her intention, and she was sure it wasn't Bill's either, but the fact remained that being here had required a level of subterfuge way off the chart. She justified her actions by telling herself she was in uncharted territory. As yet, apart from her reaction to the ankle caress in the restaurant, she had experienced no pressing need to express her feelings for Bill physically. So why had she prepared for the eventuality? Good underwear, waxed legs and all the rest.

If God, or whoever was in charge of these things, had struck a bargain with her and ruled that she could have Bill as she was having him now for ever – no sex, no cuddles in bed, no holidays, no holding hands in the street – in return for no repercussions on her family, she would have shaken the divine hand like a shot. But mortals were in charge, and this mortal mind had turned unimaginatively to the possibility of getting naked.

She had done her best to invent boundaries for herself, but she only had to look at her four boys to see how good she was at changing the goalposts. Rory's weekday bedtime was supposed to be a rigid eight o'clock, broken only in exceptional circumstances, but he was never in bed before nine. Dylan had run up such a huge bill on his mobile she had told him she was confiscating it for a week but had given it back to him after only two days. And then there was Kit.

'We care more about the truancy than we do about the ASBO,' she and Mark had told him. 'We understand why you hit Sully, it was a stupid and wrong thing to do but we understand. However, if you ever play truant again, you'll be removed from the school and sent to board like Olly Jones, we swear it.'

What rubbish they all talked.

As she made her progress along Bill's terrace, which was a quaint little side road off the main street of a London suburb, she hoped she didn't look too much like a woman with adultery on her mind. Her image of that kind of woman was a woman who bore no resemblance to Nina Wills whatsoever. Nina was not at all the woman she'd imagined, not at all the threat either. 'I was in the middle of wallpaper stripping,' Nina had kept explaining in Sheila's kitchen, but there was still the badly dyed hair and the silver nail varnish, wasn't there? In life's typically perverse way, the moment of Mark's curiosity had obviously passed. It was a pity she couldn't say the same for Kit as far as his current obsession was concerned, because if ever there was a girl capable of breaking her son's heart, it was Chloe. And nor, unfortunately, could she say the same for herself.

She almost felt sorry for Mark for not finding in Nina what he'd been looking for, for not finding what she had found in Bill. And she hadn't even been looking. Having said that, after tonight, her end might just be in sight too.

Yesterday, she and Bill had been alone in an empty university lecture theatre ahead of another talk. He'd been frantically rewriting his opening sentences to include an anecdote about how an important Van Gogh altarpiece in the Oratorio del Rosario in Palermo had been booked for an exhibition but had proved too big to fit through the chapel entrance without damage to either the work of art or the church. Mid-sentence, he'd thrown down his pen and put his hand over his eyes.

'I can't do this.'

'Do what?' Caitlin had asked, alarmed.

'Pretend.'

And that was when he'd said what she'd always known he was going to say.

'You know we're going to have to get used to being without each other again, don't you?'

The theatre was so big, and she had felt so small then, like a drop in his ocean.

'Can't we find a...?'

'I should have said something earlier.'

'Don't. Whatever it is, it makes no odds.'

'This might.'

'You're dying of an incurable disease. You're on the run. You're really a woman.'

'I'm going to Italy on Saturday, for a month, with my daughter...'

'Oh,' she had said unsurely, 'that's great...'

'There's something else.'

'Go on...'

'Lizzie's mother is coming too.'

'Your ex-wife?'

'She's not actually my ex. We've never divorced.'

'I thought...'

'She's got this idea that we should give it another go.'

'That's...'

'I know, I know.'

'I really thought you were divorced.'

'I am, all but.'

'Should you have told me?'

'I thought you might walk away.'

'You didn't walk away from me...'

'I couldn't.'

'Do you think you should? Give it another go with your wife, I mean.'

'Not until this thing, this thing between us...'

'Which is what exactly?'

'I don't know, but whatever it is, it has to be resolved.'

'And it never will be, unless we push it over the edge,' she had said.

So here she was, far from home, come to do exactly that. The gardens Caitlin now walked past were separated from the houses by the narrow track, an old railway siding perhaps. The street lights lit up neglected patches of winter grass, others were gravel courtyards or neat lawns, and every now and again, there was a slide, a sandpit, a bench, or some other vestige of summertime. She looked for the one with the blue shed and the weathervane, and there, suddenly, it was, just as she had imagined it.

The front door was propped open with a smooth stone. She was grateful not to have to knock and for a moment, she felt as if she were coming home too, just like the commuters.

'Hello?' she called, only daring to go one step inside. She drank in the details of the room: a colourful, multi-purpose space with a sofa, books, rugs, open stairs to her right, and a table behind, with more books, pieces of glass and pottery on shelves, lamps at angles, pictures all over the walls. She was both relieved and frightened by its beauty.

Bill appeared from a doorway beyond the stairs, a tea towel over one shoulder, looking domestic, a guise she had never seen him in before. He wore loose jeans and a faded red-checked shirt with unbuttoned cuffs, and no shoes, just thick grey socks.

'Good grief, you've really come,' he said.

Everything that Ali Webb had ever bought her boyfriend Rob lay in an orderly heap in the middle of the sitting room of her waterside flat. It was an enormous and costly mountain of trying too hard – skis he had used once, a music centre he was never at home long enough to listen to, a whole pile of clothes to stop either him looking like a student or her a cradle-snatcher. She had stacked it all neatly next to the shelves that were still in their cardboard flat pack, waiting to be put up. They could be used for firewood now as far as she was concerned.

Rob would see the ready-made bonfire as soon as he walked in from his holiday in Spain. The flat was going on the market tomorrow, by which time she would be sleeping in a proper home again. Her mum's home admittedly, but at least Ali had retrieved the feeling of belonging to something – a real family with its own intricate inner workings that sometimes broke down, and which, like eccentric plumbing, you could only fix if you knew how it was set up in the first place. Sheila's confession about Jan had been the missing link, the bit of crucial piping that ran under the floorboards. Ali was seeing everything in the round at last.

The bedroom that up until last weekend she'd shared with Rob, was already devoid of possessions, with a new crisp white cotton duvet cover and lilac sari on the bed, lilac candles in silver cubes on the bedside cupboards and a large stainless steel pot of silk lavender on the floor in front of the muslin-dressed window, just as the lifestyle adviser had suggested. Make it look great, the woman with the heavy make-up had gushed, and that potential purchaser might just forgive you for that lack of a second en suite.

The flat had been denuded. Rob wouldn't recognize it and he wouldn't recognize her either. Her bad fairy disguise was in the bin, along with his broken squash racquet and all the other woe-is-me crutches she'd used to prop herself up with during the last few years. It was now a matter of seeing what she could do to mend the damage and a good place to start was patching up the holes she'd helped create in her brother's marriage. The phone number she needed was on the back of her hand.

'Hi, am I speaking to Nina Wills?'

'You are.'

'Hi, Nina, I'm Ali Webb, Mark Webb's sister?'

'Oh my God, what's Chloe done now?'

'No, not Chloe. I'm, well, it's me in the wrong this time.'

'You? Sorry, I'm not with you.'

'I thought it wasn't fair to let you take all the rap for the crisis in Mark's marriage.'

'Oh, don't worry, I'm letting him take his fair share.'

'But I need to take some of the blame too. I sort of encouraged it, the getting back in touch with you and all that followed...'

'We didn't need encouragement. We were ...

anyway, nothing much did follow. It's all under control now. You needn't worry.'

'I needn't?'

'No.'

'You won't ... you and Mark, you're...'

'Just good friends.'

'And long may it stay...'

But the phone line had gone dead before Ali could finish. Nina Wills had hung up. It kind of annoyed her until she realized she didn't do annoyed any more. She heard a familiar voice behind her.

'Are you ready?' Jan de Junger said in his mechanical way at the threshold.

His car, a gas-fuelled Volvo, was waiting outside. Her own two-seater convertible was already parked in Sheila's garage, which had been emptied just for the purpose. A skip in the street outside Sheila's gate was full of rotting canvas deckchairs, rusty shears, old paint pots and a box of mouldy papers that must have meant something to somebody once upon a time. Ken most likely.

Ali was used to Jan's speech now. He put a fatherly hand on her arm.

'I'm fine,' she said gratefully. 'Really, worryingly fine.'

As they drove to Sheila's cottage in a comfortable silence which was not just through necessity, Ali tried not to wonder what the future held. He's lucky to be alive, her mother had told her. The primary goal of his physicians had been to eliminate the cancer, not to preserve his voice.

275

Some patients, Sheila said, were prepared to sacrifice the probability of their cure rate in order to increase their probability for being able to speak normally. But not Jan, Jan wanted to live, and her mother wanted to make it worth his while. The pursuit of happiness was a lovely thing, and Ali was behind them all the way.

In London, Caitlin suddenly felt incredibly tired. Her thoughts were already coaxing her back to Bristol but she felt obliged to resist them, even when they came back at her with extra sound and vision – Rory crying over his homework, Joss and Dylan arguing, Kit being dragged home by another policeman. Mark's face however, and his voice too, were in the shadows for which she was grateful.

Since coming down the stairs in this house she barely knew, her children had been at the vanguard of a new guilt. Each time they appeared, she pushed their presence away because after enticing Bill into such advanced intimacy, she felt he deserved her full attention. In an effort to appear entirely relaxed, she stretched out on his soft, bright sofa, her hands behind her head, and told herself she didn't want to be anywhere else in the world. As far as all things Bill were concerned, it was her first dishonesty

He was kneeling on the floor, wrapping a tiny Egyptian funerary figure back in its cloth, one of the last treasures he had spent the past hour showing her. 'I don't usually share these things,' he confessed. 'They belong to my own private world.' She understood the compliment but she would have preferred the cliché, the declaration of love, the desperation at their plight. Less show, more tell she wanted to cry. Her heart felt heavy.

Upstairs, before the fumbling, they had ventured into his bedroom. From a wall full of books, he had pulled out his favourites – *Moby Dick*, *The Diving Bell and the Butterfly*, *The Old Man and the Sea*. They had lain on his bed – on *his* bed – reading passages to each other. Stories of condensed humanity, he'd called them.

She had almost begged him to stop. 'Put the book down and hold me,' she'd asked. 'I just want to feel your body lying with mine, no books, please.' But he wouldn't.

'We're not going to do the predictable thing,' he'd said, pulling the hair from her face and tracing the faint grooves growing vertically from her lips.

'It's not predictable.'

'It is. It's been the inevitable outcome since we first laid eyes on each other.'

'Then why not? Perhaps it's right.'

He'd picked up her wedding finger, twisted the ring and said nothing.

'But do you wish we could?' she'd asked him, not understanding her persistence, which seemed a stronger force than any desire.

'We can't even think about it.'

'How can we not?'

And then, as if there had never been any argument about it, they had done something very

277

close to but not quite entirely the predictable thing anyway. Kisses had led to whispers that had become soft moans that had turned to pleasure. She knew enough now to imagine what it would be like, enough to know too that it would be good. But had it helped? Did they know each other any better? Caitlin didn't have any answers.

On the sofa with her boots off, she could sense their journey was nearly over. This trawl through his treasures, this sharing of secrets, was a safe place to rest before they each went their separate ways.

Bill tied the roll up with a velvet ribbon and put it back in his antique roll-top desk. At the same time, he took out a wooden box from one of its drawers, came over to the sofa and moved her legs to place himself under them. Her feet tucked themselves between his thighs.

'I want you to have this,' he said simply.

'So it's true then?' she asked. 'What you told me the first day we met, that you fall in love with things, not people? You're hopeless with women but show you a shabti and you're anyone's.'

'You didn't show me a shabti.'

'But you're not mine, are you?'

He stroked her ankles. The room's acoustics were muffled, as if someone had zipped them up in there. Her feet were almost too hot under his legs.

'What's in the box?'

'A thing.'

'Thing One or Thing Two?'

She knew he'd get the Dr Seuss reference because he was her and she was him and there wasn't a hair of difference between them.

She went to open it, but he rested his hand over it. Take it home, he said, have a look at it when you're feeling miserable. But she was already feeling miserable. She had sold herself short, allowed him to have an access to her that should have been harder earned. She had given herself away.

'My boys,' she said. 'Do you remember their names?'

Bill reeled them off: Kit, Dylan, Joss, Rory.

'Do you ever imagine what they look like?'

'No,' he admitted, beginning a careful mitigation but he didn't get as far as she needed him to because loudly and insistently, his telephone rang from the other side of the room. It was going to be bad news, Caitlin knew it. She held her breath. What if it was Mark, telling her one of the children was hurt? He could have phoned Paul, who would have caved in, revealed all. She pulled out her mobile but there were no missed calls.

Bill removed her feet from his lap and stumbled to answer it. Standing underneath the stairs with his back to her, he mumbled into the receiver.

'Oh, babe, don't cry,' she heard him say in a low voice. 'She never means these things. We can sort it. Do you want me to come over? Don't cry. Stop crying now. Of course I can, I'll be there in ten minutes. No, it's fine, I'm not doing anything...'

'Your wife?' Caitlin asked.

'My daughter.'

'So you need to go to her.'

'Kids come first and all that.'

'Of course.'

And that was it, the moment they fell, separately and in different directions, right off the edge.

Caitlin didn't open the wooden box until she was on the train where she hid in her airline-style seat with the flimsy curtain pulled against the night. The betrayal she had felt at the way Bill had prioritized his daughter was all to do with her own maternal negligence, but she was less enamoured all the same. She had risked her boys' happiness for a moment with him, so why hadn't he shown the same recklessness for her? Because clever him, he had managed to keep something back.

She lifted the lid with a certain trepidation. Regret must not come into it now. Inside the box, sitting on a paper nest, was a white-veined pebble shaped like a heart, the marble running through its grey middle like a mended break.

She picked it out and rolled it until the cold stone became warm. When she ran its smooth surface across her lips, she caught the smell of dried seaweed and salt and bizarrely, a hint of Lesley's Egyptian mummy flakes. There was a note in the box, folded into four and formed into a shallow ellipse by the pebble's long reign on top of it. She opened the paper carefully, a crumpled page torn from an exercise book forty-eight years ago. In fading pencil it said, *Chesil Beach, August 7 1960, for the girl I will love.*

A liquid tiredness washed through her so she closed her eyes and wondered why she didn't feel sad. Perhaps the relationship with Bill – now surely over – had always been going to happen. She was always going to fall in love with him in the same way that her parents were always going to be killed on the road. She had known him before she'd been born. And she gave enough of herself away to others to allow herself this, didn't she? But would she be able to climb into bed next to Mark tonight? Of course. Could she, if she had to, bring herself to make love to him tonight? With ease. Had she changed herself for ever? Not a bit. She was the woman she had always been, even more so perhaps. Her head fell back on the headrest. The rhythm of the engine passing over the tracks lulled her into something approaching sleep and for ninety glorious minutes, she thought of nothing and no one. Then, as the train pulled back into Bristol Temple Meads, she put the pebble back in the box, the box back in her bag, and shut the last four crazy weeks in with it.

Twenty-One

Mark pulled his hired transit van into the narrow space reserved for lock-up number four and tried to ignore the immediately obvious fact that he was at least double the average age of everyone else there. His gleaming white van however, looked the newest in the rehearsal studio's car park, as uncool as a pair of pressed jeans at a rave.

He squeezed between his vehicle and the next. He'd put himself on a secret diet but his twenty-year-old waistline had yet to reveal itself again. Anyway, what did it matter? Four out of the five members of Vortex had bothered to travel from all corners of the world to recreate their tornado of sound! Only Joey Bertoli and his rhythm guitar were missing.

With shades of his dead father Ken, Mark had emailed them all with the link for the AA route planner. Look for signs to the Electric Mill, I've booked it for six hours from Friday at noon. I can hire all rehearsal equipment this end. It was really going to happen. Gibb had already landed. *I'm alive and at Heathrow!* his text had read.

Young men in loose dark clothes, the crotches

of their trousers down round their knees, their heads snug under beanies, milled confidently in and out of different doors, carrying amplifiers, beer cans, guitars and keyboards. Every time a door opened, a blast of music burst out and joined the general cacophony of sound – reggae, funk, and just plain bad.

As Mark walked towards lock-up number four, which looked from the outside to be nothing more than a glorified cupboard, he strained his ears for something familiar. Sartorially but also musically, there was no denying several generations had passed him by. When the door opened on their practice, Vortex were going to sound about as hip as The Osmonds. Or were The Osmonds cool now? Revivals confused him.

'Don't worry,' Joss had reassured him that morning. 'It'll be soundproofed. No one will hear you.'

He should at least have gone home and changed out of his suit. Perhaps he should take his tie off – and do what with it? Tie it round his head like Bruce Springsteen? The only person in the entire complex he'd seen so far who could possibly have been older than him was the man behind the desk in the dimly lit reception. Mark knew his name because he'd seen the tattoo on the back of his hand.

Reg had spent ten minutes hunting for the keys and then hit himself on the side of his head and said, 'Oh, yeah, wake up Reg, someone has already been in and asked for them.'

283

'Who?' Mark had asked, looking at the stacks of drums behind him – rubber hat boxes for giants, labelled with 'Bass', 'Side Tom', 'Floor Tom' and 'Snare'. An open cupboard revealed a stash of foot pedals and cymbals.

'A bloke my age,' Reg had croaked through a cigarette. 'About twenty minutes ago. Bought a KitKat and a can of Coke. Do you need drums?'

'Might need a few accessories. I'll find out.'

He walked across the courtyard feeling the grin already spreading on his face. Would it be Lurch in there? Not Gibb, for sure. He'd be the last, knowing Heathrow baggage reclaim. Coxy maybe. My age, Reg had said, and he was fifty if he was a day.

The Electric Mill reminded Mark of a cross between an out-of-season holiday camp in the 1960s and the sort of American motel where you would expect to find someone stabbed in the shower. It hit just the sort of shabby note that Vortex had always aimed for. If it weren't for the age gap between them and the other milling musicians, Mark thought he'd feel perfectly at home.

He walked around the back of the van, took eight cans of Carlsberg lager from the transit's passenger seat, pressed the remote lock on the key fob, and with the alarm lights flashing ostentatiously at him, he walked as casually as he could towards the large door 15 feet away.

The padlock was hanging off, but the door was open, like Reg had said. Inside, the dimly lit, windowless room was empty apart from a fridge along one side wall and, at the top end, two sets of speakers and two microphones on stands. A single bare light bulb hung from the middle of the ceiling, and the place smelt of unwashed bodies or stale beer.

He turned almost immediately to go out again. He could waste a bit of time by phoning Caitlin, not that he could think of anything he really needed to tell her. He just didn't want to be caught standing in there by the others, like a new kid on his first day at school.

'Can I help you?' a voice behind him asked.

He span around to see a man with short grey hair cut close to his head sitting on a shabby sofa with his legs on a low table. The *Sun* newspaper was open at page three next to him.

'I'm sorry,' Mark said. 'I thought this was number four...'

The man stood up. 'It is four, you fat tosser!'

'Christ!' Mark shouted. He hadn't used that blasphemy since Kit was born.

'Coxy to you,' the man said laughing, 'and where's all your bloody hair gone?'

The brown towelling bikini with the gold buckle and white piping lay on Sheila's bed, teasing her. There was no way on earth she was going to pack it with her other clothes in the suitcase that lay open on the floor and yet she could feel it doing its best to persuade her.

'Don't be so ridiculous,' she told herself. 'A bikini, at my age? And what would I want with a bikini in Holland in December anyway?'

'Come to Leiden with me next weekend,' Jan had said for almost as long as they had been reunited.

'Not next weekend,' she kept saying. 'Next weekend I'm driving Kit to a rugby match in Bath.'

'The weekend after then?'

'I've promised to babysit, but I could try for the one after that?'

'What if there isn't a one after that?' Jan had asked her.

In the end, he'd given her twenty-four hours to get ready. She'd already used twenty-three of them worrying about letting him see her naked. So far, if you didn't count their younger days (and Sheila no longer did), Jan had only been acquainted with her bare feet.

She picked up the bottom part of the bikini and held it in the air. Its sides were dreadfully wide, wider even than her most sensible knickers. Had it really once been the stuff of seduction?

She hadn't actually said goodbye to anyone. She hated the fuss of goodbyes, so she had written it in three separate notes, one for Ali which she would leave on her pillow in the bedroom next door, one for Caitlin, Mark and the three youngest boys, and one for Kit, which she had slipped into his back pocket, along with a twenty pound note and a finger to the lips last night. She couldn't risk the possibility of something bad happening to any of them while she was gone. As for herself, she felt invincible.

The telephone next to her bed rang. It was Jan,

speaking through his robot to tell her he would be with her in half an hour.

'What are you using that thing for?' she asked.

'I-am-saving-my-voice.'

'What for?'

'You,' he said.

She began to pack quickly and methodically. Two sweaters, two skirts, two pairs of trousers, two blouses, one cardigan, two scarves, two new packs of not too sensible knickers, one pair of not very sensible at all knickers and a matching lace bra, a nightdress, a wash bag, a medicine kit. She lay the clothes she was travelling in – her lucky chocolate brown skirt with the kick pleat and the cream sweater with orange and brown stripes around the polo neck – on top of the suitcase and walked along the landing to where her bath was waiting.

The water was still a little hot so, undressed now, she padded back to her bedroom. Camera, make-up, hairdryer, one pair of flat shoes, one pair with a heel. The suitcase began to bulge.

Her one smart jacket was hanging on a coat hanger over the full-length, free-standing mirror. As she unhooked it to return it to its dry-cleaning sheath in the wardrobe, she caught sight of herself. Her reflex response to seeing her own nudity was to pull in her tummy, straighten her back and tuck in her bottom. She tried to imagine that she was Jan, looking at her with those eyes that still turned her inside out. How would she measure up to his memory?

'You are happy for us to share a room with

twin beds?' he'd asked. 'Yes, of course I'm happy,' she'd said. But she was nervous too. She was plump around the tummy and hips, and the triangle of hair that always used to be a glossy black had lightened to a peppery grey.

Her breasts needed help to form a cleavage these days. She grabbed the halter-neck bikini top from the bed and put it over her head, placing each breast behind the two towelling triangles, adjusting the material and clipping its white plastic flower clasp behind her. A little more help than that even. She put her hands to the nape of her neck, undid the ties, hoisted everything up and retied. The bikini bottoms were less easy to get on. Somewhere around her lower thigh, they needed tugging and as they scraped into position, the hard white piping left faint red tramlines on her skin. She wriggled into the last centimetres of spare cloth, pulled the tarnished gold buckle to the centre and took one reluctant step towards the mirror.

'Sheila?' she heard Jan call from the foot of the stairs. 'Would-you-like-a-hand-with-your-bags?'

She jumped, flew herself out of the bikini and grabbed for her dressing gown on the back of the door. Her hand grasped an empty hook. Her modesty was a useless 30 feet away, lying on the bathroom chair. What then? In a bid to snatch up the smart jacket, which was now draped across the ottoman, the mirror treated her to her reflection again. At a flash, her legs were long and slender in flight, her breasts full and soft. A towel would do.

'I'm not quite ready,' she shouted back, 'but why don't you come up?'

Mark might as well have been standing there naked too. Any member of Vortex could see straight through him so there was no point in putting on any sort of a show. The awkwardness of reunion had been miraculously short-lived, and he couldn't help thinking what superb television it would have made. No hugging, no compliments, no squeals of delight or rapid exchanges of family information like there would have been if there had been women present.

They hadn't even spent much time bothering with formalities. As each of them had arrived, they had kicked into the ancient routine of ritual humiliation.

'I caught Coxy reading the *Sun*,' Mark had told Lurch within thirty seconds of his arrival. 'Vortex's only Trotskyite member now reads the *Sun*.'

'It was left on the sofa. I was just flicking through it,' Coxy had protested.

'Well, it's better than that worthy little rag you work on. If that got any more politically correct it would disappear up its own arse.'

Mark was relieved to see that none of them had hung on to their crowning glories. Coxy's bubbly brown halo was now a scruffy grey mat. Gibb's thin curtains were a soft silky handkerchief. Even Lurch's thick black mop was no longer worth commenting on.

'Fucking hell, Gibb, how many more times do you need to tighten a snare?' Coxy ribbed, moving from foot to trainered foot. He out of all of them was the least evolved. The sight of him in his jeans and student's tee made Mark feel ridiculous in his suit, until Lurch had turned up in Armani. Gibb was in black as ever, but it was moneyed black this time, leather, wool, organic cotton.

The others were ready to play, nervous now.

'Does it still take you four hours to rig up a mic?' Coxy baited Gibb. He was referring to one infamous gig of theirs before which Gibb had spent the entire afternoon fiddling. No one ever knew what Gibb did to his drums. The rest of Vortex used to provoke him to boiling point during the tuning up. *Hasn't anyone ever told you a drum only makes one sound, mate? It's a drum, mate. Just bang the fucking thing.*

'Still keep your guitar at concert pitch, do you, Coxy?' Gibb replied. 'Got your tuning fork with you?'

Coxy was always notoriously out of tune.

'Give me a D off your keyboard, Lurch,' Mark said.

Lurch, who seemed in the intervening twenty years to have gained control of his lolling tongue, gave Mark an A.

They all laughed. Someone was going to have to start. Gibb ran to settle behind his drums.

'Come on then, you bastards!'

Coxy sprinted down to the other end of the

long room, took the unopened pack of Carlsberg off the table and ran back to set it on the floor, at stage right.

'They're Joey,' he said, as if Joey were in that rock band in the sky.

'All right!'

Lurch started with the keyboard, Coxy put a bass line over the top, and then Gibb was there too. Mark got high on the sound of his own voice, the others lost in their own tornadoes of memory. They played for a terrible five minutes before stopping and admitting they might just need a little more practice.

'I'm bloody starving,' Gibb said.

Coxy picked the KitKat he'd bought from Reg out of his shirt pocket and threw it at him. Gibb peeled back the foil. The chocolate was creased, like a sheet on a bed that needed changing, and it sported a spotty white bloom.

'Does this date back to the 1980s too?'

Caitlin and Ali sat in Sheila's kitchen sharing a bottle of wine they'd found in the cupboard. It still had the pink raffle ticket sellotaped to its neck.

'I hope she's all right,' Ali said, checking her watch. 'She said she'd phone me when she got there.'

'Talk about a reversal of roles,' Caitlin replied. She had a burgundy smile and was far too loosened by alcohol for six o'clock on a Thursday evening, but so what? 'I bet she used to sit at this very same table saying the same about you.'

'I don't think she did actually. I was always Daddy's girl.'

'If she didn't say it, she thought it.'

'You think? Not having children of my own, I find it hard to...'

Ali put on the brakes on purpose. That was the old Ali talking, the victim Ali.

'Maybe I should say not having children of my own *yet*...'

'Well, take it from this mother then. She's probably *still* thinking it.'

Ali liked the idea. 'So do you think she and Jan will...?'

'Do we want them to? They might. Sheila did have a bit of a twinkle behind the eyes.'

'I wonder what age all that stuff stops, in favour of something less...'

'Complicated?'

'I was going to say predictable actually,' Ali said.

Caitlin felt a disappointment wash over her. Ali was right, sex *was* predictable. Even sex – or nearly sex – with Bill.

'I guess that depends on how much you're still attracted to someone.'

Ali assumed it was a reference to Mark and Nina. She poured them both another inch of Fitou. It wasn't bad for a tombola prize.

'Caitlin, I feel I owe you an apology. I've been a cow.'

Her sister-in-law waved a lazy hand in the air. 'Don't even go there.'

'But I pushed Mark towards Nina, I know I did. And then there was all that dodgy history I told you about the pair of them.'

'I asked, didn't I?'

'Yes, but I enjoyed telling you.'

'Water under the bridge,' Caitlin said.

'Mark would never be unfaithful, I'm sure of that.'

'He'd never be unfaithful with *Nina* – even I know that now. But if he met someone else, someone out of the blue, someone he really connected with...'

'That sort of thing doesn't happen in real life,' Ali said, slumping a little. 'Only in the movies do strangers fall in love – usually on a train station. That's where I'm planning on spending a lot of my future time, there and in a second-hand bookstore...'

'But if he did?'

'Then you'd forgive him.'

'Even if he'd slept with her?'

'You would in the movies.'

'But does it work both ways? Would a man forgive a woman?'

'Women aren't so carnal, are they? If *we* are unfaithful, it's a bit more worrying, don't you think? We just don't have sex for the hell of it, do we? It's got to mean something.'

The conversation was teetering on a dangerous edge. Caitlin knocked back her wine and stood up. The boys needed supper and she was a good thirty minutes walk from home.

'To be continued,' she said lightly.

Twenty-Two

December 17

As soon as the last customer of the lunchtime rush wandered out of the tobacco factory bar to rejoin the pre-Christmas chaos, Chris Jones stuck a notice on the door – 'Closed for Private Function' – and pushed its three bolts shut.

'OK, boys,' he said across the room to his son Olly and godsons Kit and Dylan, who were flipping beer mats on stools at the bar. 'We're on.'

Chris disappeared through the internal swing doors marked 'Staff Only' that led to the offices of Salt Peter Productions and came back with a steel ladder.

'We've got to take these paintings down first. One of you go and get the bubble wrap from my office, will you?'

He began to lift the first of the six huge canvasses of grimy men and belching chimneys off its nails. The technician from the digital projection company who had phoned to say he was on his way had asked for one large plain wall on which to work his magic.

The space beneath him where Vortex would play had to be cleared of tables and chairs. Mark and Gibb were due back soon with the set of drums, amplifiers and microphones they'd hired from Reg at the Electric Mill.

'Do you think your mum and dad would like one of these for their birthday?' Chris called down to Kit as Mark's eldest boy came saunter-ing in with a roll of masking tape.

'*Birthdays*,' Kit said, stressing the plural yet again. He'd been on a campaign in the last few weeks, and he was winning. Even Rory had made his mum and dad separate cards this year.

'Sod that,' Chris said back. 'They're not get-ting one each.'

'Lou's already given them a joint present. A book by Nancy someone.'

'Friday,' Olly Jones said from the depths of his hoodie, returning with the bubble wrap. The filthy hems of his frayed jeans brushed the floor as he walked. Chris saw his lewd gesture to Kit and Dylan.

'You don't know what you're talking about, mate,' he told his son.

'Kit does though, don't you, Kit?'

'Grow up, Olly,' Kit said, and from his van-tage point up the ladder, Chris Jones realized that for once with these boys, it was no longer a case of the pot calling the kettle black.

Paul had brought along so many flowers for Erin's grave that Caitlin was forced to make a tasteless joke about Elton John and his legen-dary overspending.

'Yes, I like flowers,' Paul said, pleased to be

able to quote the rock star verbatim. His arms were full of purple and blue hydrangeas, which he told Caitlin was the flower of 'understanding'. She carried an exquisite bouquet of ferns, for 'confidence and shelter'.

'How do you know these things?' she asked him as they poked the stems into the holder. Her hand was shaking a little. The idea of the remnants of her parents down there in that cold earth with the worms and the rotting wood and the brass handles was one she had so far done her utmost to avoid.

Paul shortened a vivid bloom with his secateurs. With just one or two in place, the huge floral heads had a touch of the cartoon about them, more at home in a clown's lapel than a graveside vase, but with five, then six, seven, eight, they were taking on the air of a Jane Austen wedding scene.

'My ex-boyfriend was a florist. I used to suffer from year-round hay fever.'

Caitlin thought it was wonderful, on her fortieth birthday, to be in this awful place having a laugh. It was the longest she had spent here in nineteen years. Usually, she left the car engine running while she removed one dead garden bunch and replaced it with another.

'Just one more trip to the car and I'm done,' Paul said.

'I'll come with you.'

'No, stay there, have a chat, tell them your news.'

'Don't be daft,' she replied nervously.

He went and she stared at the grey polished-granite headstone, with its deeply cut rose engraving and rustic pitched edges wondering who had chosen it. She had no memory of the process. Distant relatives, executors of the will, family friends – they had all buzzed around her in those dark days after the accident, careful to seek her opinion but she had been in no state to offer one. Whoever was responsible had done a reasonable job, perhaps not to her exact taste but not so far off to make her worry about a dereliction of duty. She ought to find out and write to them, say a very belated thank you.

'Paul told me to have a chat,' she murmured self-consciously. It was all very well talking to her mummies in the museum, but this felt entirely more ludicrous.

'So, well, it's my fortieth birthday and I thought I'd come and...'

A dog barked somewhere in the distance.

'The boys break up today ... they send their ... or they would if they had known...'

She stopped, relieved to catch sight of Paul carrying a wicker hamper and two vinyl-covered foam kneeling pads.

'Lunchtime!' he called, putting the pads either side of the stone and unrolling a pristine striped picnic blanket, laying it across the grave.

Caitlin felt queasy and thought of Lesley's mummy flakes again.

'Should we be doing this?' she asked, looking around.

'Why not?'

From the hamper he took two china plates and two crystal glasses. He produced a tray of smoked salmon from Orkney and some tiny organic oatcakes and then with a 'happy birthday', he eased the cork from a bottle of champagne. It shot into the sky above them as if it had been waiting a very long time and the foamy bubbles spilled from the bottle's neck.

'Hey, how's Kit getting on with his girlfriend?' Paul asked, pouring them each a generous amount.

Caitlin caught his train of thought and acknowledged it. 'Oh, I see what you did there!' He passed her a flute and together they toasted Erin and John.

'Here we are on this auspicious day,' Paul said, 'come to say hello to you in our forties, looking good, feeling fine. Your daughter is as gorgeous as ever, even though she has used me mercilessly as a cover in her extramarital madness...'

'Which was over before it began,' Caitlin added.

'Which was over before it began.'

'And won't happen again.'

'And won't happen again.'

Caitlin downed her champagne in one, remembering the way Bill had once done the same to a glass of white wine. She really didn't need to start thinking of him now.

'Paul, this is perfect, how did you do it?'

'There's a little deli on the corner of my road called M and S...'

'Eminesse? Sounds expensive, what does that mean?'

'Marks and Spencer, darling.'

They got giggly. Paul told her about the time he and his boyfriend had nearly made love in a churchyard, she told him about nearly making love with Bill. Damn, there he was again.

'Did you hear that, Erin?' Paul asked, waving his glass towards the headstone. 'Your daughter didn't do it. She only *nearly* did it which is an entirely different thing, although in my book, *nearly* doing it is not half as good as *actually* doing it because you still have all the guilt, but not so much of the fun, and if you ask me...'

'Let's talk about something else,' Caitlin said, eating three oatcakes piled with salmon, one after the other. She thought she might have heard from Bill today – a card or a text – but so far, nothing. That was a good thing, she reminded herself. Paul dipped his hand theatrically into the hamper and opened a box of profiteroles.

'I know, let's talk about your mum and dad. Shut your eyes. What do you see?'

Caitlin squeezed her eyes tightly closed.

'The three of us in France, buying a box of peaches from a roadside stall.'

'What are you wearing?'

'Mum's in a red denim dress with a belt and no sleeves and Dad is in shorts.'

'What about you?'

'A skirt with pineapples all over it.'

'Where had you been and where were you going?'

'To a glass-blowing factory, but it was too hot and I wanted to go back to the gîte and the pool...'

And so it went on and on, with buried memories being discovered like blackberries – find one juicy one and there are always five more equally plump ones attached to it. Eventually it was Caitlin, not Paul, who declared herself full first. They packed up the hamper, gave a final tweak to the hydrangeas and ferns and stood up.

'Bye then,' Caitlin said to the headstone.

'And don't worry, we'll be back,' added Paul, patting it with his hand as he left.

In Dryhouse Lane, Chloe – fresh in from school – picked the Nancy Friday book up from its nest of shiny wrapping paper on the kitchen dresser. The cover was a sepia photograph of a naked woman touching her body in a way that had made Caitlin, when she'd first unwrapped it that morning, assume she was looking at a book about breast cancer and self-examination.

'Women on Top?' Chloe read. 'Who gave Caitlin this?'

'I did,' Lou Jones told her proudly, wiping her hands on a tea towel she had tucked into the drawstring waist of her linen trousers and reaching to the dresser for her glass of champagne. 'It's actually a joint present. Mark will enjoy it just as much.'

The kitchen units were the usual muddle of pens, mugs, keys and fruit bowls but today, they were eclipsed by an indiscriminate display of birthday cards.

Chloe began flicking through the book with barely concealed disgust, not so much at the content but at the idea of forty-year-olds having sex.

'Is it a joke?'

But she had to wait for her answer because Lou had answered the phone.

'Webb household, hello?'

She hushed the two youngest boys who were rolling into the kitchen on an end-of-term wave.

'Sorry, I can't hear you...'

She squinted into the phone as if a concentration of her facial features would help clear the line. Her travel journalist radar picked up the sounds of an airport.

'They'll ring again,' she shrugged indifferently.

'Who was it?' Vanessa asked, wandering in from the sitting room, where she'd been painting her toenails. She'd arrived home from her sixth-form boarding college sporting a necklace of love bites which Lou, despite her obsession with sex, found unpleasant to look at.

'I thought I told you to put some cover-up on those.'

'It's my love tattoo! And if you saw the guy who did it you'd—'

'I don't want to know!'

'Well, I might tell you anyway, but who was that? I've answered it twice today and someone keeps hanging up.'

'Someone phoning from an airport, maybe? I

thought I heard a flight announcement.'

'I thought that too,' Vanessa said lazily, checking her neck in the mirror. 'Are they expecting guests from Italy? I swear I heard the word "Roma".'

Caitlin walked through the door just in time to hear the last exchange.

'Italy?' Caitlin asked, fighting to keep her expression straight. She looked at the wonky ranks of sweet red peppers Lou had filled with cream cheese.

'Hey, birthday girl! How was lunch?'

'Lovely, thanks. All well?'

Vanessa took the book from Chloe in a rank-pulling gesture, turning it over to read the back cover.

'An explicit and iconoclastic book on modern women's sexual fantasies.'

Caitlin snatched it from her. 'Can't have you reading that! We wouldn't want to corrupt you at such an early age.'

Chloe laughed. Her bitten nails poked a scrumple of pink tissue paper with 'love from Paul xx' written on it, uncovering a silver frame fitted with a photograph of two people shelling peas on a garden bench.

'Who are they?'

'Well one of them is me...'

'And the other's your mum?'

'Well guessed.'

'You've both got that gap between your teeth.'

'Hers was even bigger than mine.'

'Chloe,' said Lou, 'what you need to know is

302

that Nancy Friday is required reading for the entire female race. Vanessa has read her from cover to cover.'

'Yes, but Vanessa is not going out with my son, is she?' Caitlin remarked.

'She'd better not be,' said Chloe. 'What else did you get? What did Kit give you?'

A warble rose from Caitlin's phone, but it stopped ringing before she could hit the button. 'Damn,' she said, shoving it back into the safety of her trouser pocket. 'Chloe love, perhaps you ought to start thinking about a bath if you want one.'

'Look,' said Vanessa, 'there's a card here you haven't opened.'

Caitlin took it from her with the same haste she'd retrieved the book.

'It's ... it's not a card.' She pushed it into the pocket with her phone.

'No one's sent you a bill on your birthday, have they?'

'Bill?' Caitlin looked flustered.

'You know what a bill is? An invoice?'

'Oh, no, it's not a bill. It's a note from Sheila.'

'Aren't you going to open it?'

Caitlin touched the top of a tray of muffins she'd baked at dawn, flicking the tops of them to hear the reassuring sound of crust.

'Go and have that bath,' she said to Chloe. 'Help yourself to bubbles. And think yourself lucky – only girls are allowed in my apothecary.'

'Unfair!' Vanessa shouted. 'I had to have a

shower!'

As Chloe disappeared, Lou looked Caitlin in the eye. Scrutiny wasn't the word for it. For a moment, Caitlin wondered what she was going to say.

'She's Kit's *real* present to you, isn't she?' Lou said.

The relief was a gift in itself.

From the top of the ladder, the technician positioned the projector on a high deep windowsill and fixed its focus on to the plain wall opposite. At the foot of the ladder, Chris fiddled with a roll of red masking tape, securing the mains and the signal cable that the technician had run down the wall and fed to a digibeta player behind the bar.

'Watch out for that lead,' he shouted as Mark walked in carrying a microphone stand. Gibb and Kit followed, carrying a black-and-yellow hard drum case each.

'Have you got a test tape, mate?' the technician asked.

'Kit, on the bar, the blue box,' Mark said, pointing.

Kit put down the drum case and went over to the bar. He liked being in the company of men. The equipment he'd been asked to carry was really quite heavy and it pleased him that Dylan and Olly had been given the lighter stuff.

'No, use the one next to it,' Chris said, 'without the box.'

'Stick it in the player, would you, mate?' the

technician called to Kit.

The wall behind Gibb flashed into life. His stooped body became a shadow puppet and the technician shouted at him to get out of the way. In monochrome, a girl in a cotton dress pedalled across the expanse. Her chubby knees pumped determinedly from beneath a puff of white skirt. She came to a rest in the centre of the wall and smiled directly at the camera, showing a little gap between her front teeth.

Mark was pleased. It was the first time he'd seen his film on a big screen and the quality was fine. But then the shot faded and out of the dimness came a determined-faced little boy in a knitted V-necked sweater and short shorts, sitting on a kitchen chair playing a guitar.

'What?' he shouted. 'Where the hell did you get that from?'

The boys cheered rowdily.

'Sheila,' Chris said. 'She did offer me one of you in the bath...'

'What have you done to my beautiful film?'

'Given it a little balance.'

'It's my present to Caitlin.'

'The original is still intact,' Chris reassured him. 'Now, have a drink and enjoy.'

The wall danced with images of Bristol, Dryhouse Lane, young Caitlin, older Mark, young Mark, older Caitlin, babies, boys, big old dirty dockland buildings, galleries, factories, wine bars, holidays in France, graduation days, wedding days, birthdays. An old railway station; some archive material of the working docks;

and then Dylan in armbands; Caitlin pregnant; street theatre; bicycles in piazzas against railings; Mark being pushed on a swing by Sheila; men in flat caps smoking; boats and cranes delivering crates on the harbourside; then Mark again, with floppy hair and snake hips, a baby Kit on his shoulders. Twenty minutes long, it ran on a loop and the idea was to keep it going all night.

Mark moved over to stand beside Chris.

'You're a clever bastard,' he said, 'but you better not have messed with my ending.'

'Would I?'

The image of Bristol Cathedral on the plain wall became indistinct, then faded to something human. It was the way Caitlin's legs made a tent with the bedclothes that made Mark wish she was next to him right now. There was the edge of a hand, an indistinct frame of flesh and twisted cotton and suddenly, his young wife in all her glory, a full-length beauty wrapped in a sheet, her face blossoming into flower.

'Is that Mum?' Kit shouted.

A ravishing Caitlin danced against the brick, twirling like the white-wedding bride she'd never been. When the film came to an end, the lights returned the wall to its plain stillness again. Gibb, his drum sticks tucked under his arm, nodded appreciatively. 'Looks like you done all right there, mate.'

Mark rubbed one eye and laughed proudly. Dylan and Kit looked at each other and grinned.

'Bingo,' Chris said.

In the hallowed space of the apothecary, Caitlin found towels in wet heaps on the floor, and Chloe's black cord school flares with her knickers still inside them, hanging over the heated towel rail. A hitherto unused bar of handmade soap sat congealing in the basin, its transparency turning to expensive slime. The silver shelves against the indigo walls were stripped of their treasures which lay in pots and tubes and jars with their lids off. Chloe had tried out every single potion she could lay her hands on, and even possibly made some of her own.

Caitlin didn't mind – in some ways it was a relief to have broken the spell of sealed promise after so long. Now at least she could enjoy the decadent pleasures of the Coco de Mer body lotion and the grapeseed pure retreat gel without feeling she was using something she shouldn't. Even if her private chamber had been turned upside down, Caitlin sank into the bath with gratitude. Having a bath run for you was birthday luxury indeed.

She lay her head on the aqua blue, shell-shaped cushion that Joss had given her and let her toes seek out the deeper reaches of water under the taps. Her phone, which she had been forced to smuggle into the privacy of the apothecary under the suspicious eye of Lou, was slotted precariously behind the shower head.

Her heel knocked against something hard, which clunked against the enamel and rolled away. She swept gently around to find it again, circling it under the arch of a foot when she found it, once, twice, three times, to see if she could guess what it was, reluctant to lift her shoulders out of the warmth. The hard, cold object sounded as if it were scratching the bath's surface so she leant forward and reached down for it.

It was Bill's heart-shaped pebble. Maybe it was the lunchtime champagne, but holding it in the palm of her hand again made her feel dizzy, the same rush to the head that she'd felt at the train station watching him step on to the platform.

She took in a mouthful of the steam rising from the water. Was it Cupid shooting her a birthday arrow? No, she told herself firmly. I am tipsy and he is a memory. She gave the pebble a quick kiss in the way she sometimes kissed old photographs of the children and put it back on the middle shelf. Stay there, she said to it, retreating under the bubbles. And then the phone rang.

Twenty-Three

'What do you mean, you're nipping out?' Lou screamed as Caitlin grabbed her bag and keys. 'Where? Why? We're supposed to be down there in just under an hour!'

'I know, I know...'

Lou, her hair in huge rollers, followed her into the hall. She dropped her voice.

'Caitlin, I don't know what's going on, and I don't need to know either, but Mark is my friend too and he'll need you there from the start...'

Caitlin opened her mouth to tell her the truth but it was too long a story and anyway, Lou was a leaky bucket. She would tell Vanessa, Vanessa would tell Kit, Kit might tell his brothers and the night would be ruined.

'I'll be there. I just really need to do this, Lou.'

'Do what?'

'I need to meet someone.'

'A man? You can't, Caitlin. However important it seems now, it won't be in the morning.'

'It's not like that.'

'It never is.'

'I'll tell you everything soon, I promise.'

'I'm not sure I want to know – but what do you suggest I say to Mark?'

'You won't need to say anything. I'll be there.'

'You'd better be.'

Never one to soften her words if she meant them, Lou marched back into the kitchen oozing disapproval from every pore. Caitlin opened the front door quietly so as not to alert the boys.

'Oh!'

On the step stood Nina Wills holding a huge foil-covered tray of baklava that had taken her all day to make.

'I didn't even knock!' Nina said brightly.

'I can see through things,' Caitlin said, hardly stopping. 'Oh, I didn't mean to sound...'

But Nina was feeling wildly generous. She had spent an hour getting ready for her delivery and it was Mark's wife who looked like the woman in the middle of an emergency this time. Caitlin's hair was soaking wet, she wore no make-up, her sweater had a cheap birthday badge hanging from it and her trousers were muddy round the hems.

'You didn't. Happy birthday! I bought a pudding.'

'Thank you, that's kind. I don't want to be rude but I really have to dash.'

'Of course. Is Chloe here? She's not in your way is she?'

'Yes, she is and no, she's not – help yourself to a glass of wine.'

Caitlin ran to the family car, throwing school debris from the front passenger seat into the back. Several neighbours wondered, seeing her pull away from the kerb as if she were rushing an unconscious child to hospital, which of the four boys had broken a limb this time. She caught sight of herself in the rear-view mirror. It wouldn't have been her look of choice but what mattered was that she was on her way.

The sweet pastry smell of the baklava brought Joss and Rory running to the kitchen. Lou slapped their hands away from the food, still furious with their mother.

'Hello, boys,' Nina said. 'Is Chloe here?'

'Hey, your hair isn't purple any more,' Rory said, running a finger through the nutty syrup.

'Do you like it?'

'Yes, brown is a better colour for hair.'

Through his freckles, Joss blushed and pressed his shoe down on his brother's stockinged foot.

'Ow.'

'Could you give this to your dad?' Nina asked them. Lou had yet to say hello and she felt awkward. 'It's a card saying I'm sorry I can't come to his party.'

'It's Mum's party too,' said Joss.

'Yes, the card is for her as well – there's a voucher inside.'

'Why can't you come?' Rory asked.

'I've got to go to Turkey very early tomorrow.'

'Oh, yes, Chloe said you were going to get loads of money from the bad man who gave her that scar and then you were going travelling round the world and you've asked Dad if Chloe can live with us and...'

Nina's face turned a flame red.

'A month,' she started to explain, 'I'm only going for a month...'

'This is Lou,' Joss said quickly, over his little brother. 'She's my mum's best friend.'

'Sorry,' Nina said to Lou. 'I haven't introduced myself, I'm Nina, Chloe's mum.'

Oh, I know exactly who you are, Lou thought, purple hair or not.

Rory wiggled a sugary finger at Lou and then licked it before putting it straight back into the honeyed puddle of the baklava. Lou waved a hairbrush at him.

'Welcome to the madhouse.'

'Where is Mum?' Joss asked.

'She's just popped out,' Lou told him, undoing her rollers.

Without invitation, Nina started to cut the baklava into small strips and arrange them in two sticky circles on plates. Mark and Caitlin's youngest son Rory moved next to her to help but Joss snapped at him to go and get ready, that there wasn't time to mess around. Vanessa and Chloe sauntered in, swapping stories about Kit, posturing for position.

Lou studied them all from behind her curtain of loose curls. They were their own little microcosm of the grown-up world that had been going on over their heads since October. All she needed now was for a baby Paul Moffat to turn up with yet another photo album and she'd have the whole fascinating scenario in miniature.

* * *

At Bristol International Airport, a woman who had just lost her husband was moved to tears by the romance of it all. In a wanton breach of security, a lady with a gap in her teeth had driven right up to the entrance, left the engine running, jumped out of her car and started running towards a man with thinning hair. 'I'm here,' she was shouting, waving her arms joyously, 'I'm here!' The evening's drizzle caught in the headlights of a passing taxi and a Christmas song drifted from the open window of another. The woman who had just lost her husband watched the man with thinning hair begin to run to the woman with the gap in her teeth. He had his arms open wide.

'Katie!' the woman thought he called. 'You made it!' The lovers threw their arms around each other, amazed to be together at last. The light inside their battered estate was still on as they passed and the newly-widowed traveller was left with the memory of their broad smiles. There's one family who are going to have a wonderful Christmas she thought generously, and she bowed her poor grieving head from the crowds.

The middle of the tobacco factory bar was completely devoid of people. Small groups of early guests were clamping themselves to its edges, looking as awkward as Mark was beginning to feel.

'Where's Caitlin?' he asked Lou desperately as she whipped past him carrying a cling-filmed tray full of spiral bready things.

'She'll be here in a minute,' Lou reassured. 'There was a hot water issue. Just relax.'

'Can you get me a drink? I'm as nervous as hell.'

He walked to the double doors through which more guests were arriving with more helium-filled balloons, more bottles with bows round their necks. Suzy! Ad! Mark! Thanks, mate, thank you! Jude! Ken! Hey! Congratulations! I know, I don't look a day over thirty-nine and a half! Where's Jonno? Park round the side. Come in and grab a drink.

'Where's Caitlin?' they all wanted to know.

'Slight hitch with the food,' he lied. 'She's out the back whipping up a quick round of ham sandwiches. Champagne at the bar. Help yourselves. She'll be here in a minute.'

He went to find his sons for moral support.

'That's enough beer for now, Dylan, take it steady. No I don't know where Mum is. Joss, could you go and find out?'

He tried her mobile yet again but it was still switched off and there was no answer from home.

'She'll be on her way then,' her colleague Lesley, looking Gothic in purple and black, told him when he revealed his concern.

Mark tried to look partyish as he walked to the bar where he took another glass from the tray. He slapped someone on the back, kissed a woman on the cheek and started to make his way over to Coxy and Lurch who were standing

314

with their wives – with their wives, he thought angrily – just in front of the stage.

He sipped his drink but the lead weight of his disappointment had tainted it and it tasted sour. Vortex meant so little to Caitlin that she would rather be cooking frozen sausage rolls at home than hear him play. Is that what this insensitive lateness was about? Why should it be any different just because it was their birthday?

'All right, Coxy? Getting nervous yet?' he said, picking up one of Gibb's drumsticks and jabbing it in the air.

From the other side of the bar, Chris Jones saw the gesture and recognized it as one of a man who was trying too hard. He turned to Lou.

'What's going on? Where the hell is Caitlin?'

'She left about an hour ago to meet a man,' Lou hissed. 'She said she'd be back.'

'Jesus Christ,' Chris said loudly.

'I think he's just flown in from somewhere – Italy maybe. She lit up like a Christmas tree when she got the call.'

Mark saw them muttering and monitored the situation. The empty space in the middle of the bar had disappeared and the chat and laughter levels were high. It was twenty minutes later than the invitation had indicated the party would start. Sure, he could wait a little longer for his wife to defrost a few more profiteroles, but did he want to?

'I reckon we should start it up in a minute,' he said to Gibb. 'Get the party started...'

'Your wife turned up yet, mate?' Lurch asked.

'She's here somewhere,' he lied.

In front of the stage, Kit, Chloe, Dylan, Vanessa, Olly, Rory and Joss started slow clapping. Kit put his arms around Chloe's back and clasped them in front of her tummy. The diamond in her navel touched his palm and he kissed her on the top of her ear.

'You're coming to live with me,' he said, 'in my house, where I will be able to see you whenever I like.'

'Keep an eye on me, you mean.'

'Don't count your chickens, Kit,' said Vanessa. 'She might get a better offer.'

'From who?'

'Me?' Olly said hopefully.

'In your dreams,' Vanessa shouted, pushing her brother into the band.

'Dad!' Rory called, 'when are you going to start playing?'

'Mum's not here!' Joss shouted frantically. 'Where's she gone?'

'She's doing the food,' Mark lied again. 'C'mon boys, you ready?'

'We're ready!'

Picking up his guitar which hung off his neck by his old school tie, Mark mumbled something into the microphone about new albums and forthcoming tours and a cheer rippled around the room.

'OK?' he checked with Coxy, who was fiddling with a second amp.

'One minute.'

'What do you want that for?'

316

'In case something goes wrong...'

'Get a bloody move on!' Dylan shouted. Mark said something else into the mic, this time about teenage boys and bad parenting. Thank God they were all there, within kicking distance. Caitlin clearly had her own agenda. He'd play this one for his boys. He stared out into the sea of faces and caught Lou checking her watch.

He leaned forward.

'Good evening,' he greeted to a roar of whistling and stomping.

He thought about apologizing for Caitlin's absence. There were women here who had travelled most of the day to see her. He ought to, really, despite his anger. And then, just as he opened his mouth again to find a few flippant words, he saw her.

She was coming towards him, a slinky column of emerald satin and shiny lips, weaving her way through the crowds. She had to keep stopping to allow people to kiss her and although she was finding her fallback smile, Mark could see that she was flustered. Something unplanned had happened. That was when he noticed the other figure following her. She was holding the hand of a man in an expensive suit and open-necked shirt. No one kissed him, because of course no one knew him. She can't be doing this to me, he thought.

Lou looked at Chris, Chris looked at Mark, Mark looked at his boys, his boys looked at their mother. All seven of them braced themselves for what they all knew, underneath, had been coming for a while.

'Caitlin,' Mark declared soberly into the microphone as if acknowledging the predictable arrival of a gatecrasher.

'Fuck me, it's Joey!' Gibb screamed from behind him.

'Are you fucking serious?' Coxy shouted.

Vortex's missing rhythm guitarist Joey Bertoli walked on to the stage with his arms outstretched.

'You can thank your gorgeous wife for getting me here,' he told Mark, as he gave him the same warm hug he'd given Caitlin at the airport.

Mark put down his guitar and, with a lump rising in his throat, went to her. In the crook of her bare arms, she'd already hooked their youngest two sons. There was nowhere to put his hands other than her cheeks. He kissed her on the lips.

'I'm sorry I'm late,' she said.

'I love you,' he replied. 'I really do.'

He kissed her once more and ran back to his guitar. Joey had miraculously reappeared with a shiny black bass, ordered by email, delivered by Paul Moffat.

Mark leaned into the microphone one more time.

'Good evening, Bristol,' he said to the baying crowd. 'We are Vortex!'